BELONGING

The Shifter Series:

Book I

CHANTELL RENEE

Thank you for your purchase! If you enjoy, please leave a review on the E-Book platform you bought this from or message me at, www.chantellrenee.com ☺

BELONGING, The Shifter Series, Book I

First U.S. Edition

Edited by Johnnie Bernhard

Cover Art by Elizabeth Mackey

BELONGING, The Shifter Series, Book I

ISBN: 978-1514139677
Limitless Ink Publishing©

Dedicated To:

Tomas Cantu
1926-1999

BELONGING

4

Table of Contents

Table of Contents

BELONGING

BY

CHANTELL RENEE

Limitless Ink

Publishing

Prologue

Now she had to run. Tearing herself away from the secret panel she'd hidden her three-year-old daughter in was the hardest thing she'd done in her life. Her hand touched the sheet rock in a final goodbye. She had seconds to get down the flight of stairs before the gunmen reached her floor of the mansion.

She struggled to make as little noise as possible, while hurrying down the steps. The twists of the spiral stairs seemed never ending, and added dizziness to her panic. She finally reached the landing. A hinged wall, cut from ceiling to floor, was her last obstacle to clear before her escape. The double hiding space might've worked for them both. Except the latch was never fixed and could only be closed from the outside.

She had no idea who the invaders worked for; they might be government agents, drug suppliers, or paid assassins. Assassins meant she'd never make it out alive if she stayed in the house. If she got out, she would be able to get back in under the cover of night to get her daughter.

She breathed in deep, held it and pushed. Screams and gunfire came from the second floor landing. She sent a quick prayer to the Fates and shoved the wall closed. The faulty latch failed to click shut, but the footsteps that thundered up to the third floor landing she was on told her, time was up. No one would see the panel unless they pushed at it. It was a chance she'd have to take.

She ran. Bullets hit the walls and floor around her as she raced for the upstairs bedroom. The open bedroom window loomed ahead. With just a few more steps she'd be free.

Please, let me make it for my daughter, she prayed.

The change tingled on her skin; her limbs started to shrink into the hawk image she saw in her mind. A sharp pain blazed near the base of her spine. The pain stopped, but so had the shift. She was in her normal female

8

form instead of the bird of prey she tried to change into. She fell to the bedroom floor, something was very wrong. Disoriented, she tried to get up, but found the lower part of her body would not respond. Her fingers sunk into the fiber of the rug as she pulled herself towards the window. The floor boards behind her squeaked and the clear sound of a gun being cocked evaporated what fight she had left. Realization dawned, she'd been shot, and that's what stopped her shift. There would be no escape. She closed her eyes and pictured her daughter safe, hidden and alive.

The child settled when the guns stopped firing. The little girl fell over and pulled at the stuffed bunny she'd been sitting on. Her mother had left it for her. The child curled up with the tattered animal, its gray and white fur tickled her nose.

"Sleep my girl, sleep. Close your eyes and sleep." The spirit of the mother whispered the sing song words of the familiar lullaby to the child. The little girl's eyes began to droop.

The spirit shimmered in the tiny space, relieved the child remained undiscovered. She smiled as her daughter's crystal blue eyes, so much like those of her father's, closed. She stayed for a while longer, listening to the child's soft breathing. A mother always made sure their children would be out of harm's way, no matter what. That choice had cost her life. A price she'd always been willing to pay for her little miracle.

Chapter One

Birthdays Always Suck

In four hours I'm turning eighteen. Shouldn't I be getting ready to celebrate? Any other seventeen-year-old would be in front of a mirror picking out the perfect outfit for her big day to come. Instead I'm scraping long, curly-strings of wax from the white linoleum floor of a little salon in the middle of nowhere. The bad eighties music is only made worse by the three other women here who seem to know every word to all the songs. Not the party I had in mind. Well, not the imaginary one anyway. When you have no family or friends, I guess any kind of celebrating will do.

The string I'm scraping leads up the side of the wall, its origins looks to be the mirror. Someone dripped the wax while taking off their mustache. What's really sad, is that I know that. I've worked on the spill for the last twenty minutes. How much wax do you need to remove a woman's mustache? What a great birthday this is turning out to be.

"Ann, let's wrap it up for the day."

Rude, can't a girl get some wallowing time?

The razor lifts the wax string off the wall, making it easy to pull the string all the way up to the glass. The wax on the mirror is not as thick. Getting it off will require some cleaner. The lights turn off in the shop. Guess the wax will have to wait for tomorrow.

The only light remaining comes from a small lamp in the tight room. There's just enough light for me to finger brush my long black hair, and put my ponytail back in. My dark skin and brown contacts helped me to blend in for the last twelve years. My natural eyes, sky blue, would draw too much attention. My focus is to blend in anyplace I go. Clean and neat is the only style I really have. So boring. But safe.

"Come on ladies, closing time!" That's Crystal, the owner. Better wrap it up. I think closing time is better than Fridays. You get five of them a week, but only one Friday.

All the green chips, strings, and razors go into the trash bag I carry out of the salon. The dumpster is on the way to the road. No one even says bye when they pass. Sometimes, blending in, sucks.

The pawn shop special on my wrist reads 10:38p.m. Now that I am outside, I remember why I've been thinking it's time for a change. The weather in Brownsville is typical South Texas, eighty degrees in the dead of night. The air smells of hot dirt and the humidity sticks your clothes to your skin, no matter what time of day. Winter needs to come soon. I know just the thing to beat this muggy air, a cold beer. Why not? It's my birthday and I'll drink if I want to. And with that statement, I truly need some socializing.

Around the corner stands the only bar in town. A tall pole, with one big light fixture on the top, provides the only light for the long, dirt driveway I have to walk down. The crunching sound of my shoes on the rough ground gets swallowed up by the flat open space around me. This must be what it's like to walk on the moon; so much around you, but no life for miles, except yourself. The parking lot of the bar looks full for a Wednesday night. Should be an entertaining evening. I love to people watch as much as I love to watch TV.

The bar reminds me of a log cabin. The best part being the wooden sign hanging above the door; 'Tim's Place.' It's branded on a jagged cut plaque. So Texas. I've heard the owner found the sign in the desert. Mentally I capture the image of the sign, and put it in my imaginary house I'd one day have. I think it would work best set up next to the crazy taxidermy rattlesnake statue. I'd seen it at the last bar, in the last town. My own place would require me to stay somewhere longer than a few weeks or months. That hadn't really been a possibility as a minor, but in an hour, that will change.

Eager to get the heck out of this heat, I push the wooden door open to find, Bingo Night. They don't actually play the game here, but the smokers who lost all their money at the Church Bingo, show up here to get drunk afterwards. The haze doesn't help the dingy lighting, which gives the wood walls and floor a dirty yellow tinge. I've never been a smoker, mostly because I don't want to part with my money. However, I find the second hand smoke calming.

A month ago, I rolled into this little town. I've already discovered, Tim's is the only place open past dusk. The best way to hang out here is to, sit in the back, and let the scene be my own reality TV.

A quick sweep of the room reveals the evening's *ick* factor. A few tables to my left sit a group of college boys, or C-boys, a nick name I've given all college boys. Four out of the seven wiggle their eyebrows at me. I've always been thin for my age. One day I woke up with boobs, very unnerving really. Eventually I got bigger everywhere else, but I can't seem to get my weight past one twenty. So, my big boobs still catch testosterone filled glares. Being that I'm only five foot and four and a half inches, I think I look fairly average. Plus, my sense of fashion is a cleaner version of a mechanic's wardrobe, plain jeans, loose shirts, and often a flannel or some other covering buttoned up. I suppose the fact I'm athletic-ish and seem vulnerable is all it takes for the C-boys. Who am I kidding? As long as I have boobs, I could be covered in trash, and they'd still act like cats in heat.

I give them my trademark eye roll in response to their idea of 'hello.' Just because they're in college doesn't mean they can take a hint. I move my chair to face the right side of the room, angling it away and putting them completely out of my sight. A chorus of hurt sighs and boy giggles come from their table. I'm gonna ignore that. To give them less of a view, I pull out my shirttail to cover my ass.

"Take it off baby!"

Without thinking, I turn my head towards their voices. There are big toothy grins all around. *My Grandma, what big teeth you have.* The blond hair, blue eyed one looks as if he'd eat me if I'd let him.

Wait, did I just say that?

Even in my own mind, the filter's broken. Not to worry, that would never happen. That was one mistake I HAD learned from.

A few years ago a guy like that bought me a drink, then a few shots. Later that night Mr. All American led me to a dorm room. Nine other 'C-boys' and four other teens were there. The teens, three boys and one girl, knelt naked, side-by-side. The girl looked dazed, but kept giggling at the penis of the boy next to her. The owner of the penis was tense and a little sweaty; his head turned from side to side as if he heard something the rest of us couldn't. Another of the boys kept grabbing his own ass and laughing loudly. The third simply looked at me; his eyes seemed glossed over. They'd been drugged, probably on ecstasy. That was the popular drug back then.

I picked up the half empty bottle of Jose Cuervo from the table they knelt in front of, which was made of two milk crates and a wide piece of wood, and started taking big swallows. About an hour later, I passed out. All my clothes were on when I woke up the next day. The only memory I had from the night before, ten college boys taking on the three drugged guys. I never saw the other girl that morning, or any of the C-boys. There was only me and the three passed out boys. When they woke up, I got the feeling they knew what kind of party it actually was. After that night, I called all college boys 'C-boys.' The C stood for 'closet case' as much as 'college.' I also made sure to never go home with a C-boy again.

Again, I ignore the C-boy congregation and settle in at my table. Focusing on the bar menu, and not the awful memory, I decide on the Cheek-

13

N-Basket. Being next to the border you get a lot of Spanglish. Little things like that make up Southern Texas charm. There're about twelve people in the bar, not counting the 'C-boy' crew. They don't count in my book.

"Decide on what you want, shu'ga?" I've never seen such white bleached blond hair, as that of my waitress, Pam. She's wearing bright red lipstick tonight.

"Sure Pam, I'll have the Cheek-N-Basket and a bottle of the national beer, Lone Star." She writes down my short order and glances at my I.D. I've come here close to six times, each time, giving her a different card. She never looks at them. My fake I.D.s from Texas and Mexico have various aliases. I only use them when I drink. I'm glad she pays them little mind. Under the radar, my modus operandi. I heard that on a TV show once.

When I first met Pam, she told me she had transplanted here from Denton, Texas. She said there aren't too many white ladies this far south. She walks off, nearly knocking down a drunken Mexican guy on his way to the can. He grips the wall to keep from falling. Pam doesn't miss a step. Must be a self-medicated kind of night. Most small towns have addicts. Not much else to do, or so I've been told.

The names I go by most of the time are Ann, Molly, Maria, or whatever seems easiest for people to forget. No reason to use my real name, something I learned on the streets. A good trick if you happen to be arrested. Lucky for me, that's never happened. When I was seven, I stole the only document I'd ever seen my name on from the orphanage. The page was a police report that told me my mother, Aishe Dacian and father, Juan Purez where shot and killed when I was three. No other family. When I left the orphanage at twelve, I burned that report in a hobo's fire. It was insurance that if I ever did get caught, there would be no documents as to where I truly belonged.

A basket of food and bottle of beer plop down in front of me, making me jump, but only a little.

"Anythin' else sweetie?"

Blondie is missing smacking gum for her stereotype. Instead she's chewing on the corner of her lower lip. Her eyes dart to the back door. The chicken looks crispy, fries too. The beer is cold in my hand.

"Nope, looks good."

Steam rises from the food. I start with the beer. Burning off the roof of my mouth doesn't appeal to me. In three pulls, the bottle is empty.

Pam's sugary voice is in my ear before the empty bottle touches my table.

"Want another, Hun?" Her big red lips turn up in a smile like a murderous clown, while her eyes bulge down at me.

"Uh, yes please." I'd be willing to bet her choice of drug is small town Texas vitamins or meth, the same thing. Her movements have become jittery and her hair line looks damp. She turns away, leaving my empty bottle on the table. I've barely lifted a fry and my second bottle arrives with a loud smack. Pam leaves as quickly.

This celebration isn't going as planned. No, I won't let a fit of self-pity, obnoxious horny boys or tweaking waitresses ruin my night. Food, beer and people watching, that's all I need.

An hour later I have my third beer in hand. Turns out the beer and food are the best part of my night, I think I'll call it and head back to my motel room. The outside door is pulled open bringing in the humidity. A small flare of heat lights up on my lower spine. My skin feels like it's on fire. I reach back to make sure it's not. No flames. Muscle spasm? A little flip in my stomach sets my nerves off. Doing a quick look around the room, I don't see what has me on edge. The people at the tables are basically the same.

15

Back in the left corner, I spot a table I usually don't pay attention to, being that it's usually unoccupied. Most people don't sit there because there's no light. Tonight, there's a black dusty cowboy hat and a hand with silver rings on the table's top. The shadows keep me from seeing anything more.

A shiver sends flesh bumps up and down my arms. Kind of like that sensation you get when someone walks over your grave. Okay, that's a hokey way of saying I have a creepy feeling, not to mention bringing up graves creeps me out too.

My stomach becomes nauseated and cold sweat beads form across my forehead. Dizziness makes me grab the table for support. My back gets hotter as the heat moves up my spine. This doesn't help to calm my rolling gut. My heart rate speeds up and my hands shake. There is no way all this is happening because of someone creeping me out. Maybe Pam dropped some of her 'vitamins' in my beer?

I want to run, but my legs aren't stable enough to get up. I'm not sure what to do, but my policy has always been, 'when in doubt, run.' I pull out some money from my front pocket and hope it's a twenty. I swallow and force myself to get up, ignoring the churning in my gut. *Just got to get to the door.*

"Come over here sweet thing!"

I forgot about the stupid C-boys. No, I can't let my irritation at them add to my growing attack. I think I'm about to puke.

Even from the center of the room, my pulse quickens as I get closer to the shadowed stranger. I can feel the stare I can't see following my every move. Only a crazy person would think someone else could give them this type of physical reaction. I need to get outside. Fresh air will help. I'm not crazy. No crazy here.

No one follows me out. I double-time it down the drive way, as the thick humid air begins to hug me in a blanket of calm. My symptoms all at once disappear. I'm fine now. Drugs don't just leave like that, and neither does food poisoning. The urge to vomit has totally passed too. How could cowboy hat guy create that kind of reaction from across the room? How is that even possible? What does it matter now, I'm okay and out of the hot seat, *pun totally intended.*

My watch tells me it's almost midnight, and I've been up since five a.m. I guess my new old age can't handle late nights anymore. I'm only a few blocks from the cheap motel room. Everything's gonna be fine.

Fiery heat chars at my back again. I bend down and grab my knees, until I can see straight. With my eyes closed, I can only listen for an attacker. The rocks in the dirt crunch under feet that aren't too far behind me. Finding the strength, I turn and see a man in a dusty black cowboy hat and a cream colored blazer walking towards me. All the symptoms that left a minute ago are back. My body is weak and flimsy like paper. I know I won't be able to fight him off. That thought makes things worse.

Part of me knows I need to take action; the other part is stupidly stuck on the blazer it's too damn hot to be wearing. But this isn't normal, this is bad. A new batch of adrenalin starts to snap me awake. I have to force myself upright. My well-trained runaway instincts tell me to show no fear or weakness. I gotta keep him from seeing my hands shake, I shove them into my jean pockets.

He stops. Maybe it looks like I have a weapon? If that's what he thinks, good. I shove them in further. His eyes flash down. It's working.

"Natsia kas?" His voice isn't exactly menacing, but the heat on my spine rises.

"I don't know what you're saying. Sorry, I don't have any cash." Making myself move, I step backwards getting closer to the street.

"Vitsa san nav?" He's advancing. I take another step back.

17

"Look, I don't know what you're saying, leave me alone." My last word didn't come out as demanding as I wanted. How is he doing this to me? The pain on my back, nausea and dizziness, are morphing into one big ball of messed up. This isn't like anything I've ever experienced before. Every time he speaks, all my muscles get tighter. I may not be able to keep from blacking out. I have to try something.

"Stay back, I don't want to hurt you!" My right hand comes half way out of my pocket, but I keep it in a fist. His eyes shoot down again. Not sure how much longer he'll believe I actually have a weapon.

"Rakli Maw! Atch San! Nav Ramano kas!" The tone of his voice is commanding, though I have no idea what he's demanding. The world starts to go black. A spasm of pain seizes my insides. I can't breathe. Doubled over, I manage to grab my knees again which is all that's keeping me up right. He stops a few feet in front of me, I'm not sure why, or if, I need to be more worried. I manage to lift my chin and watch for his next move.

His eyes, they are getting lighter, almost violet. The heat on my back has become an inferno but worse, it's now traveling up to my neck. Everything looks crystal clear as if I've become capable of seeing in the dark. If I didn't feel like I was about to burst into flames, I might really care, but right now I only want to get the hell away from here!

I hear the truck before I see it, which barely gives me time to jump and avoid being hit. The wheel's slide to a stop, kicking up a huge cloud of dust. The creepy Cowboy Hat had to jump further out of the way than I did. His loud cries tell me he may have injured himself. The driver's door pops open, I'm struggling to get to my feet.

"Shifter reveal! Reveal yourself to me!" Cowboy Hat's words hit me and turn my gut into a pit of snakes. Everything goes sideways.

"GET IN!" A voice from somewhere behind me yells, but the pain in my stomach is all I know. I can't stand up straight, so I move doubled over towards the shouting voice. Looking up I see Cowboy Hat is on his feet and moves with speed towards me. There is no escape. His violet eyes glow brighter. My limbs lock up, everything around me gets dim. Oh no, I can't pass out, but catching my breath seems impossible. If he would just stop, or slow down, or fall, or something, I may have a chance.

The crazed man's movements slow. I'm also in slow motion as I reach towards the truck and the driver's hand closes sluggishly around my wrists. A loud 'pop' and things are going fast again. I'm flying through the air into the extended cab then landing face down on the passenger seat. The driver speeds off, drowning out the screams of my attacker.

The smell of the truck catches my attention first: aftershave and beer, definitely a man's truck. The clinking of empty beer cans sound off around me. A moldy earth like smell, kind of a like a graveyard, is also in the mix. If I continue to inhale the awful odor, my nausea will never leave.

Chapter Two

Never Accept a Ride from a Stranger

My legs are jammed between the seat and floor board. Careful not to cause myself further pain, I maneuver each knee into place so I can straighten up on the seat.

"Sorry I didn't get the place cleaned up for ya, I didn't think we'd make it to the cab." His cocky laugh rings a bell, but I'm too dizzy to figure out from where. The taste of fried chicken lingers in my throat. I stop my ascent up to let the wave of nausea pass. I need to calm myself. Ignoring the driver for a moment, it's time to focus on my breathing. Deep and slow. Now count to twenty.

"If you're gonna stay down there, slide over and make yourself useful. Don't hit the gas leg. And no teeth!" The annoying laugh makes me want to vomit. *So much for calming my nerves.*

My legs are free. I can move onto the seat fully. My eyes open and the first thing I see is the dark night speeding by the passenger window. The truck is going fast, all I can make out is blurred treetops. My legs give me a little rebellious twinge as I move up the seat. The sore spots from my landing make themselves well known.

The truck makes an abrupt left turn, sending me flying into the window. I knock my head hard against the thick glass. There're drops of moisture on my face. *Am I bleeding?* There's no time to check on my throbbing forehead. Another sharp turn to the right causes me to fly into the driver. Then the truck jerks to a stop and throws me into the dashboard and back into the seat. The gears grind to a stop.

If I can get to the passenger door, I may have a chance. He's too fast. He grabs the back of my shirt then sends me flying out of the driver's door.

Pain flares up at the nape of my neck from a small patch of hair he ripped out of my scalp. I land on the bare ground, pain seizes my back and legs. The sharp ache in my bones keeps me from getting up and running. The driver flings himself on top of me, pressing me into the dirt, giving me no room to move.

Going still I shut my eyes and wait. The sound of my own gasps and his shallow breathing, fill my ears. The throbbing fades replaced by a fresh batch of panic. I don't want to look at him. I know what he wants-and he can have it, but I don't want to see him.

"Open those pretty little eyes, slut." He covers my nose and mouth with one hand, forcing me to do as he wants. His blond hair and blue eyes spark my memory and I know who it is without needing to see the rest of him, Mr. All-American. The rest of his C-boy crew must've stayed at Tim's.

He smiles his charming boy smile at me, then slides a hand down my stomach. I suck in the areas he touches, disgusted by him. My reactions make the crazy in his glare become more sinister. His hand loosens my jeans and he starts tugging them off. It's been many years since something like this has happened to me. I am cautious to stay out of the way of men like this.

His face darkens when he speaks, "Couldn't come over and say hi? Too good for me? Bitches like you need to be taught a lesson." He grabs at the skin around my half exposed hips, digging his fingers deeply into my flesh. I want to scream and cry out from the pain, but only manage to whimper. He grinds his pelvis into mine and bites down on my shoulder. His teeth punch through, and blood trickles down my skin. I scream. The monster looks at me with his crimson smirk.

He wasn't a guy who wanted a thrill. No, he wanted to hurt me, or worse. The maniac licks my face. I have to do something before he goes for my throat. I need to be as strong as Superman, strong not weak. He is coming towards me for another taste; I grab his shoulders and push. The C-boy flies right into the side of his truck, and drops to the ground.

What? How did I do that? The monstrous guy doesn't let the toss phase him. With the speed of a predator, he's back on top of me. This time, he presses one of my arms under his right knee, hard enough to break. The other arm is caught only by the sleeve, but I can't move it well. The expression of controlled maniac slips off his face. Instead I am seeing the true monster, a wild animal-like man. Mr. AA licks the blood on his lips. My blood.

Instead of going for my pants again, he wraps his hands around my neck. My lungs are protesting for air already from his weight on my chest. I'm like that stupid girl in those slasher movies. Pants barely on, sprawled out under the killer because she didn't get up and run.

My killer's grip tightens. His vice grip around my neck is all I know. An image of the helpless girl weakly pounding the murderer's hands fills my mind. At some point, he's slide down my body, but having free arms, one possibly broken, isn't doing me any good.

My eyes open to Mr. AA's crazed grin. An image of the slasher's butcher knife, lying just out of the reach of my good arm, appears in my mind. My killer's hands grow tighter. I look past him at the night sky, all the pain melts into a violet mist.

The night starts to collapse towards me. My fingers brush across something hard, *the knife!* My hand is thick and clumsy, but I wrap it around the handle and drive the knife towards Mr. AA's neck. But the night doesn't stop falling towards the earth. My consciousness is swallowed up into the abyss.

Chapter Three

Awakening

Where there was total blackness, bright white light is surrounding me. Blinking several times helps my eyes adjust. But nothing is forming around me, only the blinding light heats my skin. Am I alive? I don't feel dead, though I have no idea how I'd know if I was dead or alive. Maybe I'm asleep? Pinching yourself is supposed to wake you up, so I do. Nothing happens. Under my feet sand appears, and the heat of the light is from the high sun. The forest is gone. Small grains of sand brush past my swollen cheeks and stick to my bloody shoulder. In the distance I see movement, which gives my eyes something to focus on. Hundreds of men, women, and children stumble away from a burning city.

They are battered and bruised. Some are even being carried on carts, pulled by big camels. The heat seems tolerable to me, but they are already looking overheated. The men look defeated, but determined to get their families to safety. Maybe I've been sent to some crazy version of hell? The light brightens further. I throw my hand up to shade my eyes.

"We are only defeated if we die here today. Let us keep going." Says a man to the slow progression. His voice is real enough. I peek at them from between my fingers. The line gets closer to me, but not headed towards where I stand. There are men leaning on other men, both with injuries. A pregnant woman stops for a moment. She looks right at me. In the blink of an eye she's standing in front of me, her hand lifts, and she touches my sore skin.

"Daughter of my Daughters, SURVIVE." She says to me. The last word brings a jolt of electricity into my broken bones. There's a deep ache, and I hit the ground.

BELONGING

A breath puffs my chest up, and my eyelids open. The most intense bright violet light fills the air. The smell of lilacs soothes my senses. The strange light fades into a mist of rain. The water drops make me blink. I see tree tops and early morning sky. I'm back in the forest. No sand or people anymore. Something is at my side, hard and somewhat constricting my movement. I push back and turn away from the horrible odor.

I put out my forearm before my face hits the mud. The strong smell of earth and water catches my attention. The robust aroma rolls over my taste buds. There is also a smell of death and body fluids. Wait, my pants are soaked, and it's not raining that hard. Those fluids are mine.

The attack from the night before floods back, that thing next to me was a body, my attacker. Bile rises in my throat. The odors are too overwhelming. I need to get away from here. I get up and stumble a few yards away. A few deep breaths and the nausea starts to fade. Why hasn't he woken up yet?

Didn't people lose their bladder control after they'd died? Looking down at my jittery hands I think I understand, but I don't want to admit it yet. Wait, hadn't he broken my arm?

"Shit, shit, how, what? I have to pull it together." My voice doesn't sound hoarse. Hadn't I screamed at all, I can't remember. I look over my arms and wrists. No marks, it doesn't even look like I'd almost been raped and possibly killed only a few hours ago. My trembles bloom into full shakes. Had I killed him? I don't want to go back to the dead guy, but I force myself to at least look at him. He's on his side, arms stretched above his head. I've never spent time with corpses, but I don't think they are supposed to be that stiff this soon. Something is sticking out from the side of his neck.

My legs start moving towards him. At the last minute, I remember to open my mouth for oxygen in order to avoid more nausea. The body is

24

petrified, like a piece of driftwood. I push it with my foot and the corpse rolls onto its back. Another wave of nausea hit's me at the sight of him.

"Pull it together, I can't lose it, pull it together."

The talking and breathing helps clear the wave of sickness. Okay, I have to deal with this.

A black handle sticks out of the side of Mr. AA's neck. The knife is exactly like the imaginary one I'd thought up before I'd passed out, but how's that possible? There is no clue on the ground to help me figure out where the hell that knife came from. Nothing but dirt, leaves, and grass. Maybe he brought the knife to kill me? But I never saw one, except the one that was in my head. Where did it come from?

How...did this happen? The image of his crazed look and hands on my neck, reminds me of why I'd needed that knife. Tears began to sting my eyes, making my contacts move. Rage is bursting up and bouncing around inside of me, looking for a way out.

Why me? Why had this bastard come after me? Flashes of the night before appear in my head, fueling my anger. Tingles move over my cheeks and head; my foot kicks out at the ground. He had killed me or at least hurt my body beyond repair. Terror seizes me and my arms start to shake again. My legs are like rubber, I kneel and fold myself up then put my forehead onto the damp earth. What the hell is wrong with me?

"It's okay, you're safe, you're safe." I chant out loud, but even the sound of my voice can't calm the panic attack. I take deep slow breathes. The smell of the earth fills my body. The terror ebbs. With each breath, there's a wave of calming energy as I take in the scent of the ground. The earth itself is somehow calming me, which is a good reason for another freak out, except I can't. What if his friends are looking for him right now? I have to accept this, and really get safe. For now, I can be strong; later, I'll fall apart.

My face is numb, but I know it's from the hyperventilating. Sitting up on my heels, I continue to breathe deep. A fluttering sound catches my attention. I look up and see a brightly colored humming bird zipping through the trees. The blazing sun-light in between each leaf causes the bundle of leaves to glow on their branches. The colors bring life to the brown of the tree and the yellow of the sun-light. I have no words for this beauty. A cloud blocks the brilliant light, and I snap out of the reverie it had me in. The beauty of it all nearly brings me to tears.

Hysteria is at the edge of my mood. *Focus, I need to focus.* I also need to figure out what to do about the dead C-boy. With reluctance, I walk back to the gruesome scene. The truck's passenger door still hangs open, and the guy I killed is still stiff with a black handle protruding out of his neck. That knife has my finger-prints on it; I can't leave it behind.

No matter how much he deserved it, I can't believe I stabbed and killed someone. Getting back down close to the body isn't easy, but I do it. I have to pull the knife out of the C-boy's neck.

"Don't be real." I plead helpless in a whisper. My fingers touch the handle. A violet light bursts out of the shape. A loud pop echoes in the open space, and the handle and blade turn into leaves and mud, that plop to the ground. The leaves and mud remain lined inside of the unchanged fatal wound. A trained eye would see he'd been stabbed. This close to him, the memory of his hands on my throat, choking the life out of me, comes back fast and sudden. I crawl back away as if he'd lunged. A little of the tears that I'd held back escape, but only a few. The anger is stronger.

"You killed the girl you saw last night." The trees and rain are all that hear my words. In the silence, the beat of the drops fuel the anger, chasing away my tears.

"Ann wasn't really alive, but that didn't give you the right... to do what you did." My heart's pounding, but I won't let my temper flare, nor will I fall to pieces. If there is anything I know it's I am capable of survival. As Ann, that meant hiding and running. Look where that got me. No, I can do this, I deserve a life. Relief slips down into my gut, and I let a deep breath out.

I get to my feet, shaking, from anger or grief or maybe just from being tired.

"We're one and the same, her and I. We may not know where we belong. Ann may have seemed like someone easily thrown away, but we are not trash. I didn't kill you, I saved me. My name is Vivian Dacain and I am someone."

***

Several hours have passed. I made it to the bus station and got the first bus out of town, heading to McAllen. The seat I'm in helped me sleep for a bit. I'm awake now, and thankful the old lady who'd been next to me had moved seats sometime since our last stop.

"Mama that man is smelly!" The loud complaints of a seven-year-old girl wake me fully. She's squirming around, but her mother pulls her near and starts mom talking her. Out the window I see a sign that tells me we are ten miles from McAllen. Bus transportation through the Texas region isn't fun. The highways are never ending. Every hour they stop in places with a single building, with farm land for miles. I'm exhausted from walking over five miles on the interstate, in pouring rain, so I could hitch a ride to a town with a bus terminal.

The people who'd picked me up were pretty nice. They gave me a towel to dry off with, and let me keep it after I got out of the car. I had washed all my clothing in a creek in order to get rid of Mr. AA's blood. Then the walk in pouring rain didn't help. The towel couldn't get me dry enough, but it warms me up.

"Why do we have to sit so close to him?" the girl fussed. To think, I was only a few years older than her when I left the orphanage. Strange to think I've made it this far, must be luck. Nah, I was just good at hiding.

Her mother whispers, "We're almost there." I agree, the man is pretty ripe.

Sticking to my new confidence seems to be keeping me from losing it again. I'd found a thrift shop and bought a change of clothes. The old ones, and the towel, were burned up in a farmer's trash pile. The body and truck hadn't been touched by me. When they find them, my fingerprints won't be anywhere. The mystery of the appearing then disappearing knife is also on the unsolved list; not to mention the disappearing bit, broken arm, and all the bruises that attack should have left on me.

Cowboy Hat guy is also classified as unsolved, but I think that's the best place to start. He'd done something to change me or put a curse on me. A curse that heals me and makes things appear when I need them to, and then disappear when I don't need them anymore. Ugh, it's hard to keep from becoming hysterical. I need to find Cowboy Hat. This all happened after he said that weird gibberish to me. If I can find him and make him undo this, or at least figure out how he changed me, I can get back to deciding how to proceed in life as an adult. Whatever that means.

The language he spoke is the easiest place to start. What did he say again? "Natisia Kas?"

Whoa, I heard that in my ears as if Cowboy Hat sat next to me. Damn, that is wicked weird. One quick look around, no one here, but us chickens.

The bus pulls into the slot at the McAllen station. Through the commotion of people gathering their things, I exit unnoticed. My watch says it's 6:18p.m. People are out and about, enjoying the small city's night-life. A small group of women pass me; I fall into step with them.

McAllen gets bigger every time I'm here. Folks started calling it the Hollywood of Mexico, but in America. Novella actors and actresses flock to the American city for the latest hair-style they see on the cover of tabloids. From the looks of things there are new spas and nail shops I've never seen. Long dark curled hair, tall heels, glittery nails and bright colored lips decorate the windows for most of Uvalde Ave.

I always make good money here. Cleaning jobs, baby-sitting or running errands, is what I do to survive. But, I know I need to get across the border, fast. I'd also have an easier time finding out about that weird language Cowboy Hat used in an American library. There's not time to make extra cash. There's a body in the woods, and his friends will probably point their ass smelling fingers my way. I'm gonna have to dip into my sock savings. Time to ditch the girl gang and head towards the library.

***

The place looks empty, but there are a few students around. Finding an open computer among these guys strikes me as miraculous. Time for research. No Sam to my Dean for the boring stuff. The spelling of the words he'd spoken proves harder than I thought to figure out. But I get close enough and hit enter then cross my fingers.

A full page of sites, all having to do with the Romani or Gypsies, fills the screen. The second site on the page looks like a translations glossary. I click on it and another page of Romani words and their English translations comes up. At the bottom is one word, the only one he'd spoken in English, 'Shifter.'

The letters are small. I double click on the word. A new screen pops up. White circles, triangles, and star shapes decorate the sides of the screen.

The black background makes the two words, typed dead center of the page, stand out.

Shape Shifters. In large fancy writing reads, LEGENDS AND MYTHS OF THE WORLD. This disappears and yet another screen comes up titled, 'Romani,' but all the text under that is in another language that doesn't even look like the Romani language. Before I can try to understand it, the monitor goes blank. My head snaps up to see an annoyed looking girl.

"You're supposed to check with the desk, I have this computer reserved." She smirks and raises a thin eyebrow. Instead of taking the bait, I smile and step into the stacks in search of any books I can find on 'Shape Shifters' and the Romani.

Chapter Four

Romani

The van rattled over the bumpy highway. The men sang and laughed for most of the ride. Juda stared out the dusty window. Only five hundred dollars made today out of a van of six men. The amount of tourists going into Mexico from McAllen had slowed. The song became louder as they ended the familiar tune. Juda let the laughter comfort him. There were many decisions for him to make over the next few days. He thought he was ready, but spending the last several weeks with his people made him realize how much he would be responsible for now.

Of course Juda had advantages over the men; the first being, he was not human. The Fates had blessed his kind centuries ago to form an alliance with the Roma. Of course the people had no idea how much more difficult this union would make their already rocky lives. There'd been mistakes made, on both side, throughout the ages. No matter how careful, sometimes outsiders would catch a glimpse of the shifter magic. Unfortunately, the Romani's close proximity to the shifters caused the outside world to stigmatize the Roma and their ways.

All over the world, the gypsy was shunned; either for their refusal to be a part of main-stream life, or for their way of life, traveling in packs and living off the land. This usually made the group difficult to control. Juda wasn't sure if any shifter had successfully bore children with the Roma women. To share your magic with a human was strictly forbidden. There was penalty of death for both parents if they got caught. The idea that any human could control the magic without the blood that flowed through Juda's veins was moronic.

31

However, only a few groups of the Roma actually knew about the shifter. Since they were a self-contained society, there was little chance of discovery by other Romani. The ones who knew had made a sworn oath to protect the secret.

In return, Juda's kind took care of the Roma. These men and their families are part of his vitsa, clan as the townies would call them. They ate, laughed and survived as one. The shifter's ways had not changed from the old days, however. They still operated off the old monarch system, which also caused rumors and distrust for the Roma, from outsiders. But, the Roma understood tradition and supported the system.

To the human part of his family, Juda's father was known as King Shea. They would pick up their lives and relocate if the king commanded. The shifter king kept them steeled in their traditions, and soon that would be Juda's job.

As the successor, he'd not only have to care for his vitsa, but become head of the family business too. He wondered how Jared, his kid brother, would cope without him. Sometimes Juda thought he'd never see the kid if he didn't drag him to dinner every night. Juda feared losing his kid brother to the gadze world. Their father had appeased his little brother by allowing him to connect to the web. The agreement was for him to help the family business advertise. Juda knew his brother accelerated past advertising on Craigslist, a while ago.

In two years, after Jared turned eighteen, he'd have a place on Juda's council, except the kid's distance from the family might stop him from wanting the position. Juda wanted to help Jared see how much he, and the entire vitsa, needed the teen.

The van slowed. This far out of town the roads ran clear of traffic. Along this area of interstate, the woods were thick for miles. They came to a stop on the two-lane highway. An aged two by four stuck out of the ground, marking the spot that was once a gate to the property. With caution, the driver navigated through the dense overgrowth and tree trunks. If no one thought the driveway was used, no one came looking. They cleared the trees and drove for a mile. The ground became a dirt trail. A parking lot emerged.

Juda noticed a shiny black truck, its big new tires and mirrors catching the evening sun. Next to it sat a familiar old Dodge with a faded blue paint job. The van stopped and let the men out. As Juda passed the Dodge, he smiled thinking of the owner. All the men walked towards the trailers while Juda walked towards the tall grass field surrounded by the forest. They'd all been required to wear disguises, mostly extra clothing or in some cases, wigs.

No one paid him mind as he walked across the overgrown field lining the dirt lot. He pulled off each layer of clothing down to his white T-shirt and jeans. A few feet more and a small tin shed came into view. He knew Jared would be there.

Juda didn't feel the other changes he willed his body to go through. His eighteenth birthday, which happened to be tomorrow, made his connection to the magic stronger. If anyone looked, they would've witnessed a middle-aged man transform into a seventeen-year-old young man.

His hair neatened itself back to its usual tight clean haircut. All the grey that sparkled in between the blades of dark hair, became black again. His skin tightened showing no sign that it sagged with age. He ducked inside the shed as the rest of his features shifted back.

A clicking sound greeted him. He stepped to the left, letting the clothing on his arm fall onto a small pile covering the La-Z-Boy. With his back to the entrance, Jared typed away at his desk. The five computer engines hummed along with one another from their perch of metal shelves. If their father had ever come in here, the amount of technology would send him through the roof. As it was, King Shea knew the kid did more than advertising all day and night in the little shed. Juda assured him the kid was into on-line gaming. He found himself being the buffer between the two daily.

Juda plopped down on a second La-Z-Boy, they'd squeezed it in the corner of the 10x10 space. The chair faced the young boy's desk. Though he hadn't tried to startle Jared, the boy yelped.

"Very funny, Juda. I could have peed my pants, and you know dad would make me stay out here a week for that!" Red colored, Jared's cheeks.

Juda pulled himself to a sitting potion. Which proved difficult as the chair had opened slightly. "Come on little brother, I wasn't trying to scare you. You know I would help you sneak into the house anyway."

Juda stood, stepping around the small desk and pulled his kid brother into a bear hug, lifting the boy a foot off the ground.

"NOT FUN...Y COM....N!" Half of Jared's complaint got muffled by the hug.

Smiling, Juda set his complaining brother back on his feet. The boy grinned back despite his obvious embarrassment.

"I'm about to be seventeen. You have to stop treating me like I'm seven!" Jared straightened out the keyboard and the cords for the ear buds.

"Awe, I was just playing with you. What's up, what's going on in the cyber world?" As expected, the new topic smoothed over the kid's embarrassment.

"Check it out. Before you so rudely interrupted me, I was tracing a login that just happened. It came from the main downtown library."

"Okay Mr. Special Ops, I get the picture. You tell dat about this yet?" Juda shot his best grin at his brother who sat back down in his computer chair.

"Come on Juda you know *dad* doesn't listen to me. I'm perpetually three to him."

"I know you don't use our language much, but DAT is not that much Romani." Juda lifted his brows to his brother. Jared looked back at the computer screen, ignoring the reprimand.

Juda's smile faded as the kid put his ear-phones back in place and started clicking at the keys again. He knew how their Dat could be. There was nothing to say that would make Jared feel better.

A few seconds passed and the tension left Jared's shoulders. Juda walked out of the building and made his way to the house, vowing to make some changes when he became king. In the vitsa all the young contributed, but not many of their voices got heard. With the gadze world getting closer and closer to their camps, the families needed to conspire and seal the cracks. This would be the new road Juda would pave to strengthen the old traditions. The prince walked in silence to his family's home.

Juda made his way down the hall towards his father's den. He heard the men's voices. His father sat on one of his old tan La-Z-boys. He looked up in surprise, but quickly softened at his son's presence. The king's hair remained raven black like both his children. Not one gray had ever dared to taint it. His looks were aged, but not as one might think. Of course they aged differently than the gadze. A decade would pass before an adult shifter would age another year. His father was born in 1771. He looked very good for his age. Juda found himself thinking he'd be lucky to have the same strong connection to the magic like his dat had.

Next to the king sat a man who Juda knew well, the owner of the beat up Dodge in the parking lot, his favorite Uncle Nate. Nate had lighter features than Juda's father. He had more wind in his hair and sun on his skin.

Smiling at his uncle it dawned on Juda who had brought the shiny new black truck. "Sastamios! I know I shouldn't say this, but I'm happy to see my favorite kak, especially when he's bringing me gifts!"

The man smiled at Juda's welcome. Nate stood and pulled the young man into a quick embrace. "Sastamios Juda! You've gotten so tall, how long has it been? I can't believe you're turning eighteen tomorrow. Didn't I tell you Joe, he would know that was his truck! So much dook with this one!"

Juda smiled as he turned to see the king's youngest brother in the far corner of the heavily furnished room. The man wore his usual stone face and creased brows. Every time Juda saw him, he wondered when the guy would ease up a little. Juda stifled a laugh to himself. Joe always dressed the same, no matter what time of year, he had on a thick cream colored blazer and black cowboy hat.

The king cleared his throat, "Chava, I don't want you joyriding in town, you know we don't need attention from the gadze. However, your uncle wanted to give you something big. I couldn't deny him the honor."

"Yes dat I promise," Juda smiled at his dad.

Nate took the opportunity to resume the conversation between the three brothers, not letting go of his nephew as he spoke, "So Joe, how was your drive?"

The men all shared a look and in it, a decision got made. "Good parla, but I had an interesting encounter on my way in last night with a rakli shifter. I want to speak about this before the rest arrive," Joe said.

Nate pushed Juda down onto a dark gray La-Z-boy. Juda looked at the recliner like it was a talking rabbit, then he looked up at his dad who gave him a nod of approval. They wanted him to be a part of the conversation. Juda wasn't a child anymore.

"Juda," his mother called him from the kitchen. This time all the men smiled and nodded their amusement. His father motioned for him to take his leave. Juda stopped short, almost forgetting his manners.

"Can I bring anyone something to drink or take your coat Uncle Joe?" Joe stood up and shook off his blazer and handed it to his nephew.

Most of the night, the deep laughter of the men echoed throughout the house. Juda wandered in and out until all twelve of the brothers crammed into the various sofas and recliners in the den. He noticed as he saw their faces that evening, how alike and different each brother looked. All had various shades of caramel colored skin. They also all had the same dark brown irises with a circle of violet around them. This was the one unchangeable trait of the Dacian clan.

The talk became less reminiscent, and more business. His father gave Juda a look and he knew his time in the room was up. Nate smiled and pleaded for him to enjoy his last night of freedom.

Outside he leaned against the house for a quick smoke. A small group of younger boys played soccer. He noticed Jared hadn't made it back from his tin-can. If he knew his little prala, he'd be in that trailer till the crack of dawn. Lighting a clove cigarette, he took a long drag, which helped him relax.

Juda smiled thinking of his Uncles inside the house. They would all be playing instruments and dancing tomorrow night for his big party. Each had driven in from the various territories across the southern states. A few went back and forth to run the border towns between America and Mexico. Not too often were there chances to get all of them together. Though, the eldest of the eldest coming of age ceremonies was mandatory for the kings. Family or not. Lucky for the Dacians, none of the brothers had passed, and they all had successors if and when they did. Legacy was everything to the shifters.

Juda would be getting a house, choosing a wife, and start producing children. He'd been ready to start his journey since he was thirteen. Most Roma started then, but he'd chosen to wait. Of course, the shifter had different rules amongst themselves, but they tried to keep them close to the Romani traditions. Juda knew who his father wanted him to marry, but she wasn't Juda's choice.

37

Callen was a great match. Her connection to the magic was strong. But Juda
was a romantic, or at least that's what his mother said. He wanted to wait until
the last possible moment, in case someone special came along. That last
moment would be here in few days. Juda knew he was being stubborn, but
some part of him refused to completely become the stone-wall the king tried to
push him into becoming.

A hand slapped down on Juda's right shoulder startling him into the
moment. Looking up, he smiled at his Uncle Nate's familiar face.

"Reminiscing over your lost youth already?"

Juda tossed his cigarette down and stamped it out.

"Truthfully, I'm thinking of my future."

"Smart boy," His uncle released Juda's shoulder to pull out a pack of
smokes. Juda noticed the auburn in his uncle's hair as the man lit up. A gray
and white cloud of clove filled the air. Juda only ever smelled the cigarette's
scent when it was first lit.

"Say, I have a fun idea, one you will really like. Why don't you take
your birthday gift for a ride?"

Juda couldn't help the surprise that spread over his face, but he wiped
it off quickly, "That would be enjoyable." Juda was sure his uncle didn't miss
the restrained joy in his voice.

"Why don't you take your little prala. He needs some fresh air after all
that stale oxygen he breathes. He's basically living in that tin-can of his."

A plan formed in Juda's head, one he knew not to share. Nate
produced the new keys. A Mighty Mouse figurine dangled from it. Juda
laughed.

"You'll always be that chava in the Mighty Mouse pajamas to me."

38

"I'm not such a little boy anymore." Juda grabbed the keys and hugged his Uncle. Without another word, he set off towards the trail to collect his kid brother, ignoring the tisks of his great Aunts in the courtyard.

Usually a fake threat from their dat was needed to pry Jared out of the shed, but this time he only had to say one sentence, "Wanna go to the library?"

Chapter Five

Choices

Sitting in the stacks makes me want to curl up and sleep. The large translations book on my lap hasn't been much help. For the past hour, I've flipped through the long pages, but nothing on Romani, lots of other languages, but no Romani. The computer had shown Cowboy Hat's words were for sure Romani. Maybe the Internet could show more? No one has surrendered to the god of lazy and given up on their work yet. The Spanish words in the book, which compared to the mocho' way I speak Spanish, have been amusing. Basically, the book has taught me that I speak Mexican redneck. None of the other illegals I've met thought Spanish was my first language. I must've learned English first. In either case, the book isn't helpful, and it doesn't look like I'll get a crack at a desk-top tonight.

The endless supply of anxiety, I've somehow tapped into, makes me fidget. I've funneled it down to my foot, tap, tap, tapping away. My spine warms, hold on, no Cowboy Hat in sight, then why? Now it's getting hot. Whoever or whatever this is, I'm not running this time. Usually I would, but I'm not the same girl I was twenty-four hours ago. There is at least a dozen witnesses if I stand to the left of the stacks. No one stops to look at me, but I know if someone runs at me, they will notice. The large book in my hands can be of use after all, the perfect weapon.

Down the aisle a tall guy with short raven black hair stares me down. Warmth spreads through my body as we size each other up. At least the awful sickness hasn't happened again. He's pretty hot, like Dean Winchester hot. His eyes look violet, though I'm pretty far from him, and that might be a trick of light. His cheek bones fit perfectly above his strong jawline, and his lips are full. The color of his skin is darker than mine, but only a little. His smooth face compliments his clean-cut look.

All this takes me seconds to see, but it's like time has paused, so I can get a better look. A quiet whisper comes from his lips.

"Thank you Fates."

How did I hear that? One side of his lips stretches up in a sly grin.

I have no idea who he is, but the heat on my back is a clue, he has to be Romani. At least he isn't creepy like Cowboy Hat. His fitted T-shirt shows off his firm muscled arms and cuts down to his slender waist. An image of him kissing me flashes in my head. Come on now, I'm not some hormonal girl from a romance novel. *Mind out of the gutter.* To show myself how much control I have I barely glance down at his firm thighs as he walks over.

"Hi, my name is Juda Shea."

His voice is deeper than I imagined. The strange heat warms my back fully with him so close, but no nausea. I need to keep my game face on. His prettiness won't catch me off guard. How had I been found a second time by these people?

"My name is Vivian. I would like some answers." He may not know Cowboy Hat, but I figure there might be a connection. No one's going to push me into another volatile situation. For the first time in my short life, the inner strength to back up that decision straightens my spine. He gestures for us to move towards the exit.

"After you." Flashing him my own sly smile, I follow him to the exit. As we walk that way, I leave the book on a cart and discover that his backside is as firm as his upper body, nice.

We approach a younger boy whose presence adds to the heat on my back.

41

"This is my kid brother, Jared. Why don't we go somewhere we can better converse?" The tall hottie suggests. Okay, no doubt he's a sex pot, and has my heart going pitter patter. But, I can't forget these people cursed me, or something. Reiterating, *game face, game face.*

The brother is also taller than me, everyone is taller than me. He has a different energy to him though. Like he won't let something bad happen to me, no matter what. Okay, I'll go for it, but I want it to be a public place.

The coffee shop across the street, where I'd spent an hour earlier, will work. They agree, and we walk over. Admittedly, I want to walk behind Juda, safety is on my mind, but so are his assets. With Jared here, I can't give into my window watching desires. Which leaves me walking next to them, and settling for sideways glances. All good, this gives me a better view of his full arms and long dark lashes.

There has never been a shortage of cute guys to look at in my life, but there's something about this one. My pulse speeds up and my palms dampen. Strange how much I'm physically craving someone I've only known for five minutes. Taking a deep breath helps me bring myself back down to reality. There's not time for all that. Just answers. As Juda opens the door for me and gives me his sly grin, my traitorous body reminds me it has a say too.

Thankfully, we make it into the café without nudity. Juda offers to pay and I ask for an iced Chai tea and walk away to find a public, yet private enough table. The distance helps me gain further control over my hiked-up lust. Guess all of my emotions are in overdrive. I hope their answers can help me get back to normal, though my normal really sucked. Would it be possible to take this away? I'm so awake and aware in ways I've never been. This curse or whatever it is seems to be emanating from inside me. How could they have changed that? Really how did Cowboy Hat cause that? I hate to admit it, but it's like I've waited my whole life for this.

Funny thing about small Texas towns; some try to be cliché and shut down at dusk, while others went for big city and stay open 24hrs. Luckily, this place had chosen big city, probably due to all the Mexican novella stars that love the town. Sitting across from the two guys, I remember they are two strangers.

This conversation will stay in my court, "Juda and Jared. Has anyone told you that's way confusing?" I smile trying to be friendly.

"It's pretty simple to remember when you know us. But, until then remember, I am Juda, the perfect man and Jared is, just my kid brother." Juda's smile is a little less alluring with that kind of attitude. But his eyes get all bedroomy and I forget to be annoyed.

"What, please, you are only a year and a half older than me!" Jared ruffles his brows at his perfect brother. Ugh, his neck even looks sexy. Like a freakin models. Enough of the pleasantries, time for real talk.

"So Juda, Jared, what exactly is a shifter?"

The two exchange looks and Juda answers, "That's an odd question from a fellow shifter?"

"Excuse me?" He's talking crazy people.

"Vivian, let's assume you really don't know..."

"Okay, yeah do that," I say. Juda looks at me like I'm the crazy people.

"Shifters descend from Europe. Our line has been in the States for a while now. Jared and I are the sons of the shifter king, Sansella Shea, and you are in our territory. All shifters are expected to pay their respects to our father when here." My eyebrows shoot up in my best impression of, WTF?

"King?" The two of them stare at me like I'm speaking Japanese. Okaaaayyyy.

43

"Vivian, how do you know about the shifters if you don't know about the king?" Juda's suspicion is plain on his mug. How quickly cute can become condescending.

Why would I be hiding something here? He and his kind, they're hiding stuff. Both guys tense up in their chairs and watch me closely. Wait, can they sense how pissed I am? All this is aggravating, unfair, and has me shaken. I need a drink from my Chai. The familiar taste reminds me we are still on planet Earth. The younger brother speaks up, and by the look Juda gives him, that's not protocol.

"Hey, I know this all sounds strange, or at least it would if you were someone who just learned you aren't a normal person. If you don't mind me asking, how old are you?"

Okay a normal easy question, "Eighteen."

"Recently?" How would he know that? I am freaking out again and my voice isn't cooperating. My head bobs twice in answer.

"Has anything strange happened since your birthday?" Jared's personality is calming. He truly wants to understand why I'm so clueless.

The lifeless body in the woods fills my head, but I push the image away "Yeah, ok, some things have happened, but I don't want to talk about it."

Pausing, I add, "I was spoken to in a language I didn't know and I felt funny after it, like sick and all confused." A deep pull in my gut makes me stop speaking. I shouldn't share too much of that story, just yet. Okay, I don't know where that is coming from, but I'm gonna go with it anyway.

Juda's face lightens up like he'd figured out a puzzle. He sits back in his chair. "Were some of the words, Vitsa san nav?" Who knew I could be rendered speechless so often.

Juda said the exact phrase as the old man had. Again, I bob my head. If I don't start using my words like a big girl, the two of them may wonder if I've lost it officially over here.

"Yes."

The tall guy leans into the table, closing up the space between us, and sends my pulse into overdrive at the same time. "Then, you're shifter. I get you may not know what that is, that's okay. You're welcome to our compound to stay and eat as you please. Are you looking for permanent lodging or passing through?" His invite is warm enough, but way too soon.

His brother, Jared, rolls his eyes and translates into something more my speed.

"Vivian, it's obvious you've either been kept from your clan, therefore you don't know what we're talking about, or you have amnesia. What my brother is saying, we want to help you. Our Dad-I mean King Shea-will see you and help you recover your family name. He is very connected to all the other vitsa's-oh sorry- clans in America," Jared's sincerity soothes my anxiety. They are serious? Family?

I'm not an American or a Mexican citizen, not that I could prove anyhow. In my orphanage files, there wasn't a birth certificate. There was a police report with my date of birth on it, but that might have been a guess. The report said my mother and father were found in Janos, Mexico, shot to death. 'Hostile drug lord take over,' I read later at the library. That part I try not to think about. Well, the only copy of that is gone, burnt up in a fit of anger at my parents. Would these guys lead me to family? Would they know about me? Maybe the life my father led kept them away?

If I have family...I can't chance it, I need to find out. My chest tightens at the thought.

Looking at Juda first, I ask, "What exactly do you or we shift into?"

45

"Anything that's living. A dog, sheep, goat and if you are strong, larger and smaller animals as well as various human forms."

"You guys can do all that?"

"Well you shift better after you hit adult-hood, but there are some things you can do before, right Jared?"

Jared agrees, but I'm too busy thinking about the knife. Did I do that? The pull in my gut tells me I shouldn't get into that now. Okay, next round of questions.

"How did you know what that guy said? And how did you know where I was."

"Lucky guess."

The air around me thins and I can't breathe for a split second, like the feeling when you stand at the top of a skyscraper, and look down the side.

"Are you lying to me?" I'd spoken my thought before weighing it, too late to worry if I'd offend him.

Jared raises his eye-brows at his big brother. A politician's smile spreads over Juda's face. He sits back in his chair and crosses his arms over his chest. I keep my face blank, poker time, handsome. He exhales in defeat.

"I overheard one of my uncles say he met a female shifter in his territory last night. A bus ride would get you here from there, pretty quickly, so I took a chance it was you. And boy genius over here, tracked you to the library with his web site. I apologize, fair Vivian, I will not underestimate you again."

His words are flirty. Who said 'fair' anymore? None of it mattered, the violet of his eyes lightens, and for some reason I want to touch his hand. Okay, I'm really losing my focus.

I ignore the butterflies in my stomach, and the come hither glance Juda is giving me, and speak to Jared instead.

46

"So, King Shea, your father, will help me find out if there are long lost relatives out there? What's the catch? I've never met anyone who'd help me unless I was paying cash or something is expected of me in exchange."

Jared gives me a nod.

"In our culture, your culture too, it isn't uncommon for an entire family or a single shifter to receive this kind of treatment. To us, all shifters are family. You are welcome."

Juda interrupts his brother, "That's right, and you should know if you are comfortable and decide to stay, there are things you can do to contribute to the compound. Like, help with group chores. We do a lot of meals together. Or you would be able to help in the king's home, if you like. It does take money to run the place, you can work and contribute that way. That's only if you decide to stay, and I hope you do."

He turned down his charm a bit, but when his little brother looks away, Juda winks at me. Ignoring him, and the heat that spread across my skin, I think about their offer. A free place to crash and free food sounds appealing. But the offer to find my clan, family, is what has caught my attention the most. I don't know if I want that.

No, that wasn't right. I don't want to believe my parents wouldn't have made sure I'd end up with 'family', instead of in a Mexican orphanage. The anger threatens to burst out again, but I need to keep my head on straight. This may be a chance to change my life. Into what I don't know. But a chance to find out anything about family is a chance that I want. Plus, free.

"Okay, I'll come for a few days. But I want to be able to leave without question. I'm not used to being in one place and I don't trust anyone, but myself."

Juda smiles, "A true Romani." I hope the answers I got would be worth the extra time I'd be in Texas.

47

"You can be our guest at my birthday celebration."

"Oh, okay. One last question. What do the Romani have to do with all this?" They both laugh at my question, but soon realize I'm serious.

"There's some history behind it, but our kind were part of a faction of people kicked out of their homes thousands of years ago. We have helped one another survive ever since."

"Interesting. So, how many shifters will be at your party, approximately?" I ask Jared and try not to show how freaked out I am over the idea of meeting more of them.

"All the elders, kings and their immediate families. So, a couple hundred." Great, I'd be meeting three times the amount of shifters than I would've had I come a week ago. What would they think of me? Would I be welcomed? I'd spent twenty minutes with these two, and they seemed to be pretty nice. But they aren't the adults. Cowboy Hat didn't seem welcoming. The guys stopped speaking, though I wasn't sure when that had happened.

"Jared, you must be one of the most mature kids I've ever met. You said you're sixteen?"

"Yep, but only for another four months. But you know it's hard to be spoiled when you are literally raised by a village. I mean, getting away with something when you have one mom is easy. Fifteen? Impossible." The guys shared a laugh over the idea. One mom would've been amazing for me.

Okay I need to know some stuff, no more inner freaking out. I can't believe I'm about to ask this next question. "Does that mean vampires are real?" I hope the answer is no.

"There are things out there that are similar, but not exactly Hollywood." Juda looked over at his brother and continued to speak. "Vivian, it's a matter of time before your brain starts to ask the important questions. I don't want you to be by yourself later and not have an answer. Shifters, meaning you, aren't human." Juda's gaze isn't flirty anymore.

"Riiiight." I hope that came across as sarcastic as I'd meant it to be.

"What humans do you know that have a physical reaction when they are in proximity of another human?"

My heart speeds up, okay I mean I do feel the heat but...I guess there's no rationalizing that. The warmth is real. The Chai in my belly is starting to bubble, perhaps a poor choice of drink for such a discussion. But whoever expects to be told you're not human? Jared starts speaking to me, but all I hear is mumbling. I put my head down. Anxiety attack or something similar is happening to my senses. I need to focus on my breathing, and drink some water. Jared is there with a cup of ice water before I can figure out how to ask.

All the noise begins coming back to life around me. "Are we from this planet?" I feel ridiculous asking this. I want to punch something to relieve some of this tension.

"Yes we are, we go back very far in history, but let's talk about that another day. I think you need to eat some of this." Jared hands me a huge oatmeal raisin cookie. It tastes fresh and it helps.

"Okay, yeah, let's not talk about this stuff anymore. I think I've had enough mind blowing information for one night." Possibly for the rest of my life.

Juda offered me a ride in his shiny new truck but I turned him down. I needed to distance myself from the two guys. They are pretty decent and Juda is super-hot, but the time alone is calming. Juda jotted down his cell number and made me promise to call him when I'm ready tomorrow. For now, I'm letting the normal concrete road, street signs, and night sky remind me, I am still myself.

If I were a cartoon drawing, you would see my head deflate with each step. If only I could deny the existence of shifters and kings and being not human. But the memory of the knife made of leaves and mud, and the healing of my body from the brink of death, happened. My body didn't only heal, it enhanced. With every hour since I woke up in the woods, I am stronger. The thought of not being human is too much for me right now, so I'll focus on the things I can accept.

Finding out about the shifter helps me understand why I preferred to be alone and how I lived a life with so little outside connections. As they explained, our 'kind' prefers to live that way. Thinking about it, I have a few personal traditions normal people wouldn't understand. No matter how bad life got, I always found a bed to sleep in, never on the floor. In Mexico, dogs slept on the floor and I was no dog. Sometimes I'd gone for days with no sleep. I suppose some may call that pride. I call it, decency.

Shifters and Romani are a people with no nation. I'm a girl with no family. Which brings back the same old questions like, why would my mom and dad leave me alone? All this frustration, I can't help but cry. Will I ever be able to get over their mistakes? The cooling breeze whistles past my bare arms. With each stoke of the air, I calm down, almost like it pulls away my anxieties. The comfort from the invisible presences is amazing, but not normal. Mental note; ask about that at some point.

The only other reason my parents could've done that was to protect me. This thought makes me stop in my tracks. Where did that come from? I've never thought about that possibility my whole life. The brothers don't seem like some big bad threat. However, Juda's uncle did try to attack me, or at least that's what I thought at the time. Great, now I'm uncomfortable with the idea of heading into their compound. Will other shifters be able to cause stuff like that? My parents must've had their reasons.

50

However, I need to know one way or the other. Okay, I'll keep my guard up with Juda's family and if there are people I belong to, I'll tread lightly with them. Even though my arachnid senses are tingling, I'm gonna go through with the plan. But I can't stay longer than twenty-four hours. In the back of my mind, a small ticking counts down to the moment Mr. AA is found. Those seconds have to count.

The motel loomed around the turn of the road. The neon open sign settles my nerves. Home sweet home. Once in my room the familiarities of the space truly settle the rest of my nerves. There is one table, one chair, and a window unit that furnishes the tight room. Tomorrow I need to buy new clothes and maybe a gift for Juda. Tonight I'm gonna get some rest. I'll need to get as much intel as possible before making a run for the border.

Chapter Six

Father Knows Best

Jared sat outside staring up at the sky. The bench was warm from the sun-light. The spot had once been a park. Coyote attacks thirty years ago brought less and less visitors into the shallow woods. Now all the baseball space had filled in with new trees and tall grass. Jared kept the trail cleared to the only bench still standing. He usually came here late at night and pretended he was someplace else, looking up at the stars in the dark sky.

He loved his family, but he wanted to see the world. He wondered how much of the world Vivian had seen. He was excited that she'd agreed to stay. A very unique situation, outsiders weren't allowed in the compound, unless they were shifter. After all, not just any Romani could be a part of their system since not all of the Roma knew about the shifters.

His best friend and family were allowed in as traveling shifters, but that only lasted a year. David's family had been from the North. Jared had gotten to learn all about snow. The memory of his best friend caused the teen pain. They'd been blood brothers, well spit brothers. Neither of them wanted to cut their hands to perform the gadze oath. David and his parents were killed in a car wreck, leaving Jared to deal with a life of loneliness and under-achievement.

Voices rose from the courtyard, bringing the boy out of his memories. The sensation of his father's magic filled the air. Jared left the bench to investigate.

Juda spoke to their father. They stood in the commons with no one else around. Jared didn't have to see his father's face to know he scrutinized his big brother, causing Juda to fidget his hands that were clasped in front of him.

Luckily the king didn't catch it. Juda quickly laced his fingers tight. The tension poured into the night, making Jared's shifter senses prickle.

Juda explained the conversation at the café. "She was skittish, but honest. She had the right color hair and eyes, I'm sure she was..."

Their father cleared his throat, a sign of his waning patience.

"I am sure she's the one Uncle Joe saw in Brownsville," Juda snapped his mouth shut and looked over, catching his little brother's attention. A silent plea passed Jared's way. The pressure of his father's gaze hit him before their eyes made contact. Jared couldn't remember ever seeing the man and not feeling as though the king graded him on his performance as 'son.'

"Do you have anything to add to this?" The king's voice held power as both of his sons flinched. The big man turned to watch the youngest move next to his brother.

Jared squared his shoulders and spoke clinically. Like the investigators he saw on his favorite criminal investigation show, "Juda is correct, she had all the traits of our vitsa. There are no records about her on the internet." King Shea turned back to his oldest son. Without the heavy glare on him, Jared took deep breathes to calm his pounding heart.

The king looked to the sky and stood still as though he listened to the wind so it may answer his wordless questions. Jared never heard the whispers in the wind, but Juda said he could as successor. After a few minutes, he spoke to them both. Following his brother's lead, Jared stood with his hands clamped behind his back. His shoulders pulled back, giving him a militant look. The position also made concealing any nervous movements easier. His father hated fidgeting more than anything.

"Okay we will honor the invitation. I am disappointed you offered this young shifter asylum with us before taking my council, but the Fates are telling me this blunder is right. Make sure she comes. Watch her. Offer her whatever you need to: money, a car, shelter, whatever you think she would desire. I want you both to get more information from her. She may not have told you everything and if she is one of us, she would not have told you everything on your first encounter. I will talk to your uncles and decide on the next move we make. Is that clear?"

"Yes sir," They answered in unison.

The king nodded once. His scowl cut into Jared for an instant. The look wasn't unfamiliar to the kid. He figured his father blamed him for the mistake. He always did. The shifter king turned and left them without another word.

The brothers both looked at each other. Jared could see the effects their father had on Juda weren't as bad as it was for him. He wondered when his brother had stopped feeling the effects of the king's power. Jared also wondered if the kid would ever be closer to their father? The young man lived in the shadows while Juda prepared to become the successor. These days Jared felt in the way all the time. He'd leave here one day, he promised himself, and turned to go inside the house.

"Hey, wait up," Juda called.

Jared slowed to let his brother catch up.

"What do you think of her? I mean, she seems to be a Dacian, or at least one of the cousins." Juda smiled, which meant he liked her. Of course he did. Juda got whatever he wanted. But Jared didn't really care, he liked Vivian, she was older and mature. He was only a kid to her, nothing more. No, he'd put any romantic thoughts of her out of his head. She would make a good girlfriend for his big brother.

"I think she's pretty, smart, and resourceful. Not like any of the nit wits you've ever dated." Jared laughed as Juda punched him in the arm. Jared would never tell his brother how much he didn't want him to marry the girl their father had picked for him. Callen was Jared's age, but acted as if she was perpetually thirteen. Plus, there were pictures of her on the web. Side shots of a party girl in a group, or hanging on some guy, never a direct shot, but he knew it was her. And if anyone saw them, she'd be tossed out of the clan. Of course she wasn't dumb, each time Jared found one, the next day it disappeared. He got smart and started keeping a secret file of them, in case he needed to run her off someday. Juda deserved better.

They didn't say much else. They'd arrived at the house and Juda left their room to shower. Tomorrow he'd get to see her again. Now that he knew his brother liked her, he'd stay out of the way for him. But some part of Jared was drawn to Vivian. He wanted to protect the girl, which was pretty weird. Jared would have to find a way to do just that, without awakening Juda's competitive nature. Still, she may be into younger guys.

Jared laughed at himself, and lay back to check on the stock exchange from his smart phone.

Chapter Seven

Embracing the Future

"This is your 7 a.m. wake up call." The mechanical recording spoke into my ear.

I'd set up the call the night before. However, the amount of tossing and turning throughout the night, has me wishing I didn't need to get out of bed at all. There is stiffness in most of my limbs, like I'd slept on rocks. A hot shower is in my near future. Maybe if I turn on the TV it will wake me up some more. This early there won't be anything I want to watch, which is good, since I need to get to the mall for my errands. The droning of the morning news does the trick.

The water is soothing to my body, but not my mind. Letting myself pretend that everything said after I left the library isn't real, helps a bit. My denial makes me realize I need to accept this situation. After all, soon I'll meet the rest of the clan. How many did he say are human? *Breathe, just breathe.*

In front of the long mirror, with strange looking stains, I comb my hair and listen to the local anchorwoman talk. In her most desperate sounding voice, she urges anyone to come forward with information on the body found late last night. The young man was found in the woods. The brush stops midway through my hair.

"The police are asking for your help in solving this crime. If you saw anyone hitching a ride, or acting suspicious, off of interstate 77, either heading towards Mc Allen, or the boarder, from Brownsville, with in the last seventy-two hours, please contact our Crime Tip hot-line."

My heart-beat is pounding. Sitting on the edge of the bed, I watch as the camera switches from the reporter to a shot that zooms passed the police tape to the edge of the woods. On the screen is the slow progression of a tow truck pulling Mr. AA's bright red Chevy. A dark car marked "Coroner" pulls onto the highway behind the red truck. The reporter's smiling face flashes back on the screen and continues the story of the body found a few hours ago by hunters deep in the Texas wilderness.

The TV goes off. Instinctively I jump up, ready to run out of the room in my towel. My hand clutched the remote to use as a weapon, and I realize I obviously turned off the TV. Mr. AA's family would soon be notified. They would call each boy from that table and they'd all say the same thing. He left after a girl fitting my description. They would make up a story to cover for their friend. I didn't know if they'd say I left with him willingly or he came out after me and they saw us climb into his red pick-up. For sure they'd say he scored, or he would've come back.

Do I have enough time to get into Mexico now? After all of the shifter/non-human talk, I almost forgot, I'm a fugitive. If I run, I may never get to find out if there is family I belong with. Never get the chance to learn about them. But what if they found out about the fugitive part? *How welcome will I be after that?*

How bad would it be to take one more day? Surely I'd be able to get some information from Juda and his father to guide me in the right direction. Just one day, then I can get out of town and start my own search. I had to consider the offer Juda had made. When would I meet others like them again? Did human rules still apply? That was a dumb question. Of course they applied no matter what I was. However, letting myself get detained by the authorities would be worse than simply being an undocumented illegal. White rooms, and shiny medical instruments, fifty stories underground, might become my new home. Okay I'm freaking out again. I need answers more than anything else.

Whoever my family is, they should be in Mexico where my parents were found. But that doesn't mean I'd be able to find them there. The entire system is so third world. In twenty-four hours, I can get clues, if not exact locations where I can find them. What other choice do I have? One day won't hurt. I hope.

Not stopping to think about it again, I dress. My faded jeans and black gap tee would have to do for this party. Lucky for me, I was able to pick up a two-week supply of contacts when I arrived into town yesterday. The mirror is steamy, a couple of swipes and I can see. But I have to swipe a few more times, as I don't believe my eyes. Really, my actual eyes are blue, but like the guys, there's a small rim of violet around them now. The little change is freaky, but the brown contacts completely covers them, thank goodness.

I don't want to take the chance of shopping at the mall, or wandering around the streets in daylight. My watch says ten 'till nine. This place has a complimentary continental breakfast. Carbs sound good, but first I need to arrange for my ride.

"Hey, it's Vivian." I spoke up before Juda had a chance to get out his hello.

"Great, I'm glad you called. Are you ready?" Anxious much?

"Not yet, I wanted to see if one o-'clock would be too late?" I don't want to seem eager and I still need to figure out his present."

"Yeah, that's fine. Jared will be excited. He couldn't stop jabbering about you on the way home last night." Yes. But did *Juda* give me any second thoughts? Ugh, I'm bad at guyology.

"That's cool. Okay, I'm at the Comfort Inn. Guess I'll see you about one?" Really, that's all I have? Maybe I can find time to buy a low cut fitted dress, cause my mojo is obviously on vaca.

"Okay sounds great, see you in a few hours. Oh and I'm excited you're coming too." He hung up. Okay, some progress. At least one of us can use our mouths correctly. Even in my own head that sounded wrong.

After breakfast I stop by the gas station for a couple of car air fresheners and bottle of car wax. When you live on the road even this place can be a gift shop. My favorite pair of TV brothers, who know way more about the supernatural than I do, taught me that. But I don't care what Dean says, I will never eat convenience store pie.

My watch says 12:48, when I hand it over to the pawn shop guy to sell. I'd seen the small place on my way home last night. It opened early, so I figured I'd stop by and get rid of a few things. Pawn shop shows are some of my favorite late night TV. If I hadn't been so freaked out last night, I might've watched the marathon on cable. This place though, nothing like the places I've seen on the TV shows. Half of the building was dedicated to hunting supplies. Every type of head bust I have ever seen fights for wall space in the room. While I walk out of the door, I notice a little sign that reads, 'taxidermy', of course.

The dark gray of the parking lot is my only distraction. Not enough to keep my mind from pondering the shifter stuff. Besides the not human part, I wonder what rules they live by? I mean, when you can literally change into anything living, which I am still skeptical about, what would stop you from say, robbing a bank every day? Do they have the same concept of right and wrong? Would they have conscience or do what they felt like doing? The black truck pulls up and I know it's time to find out first hand.

Even with a truck window between us, Juda adds heat to my skin and a pulse in a place I'm sure would count as a sin if I went to confession, and was religious. I wonder if my motivation is coming from the need to find family or his handsome smile. Twenty-four hours, no time for boys. As I climb into the seat next to him, his scent, savory and soft like a steak dinner at the ocean, makes me want to add a few more hours.

"Hey, Vivian!" Jared's excitement makes my 'awake,' look like a coma.

"You look nice." Juda says, bringing my attention back on him. A figure of mighty mouse is dangling from his key chain. Seeing the toy makes Juda less formal somehow. He even looks less intense today, damn he's super cute. *No, no boys.*

"Thanks. You look pretty nice yourself." Oh yay, my leisure suit mojo is worse than no mojo. This may get embarrassing fast.

"Here, this is for you, happy birthday." I hold up the clear bag with the convenience store gifts. Juda takes the bag, surprisingly he doesn't make a face at the 'wrapping,' instead he opens the bag and pulls each thing out.

"Awesome. My first truck gifts. Thanks, I really love them." His smile is grateful, with a hint of hot guy added. Is he flirting or thanking me? I am pretty bad at this stuff, I'm gonna go with both.

"Give'em here bro, I'll put them in the seat compartment." Jared says, he's being helpful today. What would life be like with a sibling? What if I have siblings?

"You okay?" Juda asks.

"Yeah, I'm good. Just... meeting people... it's a bit... new. I mean, new people, new, it's difficult and stuff." Please, turn on the radio or something. I sure hope the ride isn't too long. I have no idea why I can't use words today. Thankfully, Jared asks us if we want to jam to a band he'd found last night on the web. I agree quickly, giving Juda no other choice. The ride is much better after that.

***

Nate moved through the partygoers. There were both Roma and shifter children playing a game of chase. Of course some knew the shifters

60

weren't human, but that's the reality they're used to. Like the sky is blue or the dirt is brown. They lived as one here.

The king of their realm tasked Nate to assess the danger once the new shifter arrived. His nephew had offered her asylum. Nate trusted Juda's judgment. Joe had complicated things by trying to force her magic to obey him. Only the eldest of them, the king of the realm, could tap into the source of magic and perform such a spell. The girl reacted to the 'Calling', but then fled. Joe felt bad for his blunder, but not bad enough to say he would vouch for her, which left Nate to do this task.

Nate was certain the Fates had led her here, but that didn't always mean good things. Together, they'd figure out the truth behind the mysterious shifter. The king laid an old spell in Nate's skin to help expedite the situation. Nate knew this kind of magic could be difficult for him to interpret. He'd have to do his best. Joe thought she may be a northern shifter on the run, which meant the 'Touch' should work with no problem.

A loud cheer interrupted Nate's thoughts. Juda entered the small commons area. The small courtyard had lights strung up, which aided him in spotting the little party of new-comers easily. Jared followed the young prince accompanied by a very pretty girl. Nate got the sense of deja vu. He studied every line of her face, trying to place her. His two nephews walked right up to him without Nate realizing they'd arrived through the sea of guests.

"Uncle Nate, you ok? You're all pale like a ghost," Juda laughed and gave Nate's shoulder a little shake. Nate blinked and looked at his nephew. Juda's words sunk into his conscious. Nate thought, '*Ghost... dead... she was dead. How is it that she's standing right in front of me?*' He found her eyes again. No violet rims on the brown iris, but this girl could be his sister. A deep wound reopened in his heart.

"Uncle Nate? Ah, this is Vivian." Jared did the introductions.

Nate smiled at the trio. Was it possible that much time had passed? Maybe her father's eye color effected the usual Dacian violet color?

The uncle spoke, "My apologies. I was lost in thought. I'm Nathanial Shea. Vivian, you said? Nice to meet you." He called to the magic as his arm came up, hand extended for the greeting. To his surprise she shook it, not very smart for a shifter. Skin to skin the images started to flash in his mind. A shadow, a woman with long bushy hair walked into the room. She was almost in view then the image blurred and went away completely. Nate was alone in his head once again. *Had she done that?* Vivian dropped her hand, but made no other move to indicate she'd felt the spell.

Juda eyed his uncle who turned and made his way into the main house, not uttering another word. She definitely didn't know about their magic. Any shifter who knew their heritage would've taken offense to it being done on them without their consent.

Juda noticed the human Romani smile and nod to her. They did what they did with all shifter folk; they gave her space and respect. Traditions were the glue that kept them linked as Romani and shifter. Vivian had a strong connection to the magic. Juda could sense this now. The great Aunts appeared around her and led her to the buffet. The girl was a beauty. Destiny brought them together. In this hidden kingdom he'd gotten everything he wanted, and he wanted her. The prince thanked the Fates.

Juda needed to know more about her before he'd let his infatuation grow. He laughed, and shook hands, and let her wander in and out of his people. The king would figure out her true colors. He hoped they were the same shade as his.

Chapter Eight

Callen

The skies were purple and red with the sinking sun. Callen and her crew pulled into the compound. Six years had passed since she'd spent time with Juda. King Shea had told her the invitation to live in his vitsa was standing. Her whole life she'd expected to marry Juda, but six years ago that had changed.

Juda rejected the idea of marrying someone so young. Tradition said they should have wed by the time he'd turned thirteen. Callen's connection to the magic made her the best choice for Juda. Usually the first-born married one another, but Callen's sister, Danya, could barely shift.

At the age of eleven Callen had come to King Shea's compound to marry Juda. He'd somehow gotten the king to postpone everything until he turned eighteen. Of course, he technically would be eighteen for a full ten human years. If he was still being an ass, she may have to wait awhile.

In a vision the Fates said Callen could change everything. She'd seen herself as queen, but there had been blood on her hands and her clothing was tattered. Danya had thought the dream a bad omen, but not Callen. She didn't mind treading through hardship, or getting a little blood on her hands to get what she wanted. She may even have a little on them now, but that wasn't what she wanted to focus on tonight. No she'd developed a plan after that dream. And tonight it would all start falling into place perfectly.

First, she'd gotten her father to speak to his brother, King Shea. The king agreed it was time for his son to accept the arrangement. Next, she'd sent one of her third cousins to the compound last summer. She'd reported all about what kind of girl Juda would 'date', aka, do the poke and run with. Every one of them had long hair, soft curves and a tough, can-do attitude. The last one had been Callen's specialty for years now.

Her small breasts had grown into a C cup, and her straight hips had some curve now. Most of it was natural. The last thing the young shifter did was learn to alter her body with the magic.

She'd been deflowered the day she'd come home after Juda rejected her. The boy was gadze and easy to lure. The next morning King Shea had called and said the marriage would happen, but not until Juda was eighteen. Callen had to 'fake' virginity. The best part about that was all the practice it took to really get that down. Callen had only used gadze for her affairs, her way of jabbing at Juda's rejection, even if he'd never know. Eventually, she'd found a few shifters willing to chance the eldest king-to-be finding out. But even they believed she was still a virgin. That's how good she'd gotten.

The long drive made Callen's muscles tight, but once the earth settled under her bare feet, she relaxed. She shook with desire. Callen knew the ceremony was for Juda tonight, but she hoped the king would announce their engagement and make it official. The eldest son of the eldest son would have a swarm of girls attracted to him, like mosquitos to blood. When the power passed down from the eldest, the successor practically glowed as he came into the direct connection of the magic.

Callen could taste it in the air. Instead of pushing her weight around, she'd be sly and make sure she was all that Juda could want or ever desire.

"Callen, do you want to take our bags into the rooms now or wait until after the party?" Her cousin Gonya asked her from the opposite side of the car. Her plain brown hair that needed a trim badly, hung to her middle back. This cousin was so dense, if Callen didn't pick out her outfits, the girl probably would wear a potato sack. But she was only fourteen, easy to manipulate, and Callen truly cherished that in her servants. At least she wasn't fat.

"I don't care if you take the bags in at three o'clock in the morning. It's your job so long as I have my things when I wake up." Callen let her newfound authority add an edge to her words. The girl was such a lackey. Callen had bigger things to occupy her this weekend.

For example, the Great Aunts who stayed with the king's vitsa, known for their wisdom and sticking their nose in things. They'd been run out of her compound years ago for throwing the evil eye at her while in her crib. She hadn't bothered speaking to them when she'd spent the summer here and she wouldn't bother now. As soon as she was queen, those hags would have to go. She had to concentrate on locking her prince down. Gonya started piling the bags a few feet from the car. Callen turned from the girl and moved more into the last rays of sunlight.

The entitled little shifter stretched and threw her head forward, scratching her fingers over her scalp to get the hair to move. She flipped her head, and the thick hair landed out over her shoulders, clear down to her lower back. The golden brown hair came together to form soft layering curls that encircled her slender waist. The hair was almost glistening in the waning sun rays; a side effect from pulling the magic into her form for enchantment. Not that she had to use the magic that much, but with it, her beauty out shined all others. Even the gadze noticed her. Attention fed the young shifter. She couldn't get enough.

"I think we are going to have an amazing time tonight, especially when the king gives you and Juda his blessings," Tannie said as she emerged from the VW Beetle. She was Callen's other cousin. Tannie had the shape of an adolescent boy with bright red hair. Callen would never admit to her jealousy of her natural beauty, especially the vibrant color of her hair. Both her cousins would get a chance to marry one of the boys from their uncle's vitsa. But they knew she'd be the queen of them all. Callen made sure they never forgot.

"You are right cousin. I suspect Juda will be pleased with his father's choice. I'll need an hour after the Naming to make sure he's very pleased." Both girls laughed, until the last passenger got out of the car, the daunting older sister, Danya.

"Do not speak of the betrothal. The king did not say he'd be announcing anything. Our father called us here. Come on, let's get our bags and get settled into our rooms before the party." Danya stepped close to Callen, out of the earshot of the other two. "There will be no sex or sexual favors before you wed, rakli," The older sister walked off, her rolling luggage in tow.

Callen smiled at her sister as she passed. She was thankful Danya agreed to come. Though most people saw her as a stick-in-the-mud, Callen needed her influence. Soon however, Danya would learn her real place, at Callen's back, not her side. Now wasn't the time to ruffle her sister's stiff feathers. She needed all three girls in her corner.

A few quick steps brought Callen to her sister's side. "You're right Danya, of course. I'm blessed to have you." If Danya had only known the secrets that her little sister kept, she'd probably help them carve the symbol of exile on Callen's forehead.

The other two caught up to them. The four girls walked up the dirt road towards the rooms that was prepared for them hours earlier. Callen pulled at the floating energy that the compound offered up to her. She plotted how she would play this out. With every step, her confidence grew and perverted itself into superiority. Things would change fast once she became queen.

Chapter Nine

Girl Fight

Juda's uncle had been the only weird thing about the compound, so far. Everyone in the small makeshift town gathered in the commons. I guess that name works for the large circular outdoor area. Huge slabs of different colored cut stones, some dark brown, others more garnet, but the majority pale gray, paved the dirt ground. Hanging lanterns and colorful flowers had been arranged around an ancient fountain. The fountain is made of various broken pieces of shiny stone, making a nice center piece for the space.

White Christmas lights ran across from building to building, making a blanket of tiny stars like a large enchanted bubble. Men with various instruments play at the opening to what looks like a large field. I count five in the band. All of them play string instruments and the music is magical. Any minute I expect elves to come out of the bushes and dance.

People give me nods and warm expressions of welcome when I walk past them. The joy they all share seems normal but to me, unnerving. Of course I have the family values of a nomad, so who am I to judge? A soft hand of one of Juda's elder relatives tugs me towards the food area. Paper flowers and bright tablecloths cover the tables, which are set end to end. There are five, ten-foot-long rows. Each loaded with every kind of food you can imagine. The rhythmic music has the kids and the adults swaying and clapping their hands. My elder escort guides me to the closest picnic style table and I sit. Two more elderly women appear. The three of them speak in their native tongue, and I do my best to try and understand their words.

A plate of food is put in my hands by one of the elders. The smells of potato salad, beans and what looks like BBQ chicken chunks, float up to my nose. The women move about running off anyone else at the table. Instead of facing the table, I balance my plate on my legs and pick at the food. The women hover over me, speaking to each other. From the corner of my eye, I see one using her pointer finger to write in the air above my head.

The ladies or Great Aunts as some of the others say to them in passing, speak to each other now, which gives me time to do some people watching. The differences between human and non-human are starting to stand out. A little under half of the people are humans. Their eyes are normal brown. Others have a faint hew of violet light that circle their iris, just like the brothers, and my own under my contacts.

My spine had warmed when we approached the commons earlier. After Juda's declaration of the physical reaction around one another, I figured this is the normal sensation. With so many shifters, the tingling morphed into a steady glow at the base of my spine.

The Aunts move into a semi-circle in front of me. I look up and give them a smile. They'd caught me zoning out. They stand shoulder to shoulder, blocking out the party, that I have no choice but to give them my full attention. One says something in Romani, and the other responds, then they look down at me again. None of the words make since. The smell of lilacs wafts towards me from the three Aunts. I hadn't noticed the scent earlier.

"Are you married child?" Lady White would be a good name for this women. She is soft spoken and reminds me of freshly fallen snow.

Not waiting for me to respond, the next question is asked by the lady to her right, "Do you want to marry?" This one has lovely soft caramel skin. She's younger looking than the other two. Her thin straight, graying, blond hair adds the look of sunbeams to her appearance. I will call her, Lady Blond. Again the next speaks before I get a chance to respond.

"Oh no, you have no time for it at all, you must be fierce if you want to survive." She is the boldest of the three. Her frame, much like my own, is small with curve to her hips. But her hair color is solid black and her skin has touches of softness from age. Yes, I like Lady Bold for her.

The three women speak Romani again, each looking at me then back at each other. Their lovely perfume smells stronger. A sense of calm relaxes me. Concentrating on the conversation gets difficult since their voices are hypnotic and soothing. Their bickering makes me want to laugh.

"He is worthy!" Lady Blond says.

"No, the Fates have much invested! Maw! She is not meant to wed," Lady Bold says, her words affect the other two like lighting.

"Oh pecan pie, my favorite," Lady White says, choosing to irritate the other two by ignoring their comments. My giggles draw all three sets of eyes.

"Do you understand us, child?" Lady Blond asks.

"Sort of, I'm not sure what you're talking about, but it's funny to hear you guys disagree." I'm kinda of wobbly, like I've downed a six pack of Lone Star. Strange, I can't hear the band or the crowd anymore? More laughter escapes my mouth. Their hands descend on me, touching my hair and arms. All three speak soft thanks to the Fates. I hear that a lot, I think I'll ask Jared what that means. A little hiccup leaves me, ending my giggle fit.

"The gift will be permanent by the full moon." Gift? Wait, they're speaking Romani. I can understand Romani?

My gut fills with butterflies, there's more to these people than I bargained for. My back hits the table in an effort to get some space from them and their strange smell.

"No child, don't be scared," Lady Blond says.

Lady Bold picks up the line. "You are in a place where much can be taught, but little is learned. Pay attention with your new ears."

69

My blinking responses have come back. The air is too thick to breathe. Sweat beads up on my forehead. Thankfully, the lilac odor disappears, along with my buzz.

A sigh moves past my ears, but it's not from the women. The air around us becomes less dense and the music and conversation start once more. I hadn't realized we'd been in our own bubble of sorts. Between the soft bodies of the elder women, I see blurred images of the party goers. We slide through time. Each party goer moves faster and faster the noise louder and louder. Then, we are a part of the world, again. All my strange physical reactions are gone. I'm perfectly normal.

Lady Blond places a full bloomed violet orchid, trimmed with white, into my hair. "You are a daughter and should be proud, even if others only see what their clouded minds hate." A jolt of surprise clears the rest of the fog from my head. Hate? She reaches down and takes my uneaten food.

Lady Bold pulls me into a standing position, not giving me time to freak out further. She's a good foot shorter than me. Placing her hand on the flat part of my upper chest she says, "You are the coming, the going, and the path. I am giving you our bond to keep you when your heart aches for love."

Intense cold fills my body, radiating from her fingers. As it sinks into my skin, it turns into warmth. That warmth fills the hollowness that I've learned to tolerate my whole life. I know I'm not complete, but it's the closest I've ever been. My head bows with the odd sensation. When I raise it again, they're gone. The murmurs of the people around me aren't only strange sounds any longer. I can understand each person.

Through the crowd the tall handsome Juda stands out. His perfectly dark, combed hair makes him even easier to spot. I hadn't realized I could be so attracted to the clean and neat look, but this guy wears it very well. A few people move and clear the view which gives me a better look. Strong legs, flat stomach, leading up to his large chest, and he's staring at me.

Opps, okay that's not embarrassing. Thankfully I spot Jared who turns his head in time to wave me over. He's not far from Juda. I let my legs lead me towards the teen. Jared is pulled away to dance with some girls, he looks at them with a silly boy grin. I can't help but smile, halfway through the crowd now, I come to a stop. Juda steps in front of me, making me jump a little.

"Hey," He says. He's so much taller than I am. He looks at me closely and asks, "What's with the flower?" The party-ers are pretty loud, so we are about an inch away from one another.

"A trio of ladies gave it to me." He smells like cloves. "They were like seriously old school. I felt like I was in a black and white European movie or something." I never thought a real guy could look this perfect, even his eyebrows are neat. I try not to look too long into his eyes, but I do just that. His sly smile shows back up. My hands fidget with the hem of my shirt. A good distraction for them, otherwise I may lose control and start to molest the guest of honor.

"Ahh yeah, the Aunts, they're a little pushy, but they mean well," He says, and then extends his palm in a gesture for us to walk. I follow him towards a house that's backed up to the commons, letting him lead me there by my arm at times, through the party goers. His little touches are driving my pulse up.

"I suppose you are feeling it by now?"

"Feeling?" We've almost cleared the edge of the party.

"This is the first time you are near this many shifters. The magic intensifies for shifters the closer they are to one another. And of course, the elders and the king are all here. I think I could hold up a light bulb and it would light up in my fingers." I thought about that. Physically I only had the warming of my back, but nothing else. There's a little tug at my gut, I'm guessing I shouldn't admit to that.

"At first it was weird. I can't deny it's like nothing I've ever experienced before. Amazing, but strange." There is no lie in that statement. A subject change would be best though.

Jared steps up, flopping an arm across both our shoulders. Doing his best Joe Cool impression.

"S'up?" I can't stop the laughter that comes out, but Juda shrugs the kid's arm away. If Juda wasn't grinning, I'd be protesting that move. I like the teenager; he's growing on me.

Jared however didn't take the grin as serious as the shrug. He put both arms at his sides and continued to speak sounding formal and robotic.

"Dat says we need to start heading towards the court, and to bring Vivian too." With that he turns and walks off. From the look on Juda's face, his brother's reaction doesn't faze him. There's no way I can figure out their family drama, after all how much experience do I have? I can only assume its brother stuff, for now.

We come to a stop next to the brown house we'd been walking towards. From inside the house, we can hear women's voices, and the sound and smell of food being prepared. More food? How long would this night go?

Juda leans into the wall of the brown house and crosses his arms. I face him, though I'm a good foot away, enough to not invade his space, but also not seem uninterested in invading his space. A girl steps in between us. All I see is her long curly hair and small waist.

"Hey Juda, I've been looking for you everywhere!" Without letting him speak she throws her arms around his neck, and presses every part of her body on his. Up until this moment I thought my crush was pretty small. But seeing Callen all over him has me straining to keep myself from getting a hand full of her curls and tossing the skanky girl onto the ground.

A sense of someone watching this nightmare makes me look over to see three more girls standing there with hard glares directed at me. Two of them are pretty homely looking, plain brown hair, and average height. One has bright red hair, she's tall, and looks plain but very pretty. My muscles grow tight, and a strange sensation in my gut flares to life. The skin on my arms tingles. I have no idea what this means, but I get the sense it's a shifter reaction. All three pairs of eyes are staring me down.

"Callen, I didn't know you were coming." He sounds genuinely surprised. His hands are up in the air at first, but then pat her back for a few seconds. "Oh hi, cousins, so glad you could make my birthday party." Juda moves out of Callen's octopus's tentacles. As he walks over to greet the other three girls, Ms. Bitch turns to face me. I step back from the nasty odor of coffee breath.

"You can go now. He doesn't have to settle when he's got all this." She gestures towards her tiny body. She's less than 100 pounds. Her slim body reminds me of a teenage boy, which make her boobs look fake and her hips swollen, rather than full. I must admit though; her hair is perfect. Long, shiny and wispy, all good signs it will catch fire easily. Our exchange has only taken a few seconds. The look that settles on her face screams, "Peasant."

Juda turns towards us, finished with the more appropriate hugging and greeting of his family. Callen's stiffens as he strides over and stands next to me, closer than earlier, I notice.

"Cousins, this is my friend Vivian, she is a new shifter to our compound. Actually, Callen and Danya are sisters." He gestures towards one of the plain girls, the taller of the two. But I don't care about them, for some reason his introduction of me leaves a sense of awkwardness.

73

Wasn't I more? Of course that's crazy talk. Why would I be, we barely met and he's not my anything. However, Callen's nasty glare, makes me determined to change that by the second.

"Oh hi!" she exaggerated the "I" like she's talking to a child. "I didn't see you there, so nice you are visiting the compound. When do you leave?" Her pearly white smile reminds me of a shark. Juda doesn't notice the jab in her greeting. 'Bitchy girl' is difficult for guys to clue into.

I give her the same smirk I'm getting. I can play that game. Standing straighter I answer her with the same mean girl tone. Thank goodness TV land does 'bitchy girl' characters by the truck loads.

"I'm sure you didn't see me in all your excitement to get to the birthday boy!" I nudge him with my side, he looks at me, brows questioning. "So you guys are family?" I say 'family' in a way that also says, incest much? Establishing that her queen-assiness is acting all Alabama over her own cousin, gross.

But instead of the anger I'd anticipated, my statement makes all four girls laugh. My eyes catch Juda's. He's starting to see the match in front of him. Not wanting to show my confusion, I simply keep the innocent grin on my face. Inside, my pulse picks up, I exhale through my nose to let out some of the steam, but the prickles on my skin intensify.

"Yes, Vivian, we are related." Callen shakes her head and crosses her arms. My skin crawls as I get her meaning. "But so was his parents, and my parents and all of our parents, as was yours, if you are a shifter?" The superior C U Next Tuesday look is back on her face. If you're going to use bad grammar, don't do it outside of your own head.

She steps closer to Juda, and straightens out his already straight collar. Cocking her head to the side she says, "Juda are you sure this one is what she says she is?" The chorus of evil girl laughter gets louder. Danya's eyes burrow

through me, she's sizing me up. The sight of the three strangers laughing, and
Juda letting 'mufasa hair' paw at him, has brought my anger right up to the
surface. I step from foot to foot and cross my arms. Seeing my reaction, Juda
reaches up and removes the bitch's hand.

"Callen, Vivian was not raised by our kind. She just found out what
she is." His stern look makes her lean back, the others also read his tone. This
stops the laughter, leaving only sly smiles on their faces meant for me. He's
trying to help, but in their eyes, I've become the main target.

"Oh! You poor thing! How wonderful of the king to take in the little
orphan shifter."

Callen glides over towards me, and I put my arms down ready to
defend myself. "I am sure he will find out ALL about you soon and send you
on to wherever it is you BELONG," she snarls at me.

Juda is behind her and can't see the "come on hit me" look I'm getting.
I want to punch her puffy pink lips, but I don't like the four to one odds. Guys
never get in girl fights, which means Juda won't back me up. Jared might, but
he's not here.

Her eyes lightened to a glowing purple and her face shifts. The top of
her brow sinks, both eyes grow three times their normal size and became sold
black, and her teeth lengthen into a needle smile. My arms tighten and my legs
press into the dirt refusing to attack or back down. She won't win that easily.
The flesh of my body tingles, I'm not sure why I think it, but I sense the skin
awaits my command to shift.

"Boys and girls let's get to the court. Now." The man is big, older and
somehow familiar. His presence stops the showdown like that. Callen's usual
man-ish face returns, and she turns away with a wink at Juda, making sure I
can see. All four of the girls walk towards the man. Callen's sashay is like a
slutty stripper.

"Hi daddy, let me walk with you." She slinks to the tall man's side, that's when I realize he looks similar to Juda's uncle, Nate.

Rolling my eyes would give me no relief. Maybe if I threw something at the back of her perfect head I'd feel better. Of course, that wouldn't get me the answers I came here for, nor make Juda happy. Attacking someone's family never ends well, even the low life ones.

As usual, Juda senses my irritation, "Shall I escort you, my lady?" He does a little bow and motions towards the trees that the skank gang disappeared into. The lava in me cools, and the night breeze soothes my skin further. There aren't enough pills in the world to handle these mood swings.

Chapter Ten

A Happy Birthday for a Change

The complete darkness is easier to see through with my new shifter vision. I'm not sure when I will get used to this being non-human, but seeing normally at night is pretty cool. The path is too small at times to stay arm-in-arm, so I let Juda take lead. He weaves through low hanging branches and brush. I stick close to his heels. A burning torch appears, then another. The dirt path gets wider.

Why hide this illuminated pathway thirty feet into the woods? Juda reaches over and grabs my hand, extinguishing my angst. My inner feminist is disappointed at how easily his hand calmed my nerves.

The trail makes a severe left. As we follow, a large opening comes into view. On each side, flames flickered from the wide mouths of big, metal barrels. Nine-foot tall metal walls shoot out into the forest on either side of the opening. As we pass them, I can't see a gap between the walls and the trees, it's like the walls have grown from the trees themselves. This place is ancient. The forest has claimed it as its own. We step past the doorway. He pauses. I assume so that I can take in the scene.

The clay-floor catches my attention because its rust color is vibrant. The space is about the size of a football field. Mismatched, faded bleachers, line the edges of the field, shrinking its circumference, but not quite hiding the piles of old junk cars stacked along the walls. The bleachers are colored in silver, blues, oranges, and reds, making them contrast with each other. The only light comes from the tiki torches and barrels that are scattered across the field. I can't see the metallic walls behind the cars and bleachers, but I know they are there.

Shifters of all ages stand in small groups around an empty stage, a few sit on the bleachers. There must be a hundred of them, no humans this time.

77

The usual heat comes, but instead of only heating my spine, it flies over my entire body giving each cell a burst of energy. This must be what Juda had meant earlier. The space doesn't seem that tiny now. Instead it's getting larger as the life in every shifter becomes a flicker of the energy pulsing through my body.

My hand in Juda's grip gets warmer. The connection to one of my, own shoots straight into my core. The energy gives me the impression that I can push, or pull the energy between us. Not sure how or why I know that. My curiosity gets the better of me. Thinking only to push and not take any of Juda's energy, I focus on the tip of my middle finger. Imaging a small wave move between us, I let the energy flow. Juda jumps and pulls his hand away.

"Oh! Did you feel that? I think you shocked me? That was weird." He rubs his hand. I almost laugh and ask him how I did it, but my gut tightens before the words can come out. To cover my own shock, I smile up at him letting some of my crush show in my eyes. His sly smile lightens up his face, and he moves to grab my hand again. Someone in the crowd calls to Juda, saving me from figuring out what I'd do if he was going for first base.

The people shake his hand and greet him, but never try to stop him with conversation. Not wanting to slow him down, I let his hand go and walk slower to stay out of the way. There are faces I didn't see in the commons. Many give me strange looks. Some grin pleasantly; others have open curiosity on their faces, but a few give me hard glares. They make me speed up my step, so that I don't lose Juda to the crowd completely.

A large black curtain runs along all sides of the stage. The platform sits in the center of the space. The curtain turns at a set of stairs set up to the left of the stage and continues for several feet, making a private area next to the stage itself. Juda's uncle Nate is standing at the opening, reminding me of a night club bouncer. Juda turns in his uncle's direction. I stop a few steps away to respect their privacy. Knowing I'm in a crowd where no one was human, not even me, is freaky. I understand every word being spoken around me. Impossible not to eavesdrop, but the Aunts wanted me to listen for a reason. Not looking at anyone in particular, I wait for Juda's return, and let my new ears listen.

"That is the one, look she is standing alone there. See? King Joe saw her first," a woman's voice says. Of course, you know us girls: we love the gossip.

Another raspier sounding woman speaks up, "She is the right age? Could it be her?" The din of noise swallows up the rest of her words. What was I the right age for?

"Her eye color is strange, must be contacts…"

"I think she is part northern shifter."

"Can you believe her mother? Leaving her to live such an impure life! It's disgusting. Look at her. Following Juda around like she's good enough for our prince. If I catch her alone, I am going to…"

"Hey, you havin' fun yet?" Jared appears next to me, making me jump. I don't know who said that, but I would really like to know what they plan on doing.

"Sure, I guess. What's happening next? Ritual sacrifice?" I laugh, but after hearing some of the others around me, that's not as funny as I thought.

He raises his brows and steals my move with a long eye roll. I can't let one bad egg shake me up, right? In case, I'm gonna stick with the guys for now.

Juda comes over. My awkward moment cut short, until he says, "You're going on stage with me."

No time to protest. He's pulling me forward and Jared pushes from behind. This isn't what I signed up for. The whispers are becoming full blown conversations as I'm rushed to the steps. I can't keep from going up, may as well climb the steps with what little dignity I have left, after being herded by the brothers. Both guys laugh as I make a show of jerking away and climbing ahead of them.

As I ascend, I notice the stage is made of large cubs of crushed cars that are shoved together and covered by mismatched dark rubber mats. The platform has to be less than ten feet above ground. The strange stage is twenty feet wide and thirty feet across. A large high-backed chair made of ancient wood sits center stage, flanked by different types of chairs, all modern folding chairs, on either side.

The tallest one must be for the shifter king. The royal seat isn't all padded and fancy like I've seen on TV, but more like a chunk of an old tree. Uncle Nate comes over and leads me to the chair on the right of the throne. He sits on the chair next to the one I'm standing in front of. Butterflies migrate to my stomach. Without moving, my eyes pass over the throne, my seat is right next to Juda's father. Nothing I can do now. Following Nate's lead, I sit.

Okay, I can do this. Looking out at the arena, I see the entire arena of shifters has made their way to the stage. Unfortunately, the first person I spot is Callen and her coven of bitches. The little bit of residual anger from our encounter, burns up the rest of my stage fright. Juda steps up to the other chair left of the throne. His father would be between us, my nerve wavers. He gives me a wink and smile. The troops of butterflies whirl around in my stomach, as I take a deep breath.

Nate gets to his feet and grabs my elbow, making me stand and face the steps with him. A man who looks like an older Juda climbs onto the steps. The shifters closest to him bow. He waves at the crowd. Some people applaud and others stand with their right arm folded across their chest, fist to shoulder. Nate does this and bows his head.

This must be the shifter king. His head snaps towards me as if he hears my thoughts. I give him a feeble smile. The square jaw and strong facial features make the man easy to accept as royalty. I've seen lots of TV kings, but this man's presence emanates, Royalty. He has on a dark gray button up shirt, black slacks, and lace-up dress shoes, every hair in place, but no flashy jewels or crown. His thick black hair complements his thick black eyebrows. This is where Juda gets his looks. Like his eldest son, he's in shape, not too many muscles but enough to show he works out. The nearer he gets, the more the air smells musky. I don't know if I should salute, curtsy or drop to my knees with my forehead on the rubber mat.

If Nate wasn't holding my arm, I might try and hide behind him to escape the king's fierce gaze. Other men follow behind the king onto the stage and move to their seats. They all have similar features; brothers.

Without breaking eye contact, King Shea stops right in front of me. The weight of his gaze threatens to send me running around and screaming like a lunatic. Instead, I pull my shoulders back and absorb his intensity.

He looked closer, "Sister?"

The crowd took a collective breath. Cries of shock echo in the arena. The members of his contingent step one way or another to gaze at me.

"My name is Vivian." The tingling I experienced earlier on my skin, my magic I now realize, blooms up from the center of my body. Each muscle is alive with it and making me one big conduit ready to disperse some energy. Very cool, but scary.

"Vivian." The air pressure near me gets dense. Something unseen brushes my cheek. "Your eyes are different from hers. Please allow me to take your hands." No way did I want this big bad shifter king touching me, but the argument won't leave my lips. His presence washes a sense of safety over my frayed nerves. I've come all this way for answers. The warmth in my chest intensifies as his hands come towards me. The Aunt's gift is there, stopping a sea of emotions. Why had he called me sister?

"Okay." Taking a deep breath, I lift up my right hand. The direct connection will probably knock me down, but I can't go back on my word. His hand closes around mine, then he closes his eyes. There's no big burst or shock so I relax a bit. The king lifts my other hand, then brings them to his face and breathes in the scent of my skin. A burst of heat and a strong odor are in the air between us, making me shut my eyes. The wind picks up and a soft whistling passes my ears. All the sounds of the night cease, drowned out by the pressure of her voice.

"Brother," the woman's voice whispers making my flesh prickle. "Daughter, my love..." This time the whisper is next to my right ear. The familiar sound sends my heart to my feet. Tears are streaming down my cheeks. I've lost my poker face. My warmth in my chest is back, chasing away the grief. The wind dies down, but as it goes, her last words tickle my ear.

"Leave here my child."

When my eyes open, the king's back is to me. He must've been speaking to the crowd for a few seconds already; I tune in for the rest. He addressed them in their native tongue.

"Today is a great day! Thank you all for being here to witness my son's Naming, and the return of lost blood we thought dead." Trying not to look at the crowd or the king, I spot Cowboy Hat, thick cream blazer in place, closest to the steps. His presence spikes my blood with adrenalin. Everything in me says to leave, just like the voice had said. Instead, I turn my face towards the night sky.

Tears run down my cheeks. Is she hovering in the air around me, watching? There's a slight pressure against my skin that lingers. Swallowing the cool, night air, I try and focus on the warmth in my chest, letting the spell dull out the shock and pain.

"Vivian?" My eyes open, his arm is extended out, hand stretched towards me. "Come, stand by me." Letting the king lead, I step center stage.

He starts speaking again, this time in English, "Clan, you are witnessing a true miracle. Twenty years ago, our beloved sister, Aishe, was taken. Tricked into leaving her home and the people who loved her. But today, her flesh and blood returns to us!" He'd said my mother's name. This man was really her brother?

Both his palms come up to my face.

"She told me in her own words, if only you had heard her. She's happy we've found you."

He spoke next to the crowd. "From this day forward she is a part of this clan as long as she lives the pure life and follows our traditions. We are hers, and she is ours. You shall know her as Viv Shea Dacian." Cheers erupted from the crowd. Shocked, the thought hits me: they are my family.

Chapter Eleven

Family

He didn't think I'd heard her, and he'd lied. My mother had only spoken one word to him. If the king had heard her words to me, I don't think he'd be this welcoming. No one had said he had the strongest magic, but being next to him and knowing what I'd been told about him, I doubt he has any equal. So, if I can feel, see and hear things that he can, and can't, what does that mean about me?

My shaky hand wipes my tears away. I'm hoping the others think I'm crying because of being reunited with family. Heat moves up my temples to my forehead, the anger is barely controllable. How could they know I existed and never try and locate me? Now my world has shattered into a million new questions. Losing it in front of all these people, family or not, would be seen as weakness. I can't afford that. The anger at least chased away the grief, but I take a few deep breaths to help my temper simmer.

My eyes fall over Callen who's standing with her arms crossed. Her evil girl stare down, looks way worse with the shine of the deep violet glowing from her irises. One of my eyebrows rises in response to her silent threat. I wink and let a little sly smile spread over my face. She turns and pushes past her minions towards the exit. That was easy.

Nate approaches me, bows his head to the king, and then escorts me back to the steps. Passing Juda, the familiar tingle starts. Wait. He's my cousins? Oh man, I'm lusting over my cousin?! My stomach rolls at the image of webbed feet and hands on babies I hadn't thought of having. He has to know our flirtationship is over, but Juda's expression says 'mine.' My heart speeds up, but I reprimand myself for enjoying the thought even for a second.

Callen had said family marries family, but I've seen way too many HBO shows to know, inbreeding can never be good, even for supernaturals. Sadly, there will be no fueling the flames I'd seen in Juda's glare. This is going to be difficult.

Cowboy Hat steps in my path, blocking my exit. Juda's Uncle Joe held out his hand, palm raised, in an invitation to help me down the stairs. He's not that scary for a guy who'd almost attacked me.

"I deeply regret our first meeting. Can we start again?" His flat voice gives me little indication of his emotions, but his words seem genuine. Not wanting to make a scene, I take his hand and let him lead me the rest of the way.

"Viv, I am pleased you found your way home," His voice is monotone, but somewhat pleasant. After we get to the bottom, his head tilts slightly in fare well, then he turns and walks back to his position on the stage. He couldn't have known what he drove me to that night. Maybe I would've been taken by Mr. AA or fooled into a one-night-stand, regardless. He'd given me the power to save myself from death. His actions led me here, to family.

Each face in the crowd is different now. They're all my family. Why did my mother tell me to leave? What am I missing?

Jared waves to me from the middle of the crowd. It's easy to spot the lanky boy over the rest of the shifters. As I walk to him, the men pat my shoulders, and women hug me, but a few looks give me the impression that something's not right. Maybe I'm too used to being alone to decipher their true meaning. At least I'm not getting the death stares. Really, if it were me in their shoes, I wouldn't tell the strange new girl everything. If I leave tonight, I'd be able to get across the border before daylight. Wrestling between happiness, grief and anxiety, I make a decision to let the night play out and make my move in the morning.

I arrive next to Jared in the center of the crowd. Juda would be able to see us clearly from the stage. The majority of people closest to me openly gossip about my return in their language.

"If she's returned, what happened to her mother?" Sweat beads form on my temples.

"Do you think she's truly shifter blood?" There's a flip in my gut and I swallow down my anxiety. Jared leans over and nudges my arm, like a puppy wanting attention. His thick brows scrunch together and he sticks out his tongue. We both giggle until a small wrinkled woman in front of me turns and gives us a stern look. Okay, my freak out mellows to more of a yellow alert. The kid had defused my crazy. Having Jared with me in the middle of all the strangers makes it less scary. Funny, he'd been a stranger a few hours ago. I'd never met someone like him, so easy to like. This is someone I can't walk away from, a real friend. Knowing this gives me a little jolt that's both exciting and scary. It's worth the risk of loss. The happiness outweighs that possibility. A big smile spreads over my face. Even my gut thinks this is right. There seems to be a new part of me awakening each minute I spend amongst my kind.

My eyes turn back to Juda. Apparently he'd never stopped watching me. Warmth gathers, further south than usual, and, to my shame, I don't want to deny the reaction. Maybe our webbed feet babies would be adorable?

King Shea starts speaking, it sounds like a prayer. The heads of each shifter bend in response, but I don't bother to tune in. A change has rippled through the air and I want to get ahead of whatever kind of emotional roller coaster is next. Juda turned and faced his father. The break in our stare helps remove the images of children. However, the backside looks as wonderful as the front, bringing different images to mind. Images involving feathers, and

BELONGING

possibly, hot wax. Okay, maybe I've watched one or two of the late night motel
adult hours.

The prayer came to an end and the shifter king spoke in English.
Which is great, I don't know if the 'Fates' would take offense to all the
possibilities I'd had going on in my mind. Moving on.

"Tonight family, you are here to witness the eldest son of the eldest
son, receive his birth rites. Juda, son of Marko Shea Dacian, come forward."

Juda does as his father commands. The king steps behind his son, by
comparison, a foot taller than Juda. The rest of the men on stage step up and
form a semi-circle around Juda. He kneels down with his back to the men, and
sits on his heels. Juda holds my gaze, and starts stripping off his shirt. To my
shame, the fire inside me gets hotter. With his shoulders pulled back and no
shirt on, he truly looks like a demi god. The men tower over him like
mountains. They've grown several feet in height. Not something you see every
day.

Jared put his gangly arm around me.

"Just watch," he whispers. Gladly. I won't look away until the shirts
back on anyhow.

"Juda Shea Dacian. Eldest son of the eldest son, you are the vessel to
which the Pure Source connects. From your father to his father and back to the
Great Bear, you are entrusted with the sacred duties of..." The stage under
Juda begins to glow pale lilac, "tradition," the light becomes lavender,
"protection," it deepens into a bruise dark purple. The wave of color washes up
Juda's body, then sinks into his chest.

A slanted line appears to be etching down his chest, like he's splitting
open. Violet light beams out from the deep cut. Blood trickles down his bare
chest, but only a drop or two. Juda fights to keep his face frozen, but he's
panting with the effort. The sides of his hair are wet, the king continues his

87

ritual. "...and dominion..." The line cuts up sharply then back down, "Over all those who belong to you. Do you accept this trust?" The voice of the king echoes throughout the arena, altered by the power he's channeling. The glowing line slices sharply upward. The pink of his muscles are visible, but only the few drops of blood escape the open wound.

"Yes." Juda sounds as calm as his stone face looks. In less than a moment, a deep purple mist forms, hiding him from my sight. A thunderclap sounds, and lightening hits the dense mist, illuminating Juda. Helpless to do anything but watch, his body contorts into an inhuman back bend, while electricity shakes him violently. Then all the flames extinguish at once, and the arena is dark. Through the mist, a violet glow pulsates from the stage.

Jared's hands grab me as I try and run to Juda. The mist fades giving us a better look at the stage. The light that remains comes from the seven-pointed star that has formed itself upon Juda's chest.

I wait for chaos, but there are no screams. Instead, the crowd speaks as one, "So, it shall be."

The flames come back to life in the barrels illuminating the stage. Juda's hands are curled up into fists and his head remains bent down. The star on his chest glows dark purple. The same light reflects on the stage behind him. The star burned all the way through his body. How he didn't scream is beyond my comprehension.

My body is hollow. The muscles in my stomach burn as I try to move forward; something isn't right. Jared is frozen like a statue. No, he's moving, but slowly. Turning my head back towards the stage, the action isn't as hard as it had been when I'd tried to move forward a second ago, I see Juda is also sort of stuck in time. Is this a part of the ritual? *Why is everyone else moving slowly, but I'm normal? Am I doing this somehow? Please be normal, please.* My eyes squeeze shut to block out the odd scene.

When I open them, Juda is standing and the glowing star is gone. The men of his family are back to normal. The sound of happy cries and singing fill my ears.

Was that my magic, or have I officially lost my mind? If it was magic, no one else was affected or even seemed to notice. Well, maybe not everyone. Heaviness presses in on me and I look over to see the king glaring my way. All the warmth from before leaves me. This is the man Jared spoke about, radiating an aura of stern protectiveness. If he'd seen what I'd done, there would be worse than his cold glare to deal with. Putting on the best doughy-eyed girly look I can muster, I turn my eyes towards Juda who, thank goodness, looks at me too. King Shea's glare softens, as well as the weight in the air around me, and he gives one nod to his son.

Not sure what I did, but the king wouldn't have noticed if it was nothing. Thank goodness I binge watched Dawson's Creek that one time, or I would've never known how to look so pathetically in love. It's just an act. Juda's undressing me from across the, err field, has nothing to do with it...

A lone violin note breaks our ten-mile stare. More instruments join in and soon there are dancers bumping Jared and I out of the way. Women with trays of steaming food walk in from the entrance and exiting gates. Juda appears not far from us, accepting handshakes, hugs, and bows. At some point he'd put his shirt back on, thankfully. Jared jerks his head towards the food and raises his brows in a question. I look back for Juda, but I don't see him anywhere; the two of us head for the food.

Jared got busy gushing over his big brother's ritual, but I don't get it, until he explains.

"A new successor doesn't usually connect directly to the Source of Magic on his first try!"

"So, Juda put the super in, supernatural?" Thinking of his bare chest, I have to agree. Jared smiles at my pun, and starts piling food on a paper plate. I feel sorry for the plate.

Over my shoulder I catch sight of the shifter king's brothers behind the black curtains. Nate had emerged to pull the opening closed.

"They'll be out soon. They got family stuff to do." Juda spoke close to my ear making me jump. His eyes are full of that hunger again, and I get the idea he's close for a reason, but I'm not ready yet, so instead I turn to my humor for distraction.

"What's up with you and Jared impersonating 'Blink'? One of you is gonna make me pee my pants." If his face wasn't only an inch from mine, I would've sounded a lot less girly. Juda makes a huffing sound and gives me a little shake of his head. He smiles at my joke, but I can see he's disappointed I didn't take the invitation to a lip party. When he steps back, my mouth aches from the efforts of declining.

"I have to go with them. You stay with Jared. He'll get you home if I'm not back by the time you're ready to leave." He looks up at his kid brother and gives him one nod then leaves.

"Nice X-men usage." See, the sixteen-year-old gets me. Wait, maybe that's not so good. "You gonna start making a plate?"

"Did you leave any food for me?" He grins, just as a pile of potato salad on his plate tips over, falling onto the, barely smaller, pile of sausage. I can't help but laugh, and grab some food too.

We sit at a bench, and I watch the others dance and embrace. The clothing of the older ones around are colorful, cotton, and in the bohemian style. The younger folks wore jeans and tee shirts. Everyone has a carefree look about them. Surprisingly, I find it's easy to be amongst the shifters. And once my plate is empty, I find it difficult to keep my eyes open.

After everything tonight, the only thing I want is to be alone. A big yawn takes control of my mouth. I try to cover it, but Jared sees. He's finished his food as quickly as I'd finished my two pieces of beef and scoop of beans.

"You tired?" No use is denying it now.

"Busted," another yawn takes over.

"Yeah this much magic can take it out of you. I'll take you to your place." My place? If Jared was taking me, I guess it would be safe enough.

Jared led us through the small forest to a path that brought us to a small building. The kid didn't stop talking the entire way about the ritual and the food, of course the food. I remember going through the bottomless pit of a stomach not too long ago. Of course guys had it worse at his age. I barely hear him, too tired to even worry why I am this tired. The buzz of the night, like a sugar high, left me low and groggy. As we came to the front of the building, I noticed a low brick wall running across the porch area.

"I think Juda wanted to bring you, but with the connection being made on the first try, he had too much to do tonight." He hopped over the wall. I walk around. Honestly, the teen is a wind-up toy. Jared bent over and picked up a rock from the garden next to the wall, one of those fake rocks with a key in it. He held out the key to me and I took it, while he put the rock back down.

"This was your mother's apartment. Guess the Aunts foresaw you coming. They cleaned it yesterday, and got it stocked up for you this morning. I know you probably have a million questions, but get some sleep first. You look tired." He stepped backwards, then thought better of his word choice, "I mean, we have all the time in the world now that we know you are family! You look great, really. Welcome home, I'm really glad you're here." He did a little hand wave to cover up the awkwardness and ran off.

Just like an adolescent, show your feelings then high tail it. I never got the pleasure of being the new girl in school. I basically schooled myself through the public library. Suppose this is what I missed out on.

A large breath puffed out of my lips, the only expression I could muster. Being this exhausted makes my hair hurt. Okay not my hair, my scalp, but it's the same when you're tired.

Inside the apartment, its pitch black. The smell of various cleaners hit my nose: lemon, bleach and Windex. Good, that much cleaning means no spiders. I'll be safe enough for the night. I twist the lock into position on the door and move in the dark towards a black sofa-like blob. My shoes slip off and then my jeans. There's a throw on the couch that smells of fabric softener. I wrap myself up and pull a sofa pillow under my head. A sigh leaves my lips and all the night's events empty from my mind. On my way to dead asleep-ville, a voice sings me a song I can't place, but I know the tune well.

Chapter Twelve

Love and Betrayal

Grass tickled at my plump little legs. The sun warmed the breeze. Dark curly hair blew with the wind; brilliant eyes with brown irises and a violet trim peeked at me through the strands. Rolling thunder pulled my attention up. The sky was stuffed with black clouds and a chill filled the air. A distant voice brought me back down to the ground. The field spread out around me, empty, void, of all life. I stood there in the center, unable to move from the nothingness.

My eyes lids pop open. Weight presses on my chest, and there's no oxygen in my lungs. Struggling for breath, I push back, going up the arm of the sofa I slept on to escape the odd weight. Coughing and generally freaking out, I start to catch my breath. What the hell was on me? The bright light from the window temporally blinds me. Is that a person in the corner? My head is sore; I lift my palm up to block out the light. My face is wet; I'd been crying? There's no one in the room, but me, so what the truck?

My right hand finds the back of the sofa and I settle back onto the cushion and look around, slowly giving my eyes time to adjust. The room isn't too big, giving me the sense of safety. My initial fear wanes down and my mind begins to clear. This is my mother's place. The memory of the night before, Juda and his shirtless ritual comes back. How can I forget shirtless Juda?

Knock, knock

"Oh!" my heart hits my ribs like it wants to escape. Dang it, I need some caffeine.

"One minute..." The throw I covered up with wrapped around my legs while I slept, I'm not sure where the thing starts and stops. Working the

93

cloth with my hands and using my feet to push out of it, I get free of the thing. Now, I need to coordinate my legs and feet with the task of getting my jeans back on. They go on easier than the throw came off, and I get to the door.

"Juda." He holds up two cups of coffee and a white Shipley's bag. Best donuts in the world.

"Good afternoon, sleepy head. Your hair looks great," He says, and steps in past me. My hands shoot up to check my hair; it's fine. Teasing before my caffeine isn't fair. No, we are cousins. I can't remember if I'd decided that was something I was willing to overlook. My mouth waters with the desire for caffeine, though I prefer black tea, right now the coffee will do.

In the spirit of keeping things casual, I try and sound nonchalant and sarcastic simultaneously. "I guess you've been dropping in every hour with fresh coffee?" I choose to sit at the opposite side of the sofa from where he stands. A decent attempt to give him a signal that I'm not interested.

Juda sets the cups and bag in front of me on the coffee table, he bends down and picks up the throw I'd left crumpled on the cushions and folds it into a neat square. Hard to not notice, even domestic work makes him handsome.

"Let's say those two cups are for you, if I have another cup I may not sleep for the rest of the week." I raise an eyebrow, my alternative to a sly grin. When did I get this comfortable in his presence? He turns, placing the folded throw on the opposite side of the sofa from me and then starts setting the pillows back where they go on the sofa, giving me his backside. To keep my hands busy, I swipe up my first cup of jo from the table. The coffee's hot and black. I'd like some sugar and cream, but I'll use whatever is in the bag to tame the bitter taste.

"I'm guessing I woke you up? I don't think I've ever seen someone chug coffee." He half laughs. The liquid is the perfect temperature. I turn the cup up, forgetting about the hot guy in the room and bitter taste. My stomach

however, clenches slightly, reminding me why one shouldn't chug coffee. I'm
thinking in about thirty minutes I have to get Juda out of this apartment or else
die of embarrassment. He stares down at me from where he stands. I put my
empty cup down and do my best to ignore the subtle churning in my gut.

"Kinda cold out I noticed," I say hoping to cover up my un-lady-like
behavior. The temperature dropped overnight, typical Texas winter. By
tomorrow it would be eighty again.

"And I can assume from the cold in here, you passed out last night not
bothering to adjust the thermostat, which means you haven't looked around."

"Uh-uh." Maybe I need some food in my body with the coffee?
Picking up the white bag, I peek in and discover hot, soft, glazed donuts. Pastry
in hand, I sit back onto the couch to warm up further. The first bite is like
heaven.

"I guess I'll entertain you while you chow down. Not saving me any?"
He teased me. Has he no shame? Since the folded blanket took up the other
side of the sofa, he sits right next to me. Sneaky. Stretching out, he extends his
long arm casually behind my head on the back of the sofa. Make that
shameless. He's testing the waters. Should I move or stay? The mix of his
scent and the hot donuts makes me weak. Dang donuts.

"Years ago when it was apparent your mom wasn't coming back, my
father had her clothes put in plastic bins. Those were put back in the closet for
you by the Aunts yesterday."

The crumbs from the donut fall onto my jeans. He reaches over with
his left hand and brushes them off. Just that little touch, and heat from his body
gives me an urge to move closer to him. I breathe in deep to catch his scent.
It's like savory spices, maybe a blend of his skin and there's also a hint of that
astronaut shampoo. Well maybe it's not called that, but I remember some
strange advertisements about irresistible astronauts. My eyes move up and he's

looking down at me. Tingles spread over my skin, but I push closer to the arm of the sofa and grab my second coffee. Our flirtationship needs to come to an end. Right?

Juda says nothing, only watches me. I take a drink, knowing more coffee won't make my morning any easier. When I lower my cup, he's staring at my boobs. Nope, he has no shame.

His devilish smile deserves the kick I send to his shin.

"Ow!" He fake rubs his leg as, my deadpan glare tells him I'm not falling for it. He gives up and chuckles.

Two donuts gone, one lone pastry remains. I use the napkins from inside the bag to get rid of the last flakes of icing. The stickiness of my fingers from the melted sugar sends an urge to lick each one, but in this situation, that may not be the best idea. The girls from those burger commercials pop into my mind. If I try to look sexy, I will look like a doof. Why am I being such a dork? Oh yeah, I downed one and half cups of coffee and two donuts in less than ten minutes. Sugar and caffeine: lethal combo.

Riding the high, I get up and walk around. Plus, if I stay on the couch, there's no telling what will happen. The floor squeaks as I step up to a bookshelf to take a closer look at my mother's things. Distractions, I need distractions.

"The TV was brought in last night." Juda explains to me while I look around. In the living room there's a three seater, light blue sofa, a simple wooden coffee table and a dark red La-Z-Boy. To the right, the room spills into a small open kitchen area that continues towards a short hallway, which ended at a small wooden door. Probably a bedroom. The whole place can't be more than eight hundred square feet.

He hasn't stopped talking about the new TV. Guys and their electronics obsessions. I better listen. "I know it's a big screen, but we couldn't

beat the price. Everything else is your mother's. Wow, I'm talking too much.
Really I want to ask if you'd spend the day with me, if that's okay?"

I put my cup down and walk into the small kitchen.

"Sure that sounds good." I hope I sound like his cousin rather than a
girl who's caring less and less that he's my cousin. Really hard to convince
myself that it matters when he's wearing a tight shirt. My fingers drum on the
pot holders, all rooster print. An image of a house with roosters and chickens
all around fills my mind. A woman calling them 'Yard birds' and then nothing.
The words echo by my ear, I know it's my mother talking, but is it in my head
or did I actually hear her speaking?

Juda had followed me into the kitchen, but I'm not ready to share with
him what I hear. Like a greedy child, I play the image over and over in my
mind. I don't move until the image is burned in. I know it's a memory, but part
of me knows my mother's presence has evoked it within me. I turn and find
Juda leaning on the cabinets, he's not blocking the hallway, so I walk towards
the bedroom. On the bed there's a brightly colored handmade quilt. Pinks,
purples and greens all adorn the spread in patterns that make the colors look
like they're playing catch me if you can.

Juda breaks his silence, "This was made by your mother and her
cousins." The stitching must have taken weeks if not months.

The question I can't get out of my head spills out, "Why would she
leave here?" My voice sounds far away.

"I've heard many stories over the years. The one that makes the most
sense is she fell in love with another clan's man and left to marry him. Though,
he would not have been her true mate. In our tradition, you mate within your
own clan. Sometimes some choose to marry outside to the northern shifters,
but the magic line is diluted that way. The northerners have a fickle pattern of
behavior."

Northern? That makes no sense to me? I turn to face him. This time my voice isn't flimsy. "So, why was she in Mexico if she was going to marry a northern shifter?"

"Hmmm…" Juda looks off and thinks for a few minutes.

"I don't know. Maybe she never made it, or she was sold as a slave and taken to Mexico."

Slave?

The anger on my face shows. He sees it, and holds up a finger to tell me there's more. Juda starts pacing the floor at the back of the small room.

"Our women have been fooled by the northern shifters. Sometimes they say they love one of ours, but never declare it to the king. This is how they get the girl out of the protection of her clan. Next thing you know she falls victim to their scheme."

He shakes his head. I'm disgusted by the thought and the implication that my mother had been a stupid girl. Years of hiding my inner thoughts from people keep it from showing on my face. The blood in my body rushes under my skin I need to keep calm and not let the crazy out; time for me to pace.

My fingers run over different books on the shelf that sit's to the right of the bed. Bending here and there, I act as if I'm reading the titles to buy some time. Why would other shifters sell their own kind to slavery? What was there to gain? How would it be possible that my mother fell for this when my father was with her in Mexico? It doesn't fit.

His words replay in my mind and one phrase rose above the rest: they mated with one another. What had it been exactly? Oh yeah, they traditionally mate within their own clan? My pacing stops, Juda's head snaps up.

"What is it?" The air grows dense with his magic.

"You said you mate within your own clan. Callen said something similar last night. I thought she was trying to make me feel dumb." There's no way to make that statement less odd.

Juda's laughter breaks the tense moment, like the girls had laughed at me for not knowing, but his isn't condescending. He stops pacing and sits on the edge of the bed. For some reason, maybe it's the topic, I move a step back, right into the bookshelf, which causes a small noise. A wide grin spreads over his face. Keeping eye contact, he lies back on the mattress propping himself on his elbows. His arms flex and his shirt pulls tighter over his chest muscles. Somehow I've managed to stop my mouth from falling open, but not all of my body is that easily controlled.

"Viv, you have to stop thinking you are human. Your blood is all shifter. We aren't sure which clan you are mixed with, but it means your DNA is not homo-sapien. Actually, our DNA isn't like humans at all, since we can shift into any living thing, it changes. We can mate with our cousins or siblings and it wouldn't be a problem physically or socially." I know I still lust for him, even after I found out we're related, but come on, how can I be okay with this? His words do add fire to my skin. Dang it.

"Is your mom, your aun..." I can't even say it out loud.

"She is my father's cousin. His true mate left the clan." If he's talking about my mother? I don't want to know. My cheeks puff up and I blow out the air and some of my stress. My way of stopping the, 'WTF' from escaping my lips. Not that my face isn't giving him a clue. I can't help but steal another glance at Juda, his T-shirt is slightly pulled up, and I see his bare stomach. With the slice of exposed skin, his piercing gaze, and body posture, I'm finding it difficult to catch my breath. His explanation lends power to my growing need for Juda.

The coolness in the room presses against my flushed face. Without a word, I flee for the sofa, moving the folded blanket to the middle cushion. Using Juda's little trick against him. My pulse comes down, though as he walks back into the living room, my heart jumps again. At least there's no way to mistake his intentions. Now if I can stick to my guns and not give in, I may have a chance, but as soon as I see him, I can't think of one thing I'd have a *chance* for. "We are not humans," he'd said.

Juda sat back on the couch, in my original spot. Not saying anything, he reaches out and swipes up my Shipley's bag then pulls out the last donut. In two bites, it disappears into his mouth. He leans onto the padded sofa arm. Staring right at me, he licks each finger, my heart jumps with each flick of his tongue. I can't tear my eyes from his mouth, especially as his tongue moves over his bottom lip and collects the remaining sugar.

"Okay," regrettably I turn towards the flat screen and pretend to find interest in cooling coffee number two, once more. "So, if she was kidnapped and taken to Mexico, how does it explain my father being found dead with her?" The second coffee is too much, my foot has started tapping on its own, and I'm getting too hyper.

"He must not have been your father." Was he saying my father could still be alive? Out of habit I turn on the TV and watch numbly as a cereal commercial plays.

Juda grabs the remote and hits the mute button then tossed the blanket onto the back of the sofa. He slides next to me. He maneuvers his body so that his right knee is up on the cushion, and his left leg is supporting his weight. We are inches from one another.

"First, I didn't know they were both dead. I'd suspected it, but I wasn't sure. I'm sorry for that. Second, I want you to stay. I know you don't know much about our ways. You should learn about your people. I don't know what happened to your mother and possible father, but I would like to help you find out. All I want is that you give yourself a chance to learn who you came from, and what you are. Haven't you ever wondered why all these years no one has found you, or how you survived alone? The magic is strong with you, which could mean your father was a part of the largest clan in the Great Lakes area. That's the only way your connection can be the way it is. They were in our territory around the time your mother left."

With real care, Juda slipped his hands into my own. The touch is reassuring not demanding. For once my body isn't over reacting to him. I lift my head; his eyes ask me if I can just try. This is more than a little test, my lips tingle in anticipation, I want to give in and stop fighting myself.

Something on TV is tugging at my attention. I don't want to look, but my gut clenches, and not in a too-much-coffee way. I break the moment and glance just left of Juda's head. I nearly choke at the image on the screen. In sixty inch, high-def-glory, is a black and white sketch, of me.

Chapter Thirteen

Falling

Juda turns, sitting on the edge of his cushion, and follows my gaze. The shock is obvious by the sharp breath he draws in at the image that's now accompanied with a phone number. The remote is in his hand, and a second later the sound pops on. I can hardly hear the reporter, due to the pounding of my own heart in my ears.

All the details known so far were reported by the Latina news anchor. The C-boy's name was Todd Hamon. According to certain eyewitnesses, the girl in the sketch, AKA the killer, had been seen with him shortly before he died and was needed for questioning in the ongoing investigation. The Latina anchor repeated the number and asked for anyone with information on the girl's whereabouts to call.

Juda's face is blank. The reporter finishes the story and then the same breakfast commercial from earlier comes onto the screen. Filling my lungs with air is difficult. A tightness shows at the corner of Juda's jaw. I can only assume he is pissed about me not telling him. What's the nicest way to tell the girl you'd been shamelessly flirting with, get the hell out of my life?

"Did you know this guy? Did he hurt you? Did you kill him or see who did?" Okay, he's very angry.

"I... He..." Maybe it's best I don't tell him. I know enough info now I can just head north, but Juda won't let me go without an explanation. Not after that report.

Time to face the music. "It was the night I met your uncle."

"Our uncle," He corrected me.

"Yes...our Uncle Joe. He spoke the words to me outside the bar. The guy was in there with his buddies. Just a bunch of college boys ogling me, but I

didn't pay them any attention. I started feeling sick and disoriented or
something. I didn't know what was happening. I left and then Uncle Joe
followed me out. You know about that." Juda's face is losing the tightness, he
looks sad, but his hand takes mine.

"Go on." His words are gentle.

"I tried to get away, but then a truck pulled up fast and I just…jumped
in. It was dumb. When I realized what I'd done, it was too late. This guy, Todd
Hamon, had driven us deep into the wilderness. He kept making sharp turns
like he was trying to knock me out. He drove further into the woods and
stopped. I hit my head hard on the window, and then he yanked me out of the
truck and was on top of me before I could catch my breath. Somehow I got him
off, but I didn't react fast enough. He got the upper hand and started choking
me. I was pinned down hard, I thought my arms would break. I stopped feeling
the pain, but I knew if I didn't fight I would be dead."

Tears slid down my face. Juda's expression has changed from
compassion, skipping anger, and went straight to rage. The image of the knife
appearing fills my mind. Should I tell him? The air around changes in a split
second, becoming very hot and my abdomen muscles are tight and jerky. I
cover my surprise by wiping away the streaks on my face. My mother's words
from last night float into my thoughts. "Leave here…" It sucks knowing I'm
telling an altered truth to Juda, but I know it's the right thing, for now.

"There was a knife. I didn't see him with it, but it was there on the
ground. I stabbed him in the neck with it. I couldn't fight anymore. I blacked
out. When I woke up his hands were still on my neck, but he was dead. I had
no marks, I'd healed." Shock flashes across Juda's face. He shakes his head, it
seems he's made a decision, but I can't tell what that decision is right now.

I finish the ordeal in a rush. "I grabbed the knife and wiped off my
prints. Then took it to the river and threw it as far as I could and got out of

there. After that I made my way here." Pale skin lined with dark shadows, and crystal-blue eyes, that showed the monster who lived inside Todd Hamon, float in my mind's eye. The skin on my throat seems to remember Mr. AA's grip just as much as I remember his evil stare. I'm sure Juda can tell there's something untrue in my story, but his face shows me, he doesn't care. I hope he thinks it's something I'm too ashamed to admit and not press me to reveal my little white lie.

Hearing it out loud, I realize how awful it was. The cops would never believe me. How could they? He wasn't just dead. He was shriveled up like a dehydrated plum. My stomach jerks again with a warning to keep my thoughts to myself. My back finds the sofa, and I pull my legs up to my chest. Even though that stuff happened days ago, after meeting my family, it could've been another lifetime ago. That's how different things are for me know. Losing them will make having to run worse.

Juda breathes a little heavier. That's the only clue I get of knowing his emotions. Which means, I have no clue at all.

"I don't want to bring you or the family trouble. I should go." There are big fat tears threatening to start at the thought of leaving here. Pull it together. I can do this.

"What? Go?" His words echo in the room. Automatically I move to the end of the couch readying myself to run if necessary. The stupid heavy tears start to come down my face.

"Viv, this is as much the family's fault as it is yours! The police will find you and blame you no matter what the truth is. You'd be the scape-goat for that idiot's death!" That doesn't sound like, leave here now. Is he saying I can stay?

The anger on his face is in full bloom as he starts to talk about the situation. "I can't stand that he touched you, and almost...damn it!" Juda runs a shaky hand over his perfect hair, after a few deep breathes he continues. "I know it was disorienting, but Uncle Joe awoke the magic in you. It saved your life Viv. That murderer deserved what he got."

Without warning, Juda encircles me in his protective arms. "You're safe from the outside world here. No one will find you. I know you're smart and covered your tracks." Not able to stop myself I give in to the grief, but only for a few minutes. Seeing Mr. AA's face again hits me harder than I thought it would. I don't want to pull away, but I need to speak.

"But my face is all over the city now, what if someone saw you pick me up?" He rolls his eyes. The sarcastic gesture helps ease the tension.

"We're not governed by the rules of the outside world. We're on our land and only those invited can come here. Look, all that I am trying to say is, you are safe, you are not bringing danger to us, and we won't let the outside world find you and falsely convict you."

Juda studies my face. His thumb lightly brushes my jaw line. "Vivian, I want you. I know you know this, and I see I may be trying to push you too fast. I'm willing to wait. This..." he gestures towards the black TV, "doesn't change how I feel. We're not a part of the human world unless we choose to be. There are humans in the compound, but they protect us as much as we protect them. You are safe here. This can be your home."

And like that, my grief turns into desire for the guy in front of me. He said, *I want you*. I lost most of the rest of his speech, except for the bits where I'm safe and this can be my home.

"I do feel safe, though I'm not completely synced with the non-human thing yet." I want to touch his face too, "I would like to...stay." And be yours if I can pretend we're not related. Hoping he doesn't pick up that last part I look down at my hands, then back up at his perfect face. His mouth turns up.

"Good." He runs a finger down my arm. He leans close, and I just can't, so I kiss the side of his face. He pulls away, but catches the corner of my mouth with a soft peck. A little jolt shoots through my body. Three days, it's only been three days since you've known him, settle down. When my eyes open, his sly smile is back, and I can tell he's enjoying my struggle.

"There's lunch in an hour. We are probably not the only ones to see this. I have to go explain the situation to my father. Don't worry, though. It is just so he knows the truth." He gets to his feet and makes his way to the door. "Meet me in the commons. Then we can continue our day together." He comes back to me and lifts me into a hug. This time I melt into his chest instead of resisting the touch. I really want more of his lips, but it's just not the right time.

"Will you be okay until then?"

"Juda, I've been on my own since I was seven. An hour is nothing." I pull away and give him a little push towards the door. His finger slides down my arms and he grabs my hands. Ten minutes ago I was disturbed by the idea of kissing my first cousin. Now my lips ached to kiss, and kiss him, and kiss him.

The three sixty in my mood reminds me of one more question. "Are you having crazy mood swings now that you've had your Naming ceremony?"

He laughs, "Oh yeah! Father says we have to learn to control it. Uncle Nate suggested meditation. Just keep breathing, right?" Juda gives my hands a squeeze then lets them fall. As he opens the door, he turns, twisting around flexing his long arm muscles in the process. I wonder how his skin would taste. My eyes snap to his as he starts to speak. I need to focus on focusing.

"Head right at the trail. You will find the commons. If you're not there in an hour, I'll come looking. Just leave a trail of donuts." He winks at me and leaves.

My body is tingling from all the excitement and the pep from my sugary breakfast. There is much to think about. My life has been broken into hundreds of puzzle pieces that need to be snapped back together. As tempting as it is to pretend there's nothing new in my small world, I need to woman-up already.

Okay. With all the confusion swirling through my head, I just need to pick one thing and go with that. If I'm lucky, the rest will fall into place as I go. What I have access to is my mother. After all, I'm in her place. I'm going to start by getting to know who she was when she lived here. Maybe I'll understand her choice to go, and why she wants me to do the same.

Alone in her place with time to kill is the perfect opportunity. The apartment has an eclectic feel, very much like my imaginary place I'd dreamt of having one day, when I could stop running. Her things aren't flashy, but simple and warm. A photo of her and other girls, all about fifteen, catch my interest first. My mother's dark, violet, irises held a sense of wonder and joy in the image. Swallowing down sudden tears from seeing her happy, my fingers open the back of the frame and I pull the picture out and shove the photo in my pocket.

The news report brought back the lingering sense of time running out. And though Juda did his best to get me to see that this place can be my home, the compulsion to flee is strong. At the same time, the feeling of being in my mother's presence grows the more I make my way through her things.

The bathrooms set up with new items and freshly washed towels. Time to get the three S's handled. Such a gross, yet practical saying, but even in my own head, it's poop, shower and shave, to keep things P.C.

The water pressure did a lot to soothe my nerves. I wrap up in a towel and start looking for clean clothes. My mother's clothes are simple, not girly. Her undies fit like they'd been purchased recently with my size in mind. If they didn't come to my waist like grannies, I would've been worried. I slip on the first pair of old school Wranglers, which fit just as well. We must've been the exact same size.

My hands flow down the authentic Santana concert T-shirt I'd found stuffed in the back of the full closet. Mom's taste in music wasn't so bad. There's not much to straighten up, but I do the little chores before I head out the door. The afternoon sun greets me. Another warmish day. Hopefully, there will be some breeze tonight.

Walking down the path to the right, I come to a line of trailers. Some of the doors have bunches of dried herbs or plants tacked on them. A group of children play a game of chase, while the women do house work and 'tis at them to settle down. Others stand around in loose groups, mostly men, talking. The chain smoking from them turns the air around the groups gray. Goats and chickens graze the grass patches. Music fills the air, thick with string and drum beats that bring the whole scene to life. These shifters know who I am. I hadn't realized I'd be walking through their territory. I guess I'm a part of this now. With that thought, I start to smile and nod to the few pair of eyes I catch.

The path, as Juda had said, brought me right to the commons. The first thing I see is Jared hanging out at one of the picnic tables, talking to some other teens. Callen and her hens are at the table with him. I'm close enough to smell her stink, cloves, and bubble gum. Such gross habits for a girl, but she isn't a normal girl. She's a warped one, inside and out.

Jared turned and caught sight of me. He runs up and gives me a hug, which I reciprocate.

"Viv!" He lets me go, so I can face the others. "Callen, did you meet Viv last night?"

"Of course. The lost puppy. You got all tuckered out and left. When I came back from changing, Juda was all alone. Me and him had a great time catching up. Too bad you ran off so early." I want to correct her grammar, but I don't want this day to be about the nasty words that come out of her painted up pie-hole.

With a big smile on my face I reply, "Looks like you could've used a few more z's yourself." Not letting her get in a retort, I turn to Jared, "Your brother told me this morning there was a picnic today. Can you take me there?" I step past him, turning to wait for him to lead me. Callen's face is still, but I notice the anger in her eyes. Now she knows Juda had been with me today, two points for me.

Jared gives me a guarded look, "Yes, I can." He hooks his arm through mine, and I let him lead me to the picnic area. Casually he bends down and whispers in my ear, "Nice." We both snicker under our breath.

In case I need to know the lay of the land, I make note that we are passing the brown house on the right and the wooded area we'd entered to go to the arena, is on the left.

A girl like Callen doesn't just let you get one on her without tossing one back at you. I better be on my game today.

Chapter Fourteen

Hidden Meanings

The picnic area is new to me. Once we make the corner completely, the wind picks up and I can feel the cool air that's been teasing us for the past few days. With the sun high in the sky, I'm sure we'll be warm enough for the picnic. The yards about two acres and filled with big Texas oak trees. There are also many shifters moving about between the rows of picnic tables lined up end to end. There's no humans, so I better be prepared for whatever the lunch brings.

Some of the women give me hugs and kiss both my cheeks as I pass them. Others grin and nod their hellos. They mostly speak Romani to one another. The polite thing to do would be not to listen; which is easier said than done when you don't really trust the people around you. Juda appeared in the crowd and mouthed a hello to me. As I walk to him, I notice a few shifters are watching. He pulls me into a long embrace, I'm keenly aware of the eyes on us, but after a moment I pull him closer. I forget to care who is watching.

"Cough, cough." Callen's unmistakable sarcastic words sound off behind me. The idea of not being able to see what the devil spawn is about to do breaks the spell for the moment.

She spoke in Romani to Juda, "Juda darling don't go getting too attached to her. I don't mind you having some fun but soon enough you'll be mine." In order to keep them from seeing that I understand every word, I look around for Jared. The answer to her statement interests me. I'm glad he doesn't know I can understand them.

In my pretend mode, I spot a small stage set up at the opposite end of the field I hadn't noticed earlier. Thankfully, there's already guys setting up instruments which means only music; no magical ceremonies today.

"Cousin, I ask that you keep your conversation in English for Viv. It is rude otherwise," Juda says. He doesn't show any emotion, which gives me no clue what his reaction is to her statement. He doesn't know I understood, why wouldn't he answer her?

Callen turns her nasty glare my way, but before she can say another word the Aunts appear out of nowhere. Lady Bold 'tised at Callen and her cronies. A little thrill of relief runs through me; they share my dislike of the hell bitch. Yeah, the odds are even now, though I'm pretty sure not one of those girls can lift a hand in violence towards these ladies.

Lady White and Blond grab one of my arms each and tell the boys in Romani, "We must take her now to be with the elders." I lift my brows at Juda as I am turned and tugged off.

"Vivian, you are greater than them, and don't forget that." Lady White says as they whisk me away. The three of them encircle me, with Lady Bold at my back. Today Lady White's lovely snowy hair lays in loose big waves down her back. The bright sun reflects off her pale skin. She glows in her white cotton Mexican style dress. With her soft aged fingers, she pinches the side of the dress to show me the pink and purple embroidery. She'd worn it for me. I give her a smile and find a lump in my throat that I quickly swallow down.

"His heart has not had its say. There may still be time girl." Lady Blond says with a wink. We had come to a picnic table in front of the small stage. The others were far, really far away now. How did we get all the way over here? We must be fifty feet from where Juda and the others stand. Juda and Jared seem to be in conversation, but Callen is steadily glaring towards me. Even from here I think I can see her devil horns.

"I don't know your names?" I tell the three of them, ignoring Callen.

"Oh child, we have had many, but we like the ones you chose for us," Lady White says. The three of them nod and touch my face or arms. I know

111

I've never used my nick names for them out loud, but I don't think that matters with these three.

The sharp notes of a violin fill the air and distract me from our conversation. Alone on the stage a man with dark skin, violet eyes, and messy dirty blond hair, rocks back and forth to his music. A hand rolled cigarette hangs from his lip, between notes he inhales the tobacco, and then exhales a puffy white cloud from his nostrils. The song is haunting but beautiful. I always loved violin.

"Child, I am sorry to say to you, this is your home." Lady Bold replaced Lady Blond at my right side. Her presence is full of strength. Her appearance adds to it. She wears a dark gypsy skirt and a gray peasant top, that's barely noticeable under the mounds of silver jewelry hanging from her neck and arms. The lines on her face deepen when she frowns.

Lady Blond starts to sway to the music directly in front of us. Spinning, she raises her arms making her ancient crocheted shawl, yellowed from time, flair out in a tent around her. She too wears the traditional gypsy garb or at least what I think of when I think 'gypsy.' Her twirling is faster than a woman her age should be able to accomplish. I can almost see the young lady she used to be in her smile. I want to love life like her when I make it to her age. Her jewels were less in amount but bigger in presentation. All three women wore various colored rings on every finger.

"Why are you sorry? Isn't family a good thing?" My mind switched back on.

The spinning woman stopped and the three of them gather around me.

"Oh daughter," Lady Blond sighs.

"Child," Lady Bold whispered with a hint of pity. "You aren't with your real family yet; you must seek them out. These creatures are blood, but..." her words cut off.

Lady Blond broke the silence, "Vivian, family is not just who you share your blood with. Though, not all of those you share blood with are here. It is those you share your heart with who become true family." She is right. Honestly I'd never let anyone in my heart except my mother. And I don't have any memory of my father to say if I'd love him or not. For some reason the memory of my mother's love is what sticks out in my mind. There are very few images of my father in my mind, and they are mostly a sense that he's there, not actual pictures. Wait, could she mean...

"My father may still be alive? Is that what you mean?" They look from one, to the other, but no one speaks again. The sad notes of the strings hang around us. The air is too hot and sticky, my hands can't stop opening and closing, will this song ever end?

The last note died away with some clapping and Lady Bold answered me. "Vivian, you are right, he is living, but he too has to make a difficult choice, and it may not be one you can live with. Or, live without." The wind picks up, making my hair move around my shoulders. The invisible element cools my skin. Where is he? Why had he not come for me? Was it true, did the sisters really know? All their eyes show kindness, but that does me no good. All the questions their words brought wrestle in my head. Why would I not like his choice? What if I don't want to see him? But that thought makes my pulse pick up, of course I want to see him. Oh man, I'm getting a headache.

The music starts again. The sisters part, so I can sit hard on the nearest bench. The world seems to be tilting over. I know Juda had said my father might not have been the one found with my mother, but hearing it from the Aunts, I know it's true. In my gut, I think I've always suspected it myself. Though my pulse is in my ears, and my stomach just did a flip, I need to pull it together. Deep sure breathes.

The Aunts don't say anything more. Lacing my fingers on the back of my neck, I pull my head towards my knees and breathe deep. Uncle Nate had suggested meditation, though I don't think this is how it's done. Giving up, keeping my eyes closed, I exhale and lean backwards until my back touches the table. In my mind there are bright colors swirling around; they are moving to the music. The different shades of my emotions flow out with each note. After ten minutes, my body is as rested as if I just woke up from a good night's sleep. When I open my eyes, the Aunts have gone and Jared and Juda sit on either side of me quietly eating.

The sun has fallen in the sky, funny how time flies around here. Juda glances at me in between bites.

"For a girl who's unfamiliar with her magic, you sure use it a lot," he says, chomping down on a large piece of meat.

"What?" He lost me.

"Nice light show, a little dim, but nice." It's Jared who clarifies what Juda meant. I guess my imaginary emotional colors really appeared. Crazy, but, kinda cool.

Grinning I get up and turn to sit facing the table. To my relief, the skank isn't around. Even better there's a plate of food for me. We all eat. Jared makes a funny face every time he catches my eye. His energy picks my mood up even further.

"Thanks for the food kiddo," I tell Jared in between heaping forks of potato salad.

"How did you know I got it?" He says with a hint of a smile.

"Because if it'd been your brother, he would've spoken up by now."

We both look at Juda who raises his eyebrows in a mock, *who me, well, I never.* All three of us laugh. The violinist is joined by another, and the two of them play a more upbeat song. Here and there people start to dance.

114

After we are done, I grab one of the wet naps someone scattered all over the tables and clean my sauce covered hands. These people really like BBQ.

"What did your father say?" I ask Juda, now concentrating on the dark sauce under my fingernails. Better than allowing my guilt to call up images from that night again. I mean, Todd Hamon had killed me, sort of, and yeah he was a big A-hole, but he was still a person. Did he deserve to die like that, possibly? But, being the one who did the deed has left a stain in me that I know won't come out over time. No matter how much justifications I'm given.

"He was upset, not at you of course. Uncle Joe had already left. Only half the brothers are still here. He will make sure to spread the word to those gone. They will keep us informed on how big the manhunt is for you, but he wanted me to tell you that you are as safe as your mother would be. Don't worry." For some reason his words sound hollow.

His hand finds mine and he squeezes gently. I can't help but smile up at him. So much has happened in the course of three days. I can't shake the deep connection, like I've known him for years. Logically these feelings are difficult to work out. Thinking about it only makes my head ache, but my heart gets it. Why stress? The warmth of his touch makes it all seem like a silly debate. This guy said he wants me, why should I worry about logic, love isn't logical, right?

"Viv, wanna dance?" Jared asks and pulls my arm, which also pulls my hand out from his brothers. Shaking my head doesn't stop the boy from leading me into a waltz right in the middle the other shifters. He spins, dips and swings me to the music, which follows us rather than the other way around. My feet and arms are everywhere. Elated, I can't help but laugh at the boy's moves. When he twists my arms around so he is behind me, I see we are the center of attention. After another crazy spin, I start to think they are not admirers, just smart people trying not to get plowed down by Jared's creative style.

The song ends. Applause fills the air. Jared bows and reaches up to bend me into the same position. Laughter explodes at our expense, and the music starts up again. This one must be a favorite because everyone grabs a partner and begins to move to the music. There are a few who stay seated and clap to the beat. One of the violinists starts to sing. Jared and I start to move along with the others, not as dramatic as before, thankfully. In the late afternoon sky, the moon hangs, another sign of winter. The beat picks up and Jared pulls and drops my arms in time with it, and I smile. He's the only family member who has made me feel like I may have found home. Why was I being gushy before over Juda? So, serious, we should have some fun and not worry about marriage.

Juda appears next to me. He gives us a small, silent applause, making us both laugh. The boys take turns twirling and spinning me around. In all my life, I've never known complete happiness. It's strange, but that doesn't stop me from soaking it up. I don't see the hell-hag, but even she can't dampen the mood. By the fifth song, I take a break. Pinching the front of my shirt with my fingers, I move it rapidly back and forth to cool down. The sun may be dropping, but it's pretty hot in the field. Jared follows my example, but Juda, being Juda, takes his T-shirt off and wipes his body down. I fan harder.

"Hey I'm gonna go get another shirt, you guys stay here, so I can find you when I get back." My eyes try not to dart down over his glistening form, and I manage a nod. Staying true to making me uncomfortable, Juda leans over and pecks my cheek. In response I sit on the bench with my hands safely under each leg. Thoughts of running them over his body were too strong after his lips touched my skin. The boy has a chest like a Greek God. Last thing I need is to be kicked off the property for inappropriate public groping. He disappeared into the crowd, probably laughing at me.

I recover and look up at Jared, "You can go too, I'll be fine." His shirt was pretty soaked; why boys get that sweaty is beyond me. With a nod he hurried off after his big brother. The music paused and the dancers hurried to take swallows from their bottles and glasses, jogging my memory of the cold soda Jared had gotten me. Another song starts. This one's light and fun. I wonder if I can still spin on a bench like I did when I was a young girl. My feet lift and I turn on my butt to face the inside of the table, making it in one move. The laughter stalls in my chest as I come face to face with King Shea.

Chapter Fifteen

What You Want to Believe, Isn't Always Reality

My feet hit the ground too soon. The momentum of my turn throws me off balance. I barely catch the edge of the table in time, but I am able to pull myself up right. Flushed as my face must be from dancing, I can tell it's getting redder from embarrassment.

"Good afternoon Viv." His hands clamp together on the table and he gives me a look like he's been waiting all day for me to acknowledge his presence.

"Hi, um, King Shea, sorry I wasn't expecting you, I, um..." To cover my babbling, I grab my soda and turn it up.

His eyes follow my movements. For some reason, I try to smile mid-drink and spill soda down my cheek. My fingers fumble to get the cap on the bottle, and wipe my face. "Good afternoon." Can I look more ridiculous? My left hand grasps my right, and they hold each other in place.

"I am here to ask you some questions before my sons come back. I thought we could use some privacy," He speaks as if he hadn't just witnessed my ten-year-old-self addressing him. A clear, ten-foot dome forms around us. Everything on the other side looks slightly out of focus. The smell of sulfur floats up to my nose, but it disappears fast. Not one eye flashes our way.

Magic.

"Please, yes, whatever you want to know, I mean you are my uncle. I don't mind." My left hand tightens making my right hand fingers hot.

"Thank you, niece, I am glad to hear you say this. How old were you when my sister, your mother, passed? I understand you don't think she was with your father when she died?"

My heart slowed. This isn't about the college boy. At least, not yet.

"I was three when the police found me alive in our house. I've never found my birth certificate. I assumed the man of the house was my father. He was a drug lord with a lot of land. From what I've read, my mother was gunned down along with sixty different men and women on the property."

A whisper comes from King Shea, but I can't make it out. Our eyes meet, and the images of the day my mother was killed starts materializing, replacing the late afternoon picnic, with pale yellow walls and a child's laughter.

The world wobbles back and forth with each of my toddler steps. There are men with guns laughing and pointing fingers at me, though not in a mean way. I was entertaining them on purpose. The smell of cigars fills the air. My tiny feet push against the small sandals I'm wearing. My white cotton dress has bright purple flowers hand-stitched in the traditional Mexican style. As each detail comes into focus, the sound of music fills my head. Shaking my little hips to "La Cucaracha," my favorite kid song, as it plays loudly. *NO, I have to stop.* I want to stay away from what comes next.

Blackness settles over the scene.

A deep voice fills my head, "We have to know what happened. Don't you want to know who took your mother from you?"

Curiosity overcomes my fear, I look. *Yes, I was dancing.* The floor is made up of ceramic Mexican tiles. Bright colors and patterns decorate each 4x4 square. The little moving feet hold my attention. The next image bubbles around me. *I don't want to see.*

"LOOK." The king's command brings the scene into perfect focus.

Loud popping noises are accompanied by shrill screaming. My face turns towards the ceiling for the lights that usually come after those noises. Mommy calls them fireworks. No lights are there. Red rain falls down on me.

My tiny dress has bright red droplets that start to spread slowly

119

through the white fibers. Reminding me of the honey mommy uses on my Sunday morning sopapillas.

I'm picked up.

"Get her to her mother, now!" The man's hair is thick and black. His face is dark and dimpled like the top of mommy's brownies. He looks down at me. I wish I could hide from him. He'd said he wanted a boy and that mommy shouldn't have lied that she carried a boy in her tummy. When she wasn't around, he would look at me and say he knew I wasn't his. He turns and yells in Spanish to call the men from the fields.

Whoever holds me carries me away. *NO!* The images melt away around me, a physical pull clenches deep in my gut.

Straining, I try to see the table, the grass, the dancers, but the world is morphing between those things and the past. I struggle harder to hold onto my own will and the walls start to go out of focus, the sound of violins float in the wind to my ears.

The voice of the king is back. "Vivian, I command you to LOOK."

This time the images are accompanied by an invisible weight pressing in on me. Suspended in the memory, helpless, I'm forced back into my little girl body to relive the one thing I never wanted to see again.

She got to me just as the popping got loud and Papa Juan fell to the floor. My tiny lungs ache for air as screams pressed out of them. "Shhhhh, my love. Mama has you. We are okay. I will get you somewhere safe, mi Corazon." The love in her voice calms my three-year-old-self, but I can't shut the affection out, can't stop each word from reopening the wounds losing her left behind. My grief threatens to drag me into a black sea of tears.

In some area of my mind, I sense actual restraints that hold me and force me to look at her face. Her violet eyes, her long curly hair and dark skin, just like the picture. The pressure becomes so great, I think, if the liquid sadness doesn't drag me away, the weight that holds me will surly squash me like a bug.

Mama and I climb. I can hear loud noises echoing behind the walls. Higher and higher we go, until the noise is completely gone. Mommy kisses me and tries to calm my crying. She started singing to me in Romani. I remember hearing the notes from bed-time.

My chest tightens, it's getting harder to breathe, but the pressure increases.

She sits me down. The violet of her eyes calms my fears. The pillow I'm on is lumpy and makes me tilt slightly.

"Mommy will be right back, lie down and sleep. Be safe, my daughter."

After she leaves me, the image of her smiling face plays over and over in my thoughts. Far away I can hear the fireworks, but it's only a few. A long gray ear catches my attention, it's my rabbit. Pulling at the ear, I find myself having to lie down to get it free. Together we lay in the space, and the noises stop. In the quiet I hear mommy singing, and I fall asleep.

The images start to grow sheer. An alarm goes off in my head, I push again at the magic restraints on my mind; they don't budge. The childhood memory solidifies and I am forced into a bright light.

The sudden burst of light wakes me up. I'm lifted by a man wearing a police hat. "It was a hidden door like I thought. And look what I found inside." The man shook his head.

"Guess that woman hid her here," the officer says in Spanish.

The emotions become unbearable. Though the film of my past is rolling, it slows to an agonizing crawl. The grip that holds me slips, as an image of descending stairs creeps past my eyes. I push again, slowing the descent even further before we'd reached the landing. My grief and the king's pressure become one large wave, threatening to pull me out into the pitch-black abyss of insanity. A painting of the dancing Dama lingers frozen in place, but he doesn't let the pressure ebb, instead there's a push and I see her. The body lies on the floor. Wavy, long, dark hair covers half of her face and body. My fight becomes ferocious against the persistent magic. One violet iris, frozen in death, peeks from under a curl.

"NO!" My agonized scream filled the dome and echoes off the walls.

The king tries to hold the image of the body around us, but I'm not looking anymore; I'm done. The struggle between our magic causes the world to spin around us both. The smell of sulfur increases as he tries to dominate over my will. Somehow his trick doesn't have as much effect as they had, and with less effort than before, I reach through all the chaos and grasp the reality of the world he'd taken. My pulse beats wildly in my ears. A part of me is aware the world is normal once again. However, most of me is focused on getting to the king to slap the poo out of him!

Hands tightened on my arms and shoulders as I start to lunge towards the king. My hands are so shaky from adrenalin. I can't get a grip on the other hands to pull them away.

"Calm yourself daughter! We are here to help," Lady Bold says. Knowing the Aunts have come, I am sure the king isn't going to continue his invasion. I do as they say and start to take calming breaths. This helps me to actually see that the king had gotten to his feet, his face and body tells me he was ready for the violence I'd been planning.

"You have no right to interfere here old ones. I am the king. This is my duty, step away." His voice causes the wooden picnic table to trimmer. My back presses into one of the Aunts behind me. Maybe picking a fight was a bad idea.

"You have your answers, king. And I remind you, we are elders. You do not rule over us." It was Lady Blond speaking to my left, which meant Lady White held me in place.

"The time of the elders is soon to pass old ones. I said step aside." The king's breathing hasn't slowed, and the sulfur smell, I assume has to do with his magic, wafts over the four of us. The pressure from before tries to come back, but it's gone quickly. The softer scent of Lilacs fills the space now.

"Our place in this family is earned, not given through birth. We have no use for another dead daughter," Lady White says.

The king looks at them and then to me. He reaches out as if he means to grab my arm, but the wave of magic from the three women pushes past me and forces the king back into his seat.

"We will have our monarchy put back in order," Lady Bold says from my right. The magic she and her sisters possess is amazing. The king looks as if he will turn into a red balloon. The smell of lilacs overpowers the sulfur, I get it. The king is fighting the women and losing. The power in the air nips at my exposed arms and makes me shiver. If this gets worse, I think I'll hide under the table.

"We are not here to take your crown, sir, but sometimes it is necessary for the young to be reminded of the power from which they came," Lady White whispers, and then the magic is simply gone. The sound of the king's heavy breathing fills our small space.

"You are right; I have what I need." He looks at the space behind me, not making eye contact with anyone of us. "I wasn't expecting the resistance; perhaps your wisdom is well placed. She is the eldest daughter of the eldest daughter." His head lifts and he focuses on the women around me. Without any other signs of his mood, he gets up and leaves us at the table. As he walks past the bubble, it dissolves. The crowd and music instantly solidifies.

My knees weaken, but the strong hands of the Aunts help me stay on my feet. When had I stood up? As the king walks through the crowd, faces turn up to him, their shock is easily seen from here. It must seem as if he materialized out of thin air. Never the less, his people bow their heads as he passes and move to clear his path.

"His magic is great, but ours is greater, with you here, child." Too busy fighting off all my different emotions to figure out which sister spoke, I bob my head in response. Their hands and presence slips away. I'm back in the darkening afternoon. Even though I'm out of the memory, my nerves are raw.

Turning my head up to the sky and swallowing down my tears helps, some. My chest warms, it spreads down my limbs. After a moment, I find the strength to shut the strong, metal door in my mind. The rawness of seeing the awful images disappears. My mother is right, I should leave.

Chapter Sixteen

Party Animals

"There you are. We've been searching for an hour!" Jared's words bring me out of my foggy thoughts. His eyebrows draw together when he sees the lines of stress that crease my face. "Viv, you okay? Do you feel bad?" I don't want to concern him further.

"I'm okay." The lie is obvious, so I amend my statement. "I'm not okay, but I will be." The air clears of my untruth. Jared pulls his lips to the side, giving him a look of apprehension. Will he understand if I leave? The kid and I really hit it off. He's the Cass to my Dean, and knowing that, I also know I will tell him the truth about everything. Just not, right now.

The main reason I want to stay, strolls up. The grief fades as I see his light violet eyes. If Jared wasn't standing next to me, I would run to him and let him comfort me, girl power be damned. Callen steps in front of him, stopping his progress to our table. I don't want to let everyone see me lose my composure, since that's exactly what she's counting on. I'll fight that battle another day. Too much emotional overload; I can't handle Callen on top of everything.

I face Jared. "Let's dance." I pull him into the growing crowd as the music picks up. Callen won this round. Jared smiles, and moves along with me.

Drums start to play with a chorus of musicians who hadn't been there earlier. The small group of men sing along with the beat. Jared and I sway in the crowd and watch the song come to life. The erotic music caresses my mind, taking the rest of my tension away. The words of the melody are in Romani and speak of a love the Fates would bring. Juda steps up as I figure out the dance steps with the others. Jared looks relieved. He is too young to appreciate getting lost in sound and the moment. Or maybe he only knew how to dance like the stars? Mr. Waltz.

Juda takes my hand and pulls me into his arms. His warmth chases away the loneliness that reliving my worst memory had left. The crowd moves with the beat, and we bend and sway with them. Juda's hand slips under my shirt onto my lower back. After a few turns, my entire body is vibrating. I need him. I want him. I need to let him know I want him. Can he forgive me? All that anger I'd had towards his father. Maybe the king didn't mean to go so far, or maybe it's normal to do what he did? Juda won't let me be hurt. As if he can hear my thoughts, his arms tighten around my waist. The remaining space between us disappears. He lifts my face up. I smell the sweet cloves, strong on his lips, when he starts to speak.

"Hey, why'd you take off without me? Don't you know I only want to dance with you?" Our lips are inches apart; his determination is clear.

Someone bumps Juda, causing him to pull away from the kiss. Jared gives us a look of apology. A woman behind Juda's head gives me the stink-eye. I step back and let go of Juda's hand. I am light headed, a few deep breaths and it passes. Anyway, the song's over and the moment has passed.

Juda gives his young brother a playful shove, turns and leads us to a table. Out of the heat and into an ice storm. The younger shifters stop talking. Their faces become hard and unwelcoming but Jared, as usual, changes the mood.

"Hey guys, this is our blood cousin Viv, she's living here now." I could kiss that kid. A few of the guys smile. Some lift their chin at me in a silent hello. My lips pull up into a tiny grin. Another wave of dizziness hits me, but leaves before I can react. Weird.

"They know you are cool with the king, but it's hard to accept outsiders. Don't worry all's fine," Jared says, only to me. Juda chats up some of

126

the girls at the table. I suppose he's only making conversation, but I want to rip out their eyeballs anyway.

"Jared, where's the outhouse?" My smile matches his.

"Very Funny. I'll take you, Juda, We'll be back." Juda gives his brother a nod, and me, a wink.

"I think you will get along with everyone here. Learning everyone's name is harder than earning their trust." Jared opens the house door and points towards the bathroom entrance.

"I'll wait here."

"It's cool, the party is twenty feet to the right, I think I'll be fine." I don't want the king to corner me again, but he's at the far end of the field with his wife. I think I'll be okay. Plus, I don't want Jared to think I can't take care of myself. He seems reluctant, but my raised eyebrows make him laugh and give into my request. He trots off towards the field and I go inside. In the house alone, I easily sense the power of their father. This becomes a motivation to hurry and get my business done, and I do.

Once I step back into the main room, I can't help but look at the mounted photos of the family: Juda on a horse, his father next to him, but both smiling and happy, no Jared. The photo shows Juda holding a fish, his father next to him, again, no Jared. Out of the fifteen or so pictures that hang on the wall, there is only three with Jared and his mother. Strange.

The last day-light disappeared while I was inside. The torches light my direction on the way back to the picnic area. In the five minutes I was gone, the party went from shindig to hoot-n-nanny. More men come to the stage. The line of horn players is shoulder-to-shoulder, or feather-to fur. All but two of the guys are in human form; it's shocking to see a monkey play a horn. The shimmering air seems to be violet colored. Making it majestic and hard to look away from. The brilliant purple glow of their eyes should be weird, but I find it

127

strangely comforting. Under my brown contacts, I'm sure my own irises match theirs. Well, not exactly, there is no one here with blue eyes.

In the crowd it's easy to spot the kids dancing from my table. A couple of shifters near me smile and wave me over to dance. My body gives into the pull of the notes and I'm wiggling and laughing along with the rest. No more glares or whispers, no more conversations, just us, the music and the magic.

One of the singers on stage hits a high note. As he finishes, he backs away and shifts right into a six-foot-tall stork. One of its long wings folds behind its back, while he splays out the feathers of the other wing like a large fan. He struts across the stage, bringing to mind the pickle jar bird but without a cute hat.

As the bird reaches the other side of the stage, pop, the singer appeared, hitting yet another long and high note. Even I cheer along with the crowd for that. A monkey is there doing pinwheels before flying into the air then, pop, back into one of the horn players. More cheers. Each player, in turn, shifts into some sort of animal for a few seconds. After the fourth one, it's easy to see the resemblance between the human form and animal form they chose. I'm not sure if they looked that way before or if some part of the beast stayed with them after each shift.

The excitement in the crowd has my skin tingling. Two people down to my left, an ape appears dancing and beating its chest. Throughout the crowd, all sorts of animals appear doing various forms of a jig. Part of me wants to do more than dance, but I don't know how to shift and thinking about it puts the breaks on my building excitement. Watching the crowd change is enough for now. Birds of many colors and types, circle overhead. A horn spat out a crazy off pitch noise, I turn in time to see a gorilla trying to play the instrument.

I've never felt this way, like I'm in a place that I belong. Who would've thought all I needed to do to feel normal was hang out at the zoo?

Okay, I know I'm being sarcastic, but being submerged in this world has clicked everything into place. Like I'd been staring at something my whole life, and finally, I'm getting it, I understand. Where is Juda? I want to share this with him. I can't deny our connection, not here and not now.

Off to the left I spot him with the other kids. Some of the group have cat ears or bird feathers coming out of their brows and cheeks. They look like living Mardi Gras or Carnival masks. Jared's nose stretches out, becoming a beak, but only for a moment, the kids laugh and try to imitate his shift.

Keeping my body moving with the beat and crowd, I make my way towards the group. A movement to my left catches my attention. As I turn to look, I immediately duck in order to dodge the large, tan, bear claw swinging right at my head.

The bear rears up over me, from the ground I try and back away, but its fierce roar makes me pause. This isn't one of the friendly animals I'd just seen. This bear has to be at least seven feet tall with claws three or four inches long and razor sharp teeth, thirsty for my blood.

The crowd parted, but the bear's focus is on me, and no one is trying to help. Until Juda, like a knight without armor, steps between me and the brown bear, yelling. My legs finally remember how to work. I get up, ready to help Juda if I can, but I realize he's speaking to it in Romani. The bear is a shifter who tried to take off my head. Jared stands by me, helping me dust off my legs and back, after a second, my blood pressure calms and I can understand the ranting between my knight and the now tame animal.

"This is not acceptable Callen, we don't do this kind of thing in our clan. If you can't follow the rules, I will have you banned until the nuptials!" Juda crossed his arms. He shouted it in Romani. I can't let them know I understand. In order to mask my anger, I look at the crowd. It's hard not to notice how the guys my age look at the bear with awe. *Someone here is marrying her? I sure feel sorry for that idiot.*

As I watch, the bear morphs into Callen. Unfortunately, unlike the others, she doesn't maintain any of the bear's attributes. Instead her skin is flush and youthful, and her boobs actually look a cup larger, but still perky. At second glance, her long wavy hair stayed as light brown as the bear's fur. I hope it smells as bad too, if only I could slap that snarky grin off the pretty little psychopath's flat nosed face.

"Oh, I am so sorry Viv, I was only dancing. I forgot you're not use to our ways. You're okay right?" She flutters her unusually long lashes at the crowd, "See, she's okay." Some laugh, but a few 'tis at her. The music starts and we are left to work out the issue ourselves. Before I get my chance however, Little Miss 'oops' turns and trots off, with her hag gang trailing behind. If I could shift into something big and rip off her head...but Juda stayed with me instead of following her. Maybe it would be offensive if I did retaliate? Sucks to admit, crazy skank is right, I don't know their ways. Juda turns and takes my hand. The anger melts. His lovely light purple eyes penetrate right through my hurt pride. None of it really matters.

"Dance with me." He kisses the back of my hand. Callen who?

Chapter Seventeen

Look, Don't Listen

We danced until the last viola player lingered, serenading the moon. Juda and his brother both offer to escort me to my mother's apartment. I don't mind, but I wish it was only Juda and I going. With the kid by us, I restrain my need to get closer to Juda. To be honest, I'm euphoric already from having so much contact with him. Except, I am disappointed that we danced for two hours, and there hadn't been anymore attempt at my lips. Without him touching me, and his lack of public affection, I'm starting to get a sinking feeling about the 'nuptials' he mentioned earlier. I want to ask about it, but he may wonder how I know about the pending engagement since they spoke about it in a different language.

"Hey, my father has me scheduled pretty tight over the next week. I may not be able to spend too much time with you, but Jared here volunteered to be your tour guide." The smile on my face is weak. Thankfully, there is only moonlight out here. I don't answer him until I see the apartment a few feet away.

"Yeah cool, I'd like that." The sinking feeling turns into disappear. How can he want to marry that hag, with the connection between us being this strong? I mean, he said he wanted me right? Maybe I'm his last hoorah before he settles down?

"Hey bro give us a minute." Jared pauses, then turns, and goes back up the trail a couple steps, and stops. Juda looks at his brother's back and shakes his head.

"Okay, I guess that will do. Viv, I wanted to apologize for Callen's behavior earlier." Great, he's already taking *her* side.

131

"You don't need to, I get it. She's young and stupid." Okay, I should be a little less childish, but thinking of her and him together, makes my brain boil.

"Viv, there's a lot going on, and as soon as I can piece somethings together, I will sit down and explain it all to you. Don't give up on me, okay?" At some point in all, this Juda has taken my hands, his warmth calms my sadness.

"Thanks for tonight, I had a great time." In case he's not paying close attention to what my body is screaming at him, I step in closer and lift my chin. For a moment the electricity between us amps up a couple notches. His lips move closer and I close my eyes, and move in too. Soft warm lips touch my cheek. I hesitate only a moment before I kiss the side of his face.

Juda pulls back and lifts my hand to plant a kiss on the inside of my wrist. As disappointing as the cheek kiss was, this one action sends sparks throughout my body. Thoroughly confused, I can only smile at him, and watch as he walks away with Jared close to his heels. They go back up the trail, and away from me.

The clock on the mantel says ten-thirty, when I wake up. Jared won't be here until after one o'clock. Most young guys sleep super late. They need like sixteen hours of sleep, or something crazy. That gives me time to catch up on some TV. There are three, back-to-back episodes of my favorite brother duo on, and I've seen all these episodes already, but who doesn't like some eye candy first thing in the morning? The old Seventies rock and Sixty-Seven Impala brings back the sense of who I've been. Strange, it's almost like I was outside of my own body last night. I know it's crazy, but that's how it feels when I think about it.

I need to get my head on straight. I know I like Jared. He and I will always be close, no matter where I end up. And Juda, he's a sexy, handsome guy. I like him, but, I don't know, it's too confusing to figure out how I really feel towards him. Whoa, the living room tilts dangerously to the right, and then straightens back up before I face plant from the vertigo. What is going on? I get in a sitting position and take a couple deep breaths. Maybe I'm getting bad allergies? Everything is back to normal. Did I imagine that? I'm good, what was I thinking about? Oh yeah, a plan. I need a plan.

Well, there's never been a time in my life that I didn't have a plan. Knowing the cops have a sketch of me up makes it hard to keep doing what I've done. However, if my father is alive. Maybe I can find my father. That feels like the right idea. Except, if I leave, will I be sealing the deal between Callen and Juda?

Sixty inch Sam looks at the camera and flares his nose. A sign the episode is about to get serious, so I turn it off. Dean and Sam always make with the funny, but I can't get into it with my real life being so off balance.

What I do know about any relationship is, if Juda really wants me, he'll wait for me. And not marry the spawn of evil. Isn't that how love works? I mean *love*, way too soon, but still, that's the idea right? Plus, I stupidly made excuses for the king last night, but his highness and I need to have a boundary talk before I fully get on the Juda train. I can go, find my dad, and get some answers that only he can give me. After that, I can consider settling down here. If my dad turns out to be a jack-hole, at least I made the effort. I mean, he can't know about me right?

Not to mention, there has to be a reason my mother wants me to leave. Perhaps to find my father, or it could be something more sinister. According to some lure, ghosts stick around for unfinished business. Well, maybe she left something in this place to help me understand what's motivating her to get me to leave. Not sure what to look for, but there are loads of cubbies and storage areas to look through. Okay, now I got a plan.

An hour and forty-five minutes of searching, and nothing. Not nothing exactly. I did discover, while I was out yesterday, someone came in and stocked the place with food and cooking supplies. I appreciate this, but it's kind of creepy. Maybe I want to go out for food? That will be a good excuse I can use when I go, and I want to go, tonight for sure. In the meantime, Jared will be here soon. May as well put this food to good use.

The cooking channel is one of my favorite pass times. Every now and then I'd stay in one of those places that came with a small kitchen, so I could try out the recipes. One of my favorite meals is chili. I know Jared isn't a vegetarian by the crazy amounts of meat he's eaten. If the coffee shop had served links, that kid probably would have eaten his weight in them the first night we'd met.

"Hey Viv! What's that smell?" Jared says, as he barrels past me to the tiny kitchen. His bowls full, and he's adding cheese from the package I'd laid out on the counter, before I can offer him lunch. Teenagers, insert patented eye-roll here. I serve myself food then carry my bowl to the fridge, stack two cans of soda in one hand, and meet him at the table. Jared has eaten half the steaming bowl of meat and beans in that short increment of time. I deposit one can of soda in front of the non-human vacuum cleaner, and take the seat across from him.

"You want some lunch?" His eyes flash up to mine, we both laugh. The chili smells amazing; I understand why he dug in so quickly.

"Sorry," he swallows a spoon full of the spicy sweet concoction, "I'd just woken up, and well it smelled good. You're a great cook!" He shows his appreciation by getting up for seconds before I have even had a bite.

"It's cool. I was your age once. Speaking of, you know it's almost three in the afternoon."

"I would've been here sooner, but I had to do some stuff on my computer. You do realize you're only two years older than me!" He says as he returns to the table, blushing.

"Yeah, true. Well girls are like five years older than their age and boys are like five years younger than their actual age, so I am more like, twelve years older." My bowl is empty. I work on the soda.

"What kind of caca-mammy logic is that?"

"Uh, my own obviously. And who taught you that word? Caca-mammy." I raise an eyebrow at him. He shakes his head and continues to wolf-down his chili. The bowls are big.

"I'm full." To prove it he belches, loudly. "Complements to the chief."

"Jared. Gross!"

"Better top than bottom!" He escapes my sour look by snatching up the bowls and starting to clean for me. This time I actually roll my eyes.

After the food is put away, we decide to walk around outside. Jared tells me all about the land, and how his family found it and eventually bought it generations ago. There are chickens, and roosters everywhere. Jared tries to catch one when I mention to him I make a great chicken-fried-chicken breast.

In between my gut lurching fits of laughter, I say, "Hey, I can defrost a pack of chicken you know?" He dramatically throws himself to the ground, chest heaving, long legs sprawled out, arms the same.

"Now you tell me."

After he's caught his breath, Jared leads us back to the apartment. When he and I are together, I can be myself. With Juda I'm less worried, and strangely euphoric. He has a weird effect on me. Is that what falling in love is? I wish I could talk this out with someone. Jared is a friend. Looking at him

135

smile, and talk about the different types of trees, I know he'd listen. What's the point? If I start down that road, I will have to admit I know Juda is engaged, and ugh, my head hurts.

"Viv, you okay?"

"Yeah, I'm fine. I think I need to take some sort of allergy pill. I've been having some pressure for a day or so now." Except, the pain disappears as I say this. I am falling apart at the ripe old age of eighteen.

"I'm fine, really. Let's just walk some more." He gives me a look of concern, but he continues down the path. I want to tell him my plan, and that I'm leaving tonight. Jared is great, and I know he'd try to talk me out of going alone. Well, that might be a way to ask if Juda would accompany me, but I wouldn't want that question going through Jared. Plus, if I ask him, he'd have to come clean on the Callen/marriage thing.

"Callen is probably still asleep." What? Is Jared a mind-reader now?

"Callen? Why would I want to talk about Callen? She's not on my mind or anything." There, now I sound like a crazy person.

"I'm just saying, it takes a lot of energy to change into something that big. You know the energy to change our body's weight and height has a consequence. Unless you have a direct connection to the magic, or a very strong one. I thought you'd be interested is all." My mind thinks back. Callen had been leaning on the other girls. Good. Maybe I'd get a break from her today. Jared is on my side, no doubt.

If I can't talk about my plans, maybe I can ask him about his father's actions from yesterday? Will that be pushing it though? No, I can't do that to him. It's not fair to put pressure on the kid, even if he's my only ally.

"That's interesting. Maybe you can start telling me about the magic stuff tomorrow?" The sun sinks low, and I don't want to keep him from going home early. I'd heard Juda tell Jared he needed to be on time for dinner more. Of course that was in Romani.

"I guess it is getting late. The winter is awesome, but night time does come sooner. Look, we came full circle." In the setting sun-light, I see the outside wall of my mother's apartment.

"Okay, well thanks for today. See you tomorrow?"

"You're on, my friend!" He turns and wraps his arms around me. His long limbs pin my short arms to my sides, but I do my best to return the hug. He releases me and runs off.

"Bye," I say to the retreating Jared.

Inside, I see it's not quite six o'clock yet. Good, people will be sitting down for dinner, no one will bother me when I head out of the compound. I hate that I won't be here for Jared tomorrow, maybe I'll leave him a note. Better yet, I'll call Juda tomorrow and fill him in on my heading north. I will also need to get to a convenience store for some hair dye. If I go as light as possible, and take out my contacts that should make me look different enough from the sketch. If there wasn't such a pull from my gut to go now, I would wait until I knew how shifting worked, but the nagging feeling, coupled with my mother's words, is too strong to ignore. Yet another emotion I need to control.

After a shower, and putting on a pair of my mom's jeans and an old school Mexican style shirt, I tuck her picture and my extra contacts into a small shoulder bag. The bag definitely came from Mexico, its thick woven string is the colors of the national flag, red, green, and white. She has a few well lined jackets, but they are all too large, and bulky. Instead I select one that's thick cotton, and black.

In case anyone is outside, I stick to the tree line. The trailers end, I see the parking lot with Juda's truck and some vans and cars, all sans people. If I want, I know I can walk out, but I stick to the dark part of the field. The cars

137

are to my left. A noise stops me. In a yellow bug, I see a guy. He's laying back, but not completely reclined. I think the guy is one of the teens from the table last night. He'd given me dirty looks all night.

As I approach, I kneel down to get a better look, a head appears from his lap, long crazy curls shake, as the girl pulls her hair over to one side. It's Callen. She tugs on the guy, and leans towards him. They start to kiss. Gross, she'd just been, oh man, that's gross. His hand appears, he pushes her head back towards his lap, and all that I see is bobbing curls.

That bitch. She's blowing some guy, and saying she's going to marry Juda? Will my phone call be enough to keep him from making a big mistake? I can stay and talk to him tomorrow in person. Tell him about what I saw. I know I'll have to tell him that I am going to leave, which will probably piss him off. However, it's the right thing to do. My gut, and mother will need to give me twenty-four more hours. A twitch in my gut tells me, it's not happy.

I back away, being slow about it, but too slow. Callen's head comes back up, I stop, and sink lower. She climbs on top of the guy, and starts to ride him. I am too disgusted to worry if they see me anymore. Quickly I get away, and make it back into my mom's apartment.

How can she do that to Juda? Worse, anyone can see her out there. What a total slut. Juda will be the laughing stock of the shifter world if he marries that hag. I may not be in love with him, but I sure as hell care about him more then to ever do something like that. I hope Juda will believe what I tell him.

Ignoring the voice in my head, telling me that's not going to be easy, I change for bed. I sure could use some late night TV to calm my nerves. Huh, if hunters were real, I'd be on the list of prey. So strange how much of my tiny world has changed in the course of four days.

Chapter Eighteen

Truth

Daylight peeks through my mother's bedroom windows. The clock on her night stand says, five-till-seven. This is why I hate winter. Usually my inner clock wakes me up at six. And then, I promptly turn over and go back to sleep, still, I get all grumpy when I'm feeling wonky. I'm sure if I look at the calendar, time is due to fall back this coming weekend.

My body is stiff from laying in the same potion too long. I guess all the crap from yesterday, stayed with me while I slept. Great, now all I can think about is Callen's nasty show, and how I'm going to tell Juda about it, without sounding petty. Plus, I did promise Jared a big lunch. I haven't decided to tell him about my *head north* plan. This day is already too stressful. Maybe, I need to sleep through it instead.

A big stretch pulls my body in strange directions, and there's no going back to sleep after that. Fine, I need some caffeine anyway.

After my shower, I make a giant cup of black tea. Almost five spoons of honey and some milk go in, it's much better now. In the front room, I click on the TV. The family I'd hitched a ride with appears on the screen. Damn, I'd hoped they wouldn't go to the cops. The volume goes up, and I listen to the husband talk to the camera.

"It was strange to see a young girl like that wandering in the rain." The same anchor woman with the light orange/blond hair comes on the screen, cutting off the rest of the statement.

"The couple said her name was Pam." The sketch of me is behind the reporter's right shoulder. The wife appears next. I see her little girl, and she'd been so sweet. Her mother had called her little flower. Right now, little flower looked irritated.

"The girl was soaking wet, my husband and I picked her up. Her car had broken down and she was walking on the side of the road." The image of the stretch of highway I'd been on appeared on the screen for a second. The mother doesn't sound upset, which is probably why they aren't showing her face. "Pam looked like a normal girl, quiet until my five-year-old started talking to her. She'd been right next to my daughter the entire ride. We couldn't believe she'd just killed someone..." Her words are cut off, then the reporter comes back on.

"Police have been running leads, but have no new information," Say's the reporter. The sketch of me is back. Now I am the killer, not the suspect.

There is no way to plea my case. I'd be arrested and spend my life in prison because some guy thought he had the right to do awful things to whoever he wanted. He was good looking. He could've had any girl with some nice words and attention. There's really no understanding why crazy does, what crazy does. I've had enough TV for the day.

My gut does a flip. Adding time to my plan makes things harder to deal with, mentally. After hearing the latest on my manhunt, it's going to be very difficult to travel from Texas to Michigan. I may need some shifting lessons. If I must stay, may as well get Jared to give me some pointers. Though I can't really wrap my head around the thought of turning into one of the animals I'd seen dancing. Well, I'm pretty motivated to try at least. Right now, my grumbling tummy is what's motivating me; time to eat.

Whoever stocked the kitchen left me small boxes of various cereals, like the ones I usually get at the continental breakfast buffets. All carbs and sugar, but those are two of my favorite food groups. I pick a random box, fill up a bowl and sit at the table. Oh, I almost forgot to get the chicken out. There

140

are at least twenty small packages of different types of meat in the freezer. I take out a pack of three chicken breasts and place it chicken side down, in the sink. The porcelain will help it defrost faster. The cereal disappears, guess I was hungry.

Knocking sounds off at the door. It's only eight-thirty, I know I promised the kid lunch, but I didn't say anything thing about breakfast. I peek into the small magnifying whole, and see dark straight hair. Okay. I leave the chain on the door and open it up.

"Good morning Viv. I thought I'd come have a word with you," Callen, the gross says. For some reason, she's wearing her hair straighter, and it looks darker. Actually, it looks a lot like my own. I don't see anyone else around, so I shut the door, take the chain off, and open it back up. No way do I want her inside with me. I step outside, closing the door behind me and stand with my back to the door. I'd thrown on the same clothes from last night, the thin cotton shirt makes me feel too exposed. Not speaking, I cross my arms and wait for her to speak. I am sure she'd seen me last night, why else would she be here?

"So, I wanted to fill you in on what is happening here." She moves to the small two foot wall that runs along the front of the house, and pulls herself up to sit. "Juda and I are engaged. We have been since he was thirteen. I realize he's very attractive and charming, but he is not available. I thought someone should tell you before you go making a fool of yourself." Okay, a direct approach. Still, I don't trust her.

"Callen, I appreciate you telling me your point of view, but honestly, I don't believe you." I don't want to sound like I'm in denial. "What I mean to say is, if that *was* what someone like Juda wanted, wouldn't it have happened five years ago?" She flinches at my words. I hit a nerve. Before she can turn into another blood thirsty animal, I continue, "Look. Let's say you have some

141

sort of old agreement, for argument sake. And you came here because you want to rekindle this old idea. Then why were you having sex with another guy?"

Callen's face goes blank. She didn't know I knew. She hops down from the wall, opens her mouth, and then shuts it again. I want to tell her off, really act like a stupid teenager, but that will only give her a reason to do the same. Instead, I let her turn it over in her mind a few times. I lean on the door, casually keeping a hand on the knob, in case she decides to charge me. The girl can shift, and I can't, there will be no fighting for me.

"I see. You want to play it that way? Fine, I have a witness to where I was, and who I was with. My sister, she has become very good at playing around with the truth. Here, you are alone, no one is in your corner. How will you explain breaking your vow?"

"What?" Vow? Huh? The confusion doesn't' do much to calm my anger, but I'm not going to let the little hell bitch coax me into losing my cool.

"Oh, you haven't taken the vow of purity yet? You have zero chance with Juda if that hasn't even happened." She turns and starts to leave, but stops and twist around, one hand on her hip. "You don't got me fooled, Viv," she says my name like it's a bug that needs to be squashed. "I know you know what you are. Juda may be holding out hope your mothers little secret was only the mistake of conceiving you, but I can tell, you're *wrong*. And soon, Juda will know it, too." What I am? My mother's secret? Callen isn't only crazy, she is paranoid. She walks off, leaving me confused and annoyed.

Safe behind the closed door, I lock both the knob, and dead bolt. Out of frustration I kick the sofa. Damn it. I have no freaking idea what that crazy hag is talking about. Worse, she is right. Who's in my corner? Jared? Would he believe Callen's sister or me? Didn't some of the other shifters say something about my mom, and why she left? I can't remember, ugh, I need to sit. The

142

sofa is closest. Sitting down doesn't help since all I can see is the large TV, which reminds me of Todd Hamon, and all that mess.

As much as I really think Juda and I can become something more, is it really possible? What the heck is Vow of Purity? I'm a long way from virginity, not like that far, I've only had three partners, by choice. Callen isn't a virgin; how would she pass? Why am I letting that slug get to me? As much as I want to tell myself she's just a manipulative liar, I can't help but think about what I've heard since I came here.

What is my mother hiding? If it's something about what I am, then it would probably have to do with who my father is. What did the Aunts say, my father has to make a choice? One I couldn't live with or live without? No, not live without, she'd put emphasis on LIVE, am I in danger here? But from who? Would Juda want to hurt me? No, I don't believe that, no way. But the king... if I run, he would send people after me. If the Aunts hadn't come to me, what would he have found out in my mind? If I there's any clue as to who my dad is, it's not just hidden in my mind, but it's straight up alztimered away.

I need someone to talk to about this. As much as I want Juda to be that guy, my gut is saying he's not, which is all too weird since I want to kidnap him, and run away to a Vegas Elvis chapel every time I touch him. I will confide in Jared. He's my guy, he won't freak, and maybe he would know what the hell crazy-town was talking about. I will chance him not believing me about what I saw. Maybe I don't even have to mention it? Okay, I will pull myself together, and figure out what to say, while I get ready for our lunch.

The clock says its ten fifty by the time I shower, and sift through my mom's closet. She has a pair of Doc Martins that are now mine, mine, mine. Time to start lunch. I've decided to tell Jared everything, even what I suspect about his father. It's a gamble, but how else will I figure everything out?

143

Cooking usually calms me completely, not today. With every minute, my stomach does a flip. I place both plates, filled with crispy golden chicken breast, light whipped potatoes, and a good serving of white pepper gravy, onto the little round kitchen table. A knock sounds at the door, noon on the dot.

"Wow, no wonder the kid wants to hang out with you." Juda stands in front of the open door, even I can smell the food from here, but it's not the company I was expecting. I need to talk to Jared first. Words are too difficult to form, so I step aside and smile. He comes in, his nose sniffing the air. Thank goodness guys are easily distracted. I need to rearrange my plan of action, I can't spill to Juda, not yet. A little spasm in my gut confirms my thoughts.

"He was right. I owe him big time." He grabs the back of one of the chairs and sits down. He doesn't even give me time to join him before the first bite is in his mouth. My chair is opposite side of the table, but before I can get there, Juda stands, pulls the chair over and places my plate next to his. Why am I over thinking this? All I have to do is smile, and enjoy his company. Callen's wrong, there is a real chance for Juda, and I if we get to know each other better. You can't collapse a house with a strong foundation. God, I love Jerry Springer right now.

"Hope you're not too disappointed to see me instead of my brother." His sly smile tells me he knows the answer to that. The warmth he's giving me truly starts to calm some of my anxiety. I know better than to think it's fully gone, but here and now, I can let go a little, for him.

"Well, he did promise to tell me all about hacking and creating front doors or back doors? You'll have to figure out some way of entertaining me." His smile gets bigger, and I realize the insinuation. "Drink?" Getting up fast, I head to the fridge.

"Sure, I'll take whatever you give me." God, he isn't going to let me off the hook that easy. I grab two bottled waters and bring them back to the table.

The three pieces of chicken become six once I cut them in half. Juda eats as much as Jared, four pieces, and a second serving of potatoes. All his compliments are fused with sexual innuendos. Stuff like: "good breasts" or "I have too much creamy gravy, want some?" Once the lip licking starts, I decide to steer the conversation off the meal.

"Are both your parents from the south?" He's taking a drink of his water, while keeping eye contact with me. The mention of parents makes him spill the water down his purple and yellow striped shirt. No one wants to think of sex and parents at the same time. Juda laughs at himself, and bobs his head up and down. I'm sure he sees my cleverness in getting us away from the sexual innuendos.

"Yes, they are. I think our Uncle Lu married a northerner. It's hard to keep track." He leans back into his chair. He's trying to be cool, but I see the food-baby poking out above his jeans. Even with that, he's still quite beautiful.

"How's things going with your new family role?" There's not much left on my plate, so I do the lean back too, but not before I pull my jeans over my own full belly. If I can't talk to him about what I saw with Callen, maybe I can strengthen our connection instead. I want us to get to know each other beyond our obvious attractions.

"Not too hard really. There is a little more to it then I considered I'd be doing. Mostly learning inventory and what not."

"How are you getting along here?" He leans onto his elbows and strokes the top of my hand. The light touch sends shivers over my body, but when he lifts my fingers into an awkward hand hold, all tension evaporates. I really need him to know how I feel. He has to know.

145

"Wait, what did you ask me?" I can't help but giggle at myself.

"How was your day yesterday," he laughs along with me, and ran his thumb over the side of my finger.

"Awesome, I mean, it could've been better with you here, but Jared and I enjoyed the chili I made, and walking around." With each word, I can't help but be embarrassed at how childish I sound. What would he find interesting in me? I'm feeling a bit lightheaded. Regretfully, I let loose of his hand to study myself by holding onto the table's edge.

"You okay Viv?"

Focusing is difficult, but wait, no, I'm fine now. The strange feeling is gone.

"Yeah, I've been having some dizziness and headaches the past couple days. But it leaves me quickly." I look up to see a frightened look on Juda's face, but he smooth's out his expression when our eyes meet.

"Sorry, I mean, I hate that's happening to you," he says and stands. I had been wanting to tell him something, but I can't really remember now. Juda gets up and walks to the fridge, getting out two more bottles of cold water.

"Thanks." Breaking the seal, I take a long drink. If only this area had windows, my skin feels all flush.

"Why don't we go for a walk?" Juda offers. Again, he seems to be reading my mind. Thankfully, I follow him to the door, he stops as he opens it, and turns towards me.

"I know it's not cool, but I think it's going to rain in a bit, why don't you grab a jacket or something? I'll wait for you on the porch." He gives me a Juda smile and steps out. Okay, well I had that jacket, oh, I remember. I grab the dark hoodie I'd had on last night from the floor behind the sofa. I'd tried to toss it on the sofa, guess I missed.

Juda's washing his hands with the water hose when I walk over to him. He's saying something, but it's too fast for me to get. He stops as I get to him. Without a word, he turns off the valve, and places the hose back onto the rest of the rolled up green coil.

"There's a sink in the apartment you can use to wash your hands."

"I was already out here. Ready?" I laugh as he takes out an old timer handkerchief. He folds it up and stuffs it into his front jean pocket. "Shall we?" He tips his head towards the trail. I go, and he follows.

The day is warm. You can feel the gulf air struggling to stay dominant in the face of on coming winter months. There should be rain soon, which will make the nights cooler. The trail we walk down is lined with large Texas trees. Several might be pecan, but if they've dropped their fruit, the family must pick them day and night. There's only dirt, leaves and small branches on the ground. Jared and I walked a different way, therefor nothing's familiar.

We come to a smaller version of the commons. Instead of a dozen tables, there are only four, and no lights strung above our heads. People mill around, talking in Romani and smoking, but when they see Juda, they start to wave and greet us. Half empty Styrofoam-cups litter the tables. A woman walks over and starts to clean up the mess. She is older, maybe sixties, and when she smiles, I see she's missing a tooth on the right top side of her mouth. Once she gets the table cleared, Juda sits down and I slide into the seat across from him. I would like to sit next to him, but who knows what the human Romani would think? Which reminds me of the 'vow' Callen had mentioned. Maybe I can work that into our conversation.

"That was nice of her." My eyes continue to follow the lady as she instructed a young girl, probably thirteen or so, to sweep the area for the prince. She moved past our table, and sat a pack of chewing gum in front of me. The older woman never paused in her cleaning.

147

"They do that sometimes, when there's a new shifter around. She likes you, it's a gift. You should chew one now that way she sees you accept it." The pink squares smell like bubble gum. I offer one to Juda, he accepts one. The woman, isn't facing us, but she can see us in her peripheral vision from that angle. She must, because a second later a wide smile spreads over her face, and she starts to sing in Romani. The others at the table around us start speaking again, maybe they'd been waiting to see if I would accept the gift.

A movement behind Juda's head catches my attention. At the edge of the trees, I see Jared. His eyes lock with mine. He puts a finger over his mouth, then gives me a stiff wave and disappears. Why didn't he come over to sit with us? Juda hadn't seen any of this; his attention is on some men who play checkers at one of the tables. From this side of his face, it's hard to not notice the curve of his lips, and strong line of his jaw. So handsome, but I really want to know more about him. Mostly, I want to know if I should care enough to get involved with all the family politics.

"The majority of people can't handle the truth of the world around them. These people, however, have had no choice but to face the truth."

"What do you mean?"

"The Romani had their land stolen from them. Cast out to fend for themselves hundreds of years ago."

"Is that why they chose to stay here with the shifters?"

"Yes and no. Over time, we became one. If it hadn't been for shifters, none would survive the odds back then." This is the history lesson I'd missed out on not growing up in the compound. "Anyway, out there, we are instantly labeled as soon as the word 'gypsy' is mentioned. Our women are diseased to the outsiders. Our men are thought of as thieves. The entire culture is damned by dark magic. In reality, if it weren't for our talents we'd make no money.

Does a man not have a right to earn money?" He didn't say it like he wanted an answer.

"You are so passionate about the people here. You know, I have no idea what kind of things I can or can't do here, I wouldn't want to offend anyone." Juda smiles and reaches across the table to squeeze my hand. His skin is warm and soft, and his eyes focus on mine, telling me I'm all he's thinking about.

"Well, I did hear you were out walking around last night." My heart stopped. Did Callen go on the defense?

"It's alright, calm down. One of the men saw you, he wasn't angry or offend, just curious. I guess we need to cover some basics. I didn't want to tell you before cause I was worried you'd find the rules odd."

"Okay. I hope none of them involve shaving my head cause, I just got my hair long enough." He smiles at my bad joke, even though I really mean every word.

"No, but you may have to give me your first born." I know that was a joke, but he's still adding too much heat to his words. "We don't usually let new people have free roam at night. Shifter or human. If you are going to be leaving the compound, we need someone to escort you out. And if you decide to stay, there are stricter rules, but that's only when you decide."

I really want to know about the stricter part, but I also don't plan on staying, coming back yes, or so I think. I am fooling myself to think Juda would ever leave this place. If I want Juda, the life he has will be a part of the package. I could tell him that I think an 'us' is a good idea, but I also need to find my father. Telling him yes and no at the same time probably won't work to my advantage.

"Hey, enough of this talk, there's a dinner coming up at six, want to go? I promise no bears."

"Yeah, that's cool. And sorry for the late night stroll." Telling Jared about my plan first is right; I'll get him alone at the dinner.

"Okay, that's settled. Now, what to do until then." Juda's eyebrow shoots up in a question. But his eyes have the answer, not yet handsome prince.

Chapter Nineteen

The Birds

"How about some checkers?" I say, which brings a smile to his face. He nods in agreement. Did he really think I would make the first move? Please, I'm not that kind of girl, a quick look at his angular jaw and dark features has me questioning the validity of that statement.

For the next two hours, he only wins two games out of a dozen or so. By the time we leave, the men of the camp are playfully teasing Juda. The women say that Juda hasn't smiled this much since he was a young boy. All that was in Romani, which Juda only translated some of the jeers and gossip. Callen's name was never spoken, but I'd have to have rocks for brains to not grasp their meaning, Callen may not be the right bride for their future king. By the time we got up to go, I had two more packs of gum and some dried herbs for my mother's apartment door.

"How about I hang those for you before we head to dinner?" Juda offers. His fingers brush the hand I'm holding the herbs with.

"Okay, yeah, that would be great." Our afternoon went by with ease. With every story about his life, I found I wanted to hear more.

"You know, I told you about my entire childhood…" His voice goes up with the unspoken question.

"I don't think a trip to the zoo, a temper tantrum, and your first car qualify as your entire childhood." I don't want to tease him, he had told me a lot with those stories, but…

"Come on, you gotta give me some credit? Okay, how about you tell me about you? I know you were young, but do you remember my aunt at all?" His words strike me strangely. I hadn't considered my loss would also be his.

"Yeah, somewhat. She liked chickens; she cooked often. Really, there's not much I can remember, just flashes." It's nice to talk about her. I've gone so long without doing it, sometimes I forget I even had parents.

"How about your dad?" My gut gives a little twist. I don't know if it's to stay quiet about my plan or to come clean.

"I don't have any kind of memories of my real father, but if he's out there..." The pang in my stomach nearly sends me to the ground. I cover my stop by adjusting my pant leg over my boot. Okay, no telling him, got it. We don't say anything until we reach the apartment.

Juda hangs the herbs by the paper string that's tied around the small bundle. There's a hook above the door that I hadn't noticed.

"There, now if they walk by, they will see you are protected." If there is any bland food trying to attack me, I can see a use for the herbs, otherwise, I don't get it. "I know it's a strange tradition, one I will gladly explain on our way to dinner. We are late." Juda reaches out and takes my hand, then leads me back up the trail, taking the right fork this time.

He doesn't let go of my hand. Touching him is too distracting to pay attention to the tale of the herbs. I try to listen, but only catch that the tradition goes back centuries and that each herb has different qualities.

As we approach the end of the trees that opens up to the commons, he stops and pulls me into a hug. My breathing seems loud. I know he can feel my heart beating through his own chest. My mind is aware of the location of his lips, just behind my right ear. He licks them. Is he about to kiss me? In case, I pull in my own trembling lips, to moisten them. He pulls back, but not away.

"Viv, can you see yourself being mine?" He runs a finger down my back. Vibrations spread over my entire body. Our connection is stronger than it had been.

"Yes, I..." He kisses the side of my lips. The current of electricity the small kiss sends through me, makes me catch my breath, and drives my heart rate up. His breathing is rough, but he stays an inch away from my lips. Our bodies are close enough that I can tell he wants me, but instead of kissing me fully, he puts his forehead to mine.

"I can't..." His words are nothing but heavy breaths.

"Juda?" A woman's voice calls out his name. My fingers grip him, but his eyes are closed. I don't understand.

"Sounds like my mom," he says, but pulls me a little closer. Our bodies press together. This is it, he's going to kiss me. I know it.

"Juda?" Why is she calling him now? He sighs, but lets me go. Maybe if I stay close, I can distract him further.

"I know you're out there, Juda?" She's in the commons, I can hear the difference of her calls. She's walking around and looking for him. There are small houses that line up on either side of the commons, which we are behind. Any minute she could step around the corner and see us here.

"I'll be right back. Why don't you grab us a table?" He kisses my forehead and abandons me, disappearing around the corner. Before I can walk, I take some deep breaths to steady my pulse. With him gone, I can breathe steadier. The dizziness passes. It's not as bad as it has been. The idea of little birds with ribbons and animated hearts, circle above my head. Puppy love perhaps?

Lucky for me, no one is in the commons to witness my nearly tripping on untied bootlaces. I plop down on the closest table. I thought girls were supposed to be the emotional ones. He is like a freaking light switch, and I have no idea when he's on or off.

The planets are clearly visible in the darkening, South Texas sky. I focus on them and clear the rest of my Juda worries from my mind.

"Lovely, isn't it child?" The soft voice startles me.

The Aunts stand ten feet from my table. A warm smile spreads across my face. When they move towards me, it's as if they are one, each step reminding me of water flowing down a river. Soundless, like mist. The familiar perfume, lilac, fills my senses, calming my mind further. I'd come to associate the scent with their magic.

"You are the daughter no one expected to come," Lady Blond whispers. I'm not sure her lips moved. Another sister speaks so close to the last, I hardly have time to register what they are saying.

"Your journey is only beginning. Distractions are clouding your eyes, do not let the unworthy too near." The words of Lady Bold are unyielding. Lady White picks up the line of words as if she spoke the sentence herself.

"You are much more than a daughter, now." Their voices are similar in pitch, and not one moves their lips when they speak. "And so much more than a lone wolf!"

Three pairs of eyes grow larger, black starts to spread over each face, "You will bring forth the birth of the new. Be wary of tricks and falsely given affections." These words are spoken out loud, but hardly sound human. Black spreads over each woman. Arms and legs disappear. The loud sound of talons on stone draws my eyes towards their feet. Large, dark, orange bird legs and claws are where their legs and feet should be.

"Our time is done, for now." Large black wings spread from around black feathered bodies. Their shift complete, each abnormally large crow jumps into the air one after the other. In mid take off, each body shrinks to normal crow size. The sky had been pinks and purples when I sat down, but night has come and the three black birds get swallowed up fast, disappearing into the black sky. The emptiness of the large sky presses its hollowness into my chest. No one is here but me, like it's always been. The fuzzy, goofy feeling Juda left me with is gone.

The Aunts are my only-go-to when things get confusing or threating. Funny how you don't even know when you start counting on someone, until they aren't there anymore. Sadness tries to settle in my heart, but the gift of connection. The Aunts had given me, blocks the emotion, warming my chest, chasing the cold loneliness away. They may be gone, but the magic stayed, giving me hope they are not too far away.

Time to head towards the picnic area. Their words of praise and warning stick in the back of my mind. Though the message is a little unclear, I can only assume they mean the king and some of the other shifters, shouldn't be trusted. I will not fail them. After all, I'm more than a daughter now. Possibly, a queen to be.

Both humans and shifters are gathered at the tables. To my genuine relief, it's not BBQ. There is salad, roast beef, and various types of rice and other veggies in large aluminum pans. People laugh and chat with each other. No one shoots me nasty looks, which has a lot to do with me not seeing Callen and her hags. The king, and his brother Nate are at the head of very long tables set side to side. I count at least six tables in total.

Juda appears as I'm picking out a table for us to sit at. He puts his hands on my shoulders and steers us to the middle, where his younger brother and friends sit. We are very close to King Shea's table, which makes me uncomfortable. The reasons I'd come up with earlier, for the king's invasion of my mind, are more like justifications. I believe it's time to prove to everyone, including the king that I belong with Juda, and there for, I belong here.

I do what I do best, I blend. Keeping the conversation light with the others around as I mill around, never making anything about me, including not trying to steel Juda's attention. Then I mimic body language. Soon, people relax and start to crack jokes.

"Hey Juda, dat wants us to help in the toast, come on," Jared says.

Juda turns and gives my shoulder a squeeze, "We'll be back." The kids and I listen to the family toast, mostly stuff about keeping together. It should make me happy this invitation to dinner. Doesn't that prove some sort of acceptance on their part? Though, there are faces around me that say, why is she here? The toast is quick, but the guys are stuck talking to the people at their father's table.

"Hey, you're in my seat," Callen's familiar voice shatters my concentration. Her long golden, brown hair seems to glitter in the dark. She stands across the picnic table, her bright pink, tight fitting dress, shows off her exaggerated curves, even bigger than the first night we met. Necklaces and bracelets cover her up like some glorified club girl.

No sign of her hag gang. One of the shifter kids, a guy named Trip, I think, moves when she flicks her claws at him. The skank sits directly in front of me. Her brown/violet eyes size me up. I don't care if I'm only in a T-shirt and jeans, because all my curves are real. I hope by meeting her gaze, she realizes all her threats this morning are pointless and hold no power over me.

"It's fine. There's always a seat reserved for me." That sweet, grotesque smile spreads over her lips.

"What happen to your fan girls?" I mimic the same smile she's so good at. I wonder if the others around us can sense the air thicken, like I can.

"They're around. I wanted us to have some girl time. I mean, so far you've made no friends." She reaches over and grabs my hands off the table. "Nice to see you tonight, not sculling in the shadows?" A few eyes glance our way. The lump in my throat goes down easy, her words ignite fire and that primitive part I've been getting to know the past few days.

156

"I've made friends. And this place, isn't yours. Aren't you from New Mexico or something? Why don't you go annoy those people?" My voice stays calm and cheerful. I won't even bring up last night, no use I'm sure that's what she wants.

"I know; you're sticking around for the wedding? How nice. Maybe you can be my something old."

One quick tug, and my hands are free. I can't stop myself from fidgeting in my seat.

She laughs and continues, "I don't know why the king is taking so long in announcing the ceremony, but know, it's going to happen. I can only guess my fiancé is confused by you showing up. I suggest you leave. I'd hate to bitch slap you out'ta the way. But, I will do what I have to do." Her bitchy words won't lead me into an out and out explosion.

Steady, take her down one notch at a time. "My mother was the king's only sister, I belong here. Juda isn't confused about anything. He's sees there are options now, he doesn't have to settle." She's used to manipulating people. By addressing each sneer, I will stop her from making the others think any truth is in what she is saying.

"Please, for all he knows your mixed blood would taint his clan. Face it, girl, I'm a better match. My magic is stronger, I know all the traditions of our people and I'm willing to kill to protect what's mine. Are you?"

Even though our exchange isn't louder than any of the other conversations around us, the people closest are silently listening. The little fire from earlier starts to blaze, and I'm done.

"Callen, you should save yourself from further embarrassment. I can learn all those things. The elders are on my side. Your attempts to scare me are a complete waste of time. Go throw your temper tantrum for someone who gives a shit." Tendrils of cold sureness, spread though-out my entire body and douse out my apprehension. The air stirs around us, I get the sense that it's waiting for me to tell it what to do. What I need is to know how to make this girl stop her attacks.

My own eyes are starting back at me. What has Callen done to me? Wait, the table looks different, I'm sitting where Callen should be. I am Callen? No, I can hear her thoughts and still know my own, I'm in her head.

Why is she looking at me? Did she tell Juda about last night? Impossible, she wouldn't chance it. Callen's thoughts are exactly like I'd expect, simple and full of self-importance.

A strong urge to be cruel slithers through her head. An image of a hand, with familiar red nails, slaps a woman's face. 'You were never worthy of my father's love.' Callen's mother only had enough magic to shift every now and then. Why would he marry a northern?

How could she be disgusted by her own mother? I don't want to be in her head anymore. And like that, she's gone. The beady eyes of one really twisted girl stares from across the table at me, once again. There is serious crazy living there.

"It won't be so easy to bully the people here. They aren't your father, spoiling and ignoring the monster growing inside of you." To prove my point, I imagine there to be an invisible hand made from the air itself. Not too hard, I use it to push her back. She moves in her seat, to anyone else it may look as if she jerked on her own. A look of shock appears on her face, but is gone fast. That had been enough, no need to expose the girl's sexcapades to all here. If she comes at me again though, I won't hesitate. After all, once the words are said, they can't be unspoken.

Callen's smirk fell slightly. She looked down and over to see if anyone had touched her, though I'm pretty sure she knows it was something I did. Maybe the look wasn't to see if someone had pushed her, maybe it was to see if anyone else noticed she'd been pushed. Seeing that no one looks shocked, she turns her full attention back to me. For another second, I see the little girl she really is, fear, confusion, but those emotions disappear as the mean girl flips back on, "Your blood is wrong, you're not right." The words are more of a whisper, but I hear them fine. She gets up. I stand to face her.

"Leaving so soon? Isn't there more seats for you to steal?" I try to mimic more of her mean girl snarls laced with sugar.

A few people laugh. The small sounds catch her attention. An audience usually feds her bitchiness, she so loves to be the center of attention. Callen steps away from the table. The air around me warms, I look over to see the king watching. Is that his magic or hers?

"We'll continue this conversation, later." Callen turns and twitches off. More people openly laugh at the retreating girl. Trying not to show my annoyance, I sit back down. A second later, the air cools, becoming the normal night breeze once again. Taking a chance, I glance over at the king's table; he's eating and talking to his family, as if he'd never noticed the girl fight. It's petty, but it sure felt good to put her in her place.

After that, everyone only spoke English. I'm not the only one who doesn't care for Callen. Many of the girls around me whisper to me; they've always wanted to tell her off. No one tells the guys about the spat, I'm glad. I'm not sure if I want Juda to know, that I know about his betrothal. Or at least, not tonight.

During dinner, the kids start to ask about the gadze world. After a while, I'm no longer trying to fit in, I just do. Music plays, and I join in with the dancing and singing. No one changes into safari animals. A normal family gathering. Well, as normal as I'd ever seen.

No one brought up the Aunts the entire evening. The words they spoke never leave my mind. There seems to be no end in sight for the party. Time to cut myself off.

"Hey, I'm pretty tired. Jared, you up to walking me home?" Down the table Juda chats with one of his uncles. I know it's bad to take advantage of the distraction, but I really want to talk with Jared alone.

"Yeah sure." I wave to Juda as we head out of the party. A strange look comes over his face. His brow wrinkles, his head tilts to the side, but then he smiles and gives me a wave back. I can't decide if he is angry, confused, or relieved that I didn't come up and demand for him to leave the party with me. I want him to know, I'm not some selfish girl. I respect his duties. At least I won't have to work out some sort of excuse to get alone time with Jared. Nothing like winning a guy over by demanding to be alone with his taller, younger brother.

Chapter Twenty

Jared

Jared watched as Juda tried to conceal his jealousy with casual nonchalance. He'd studied his brother from afar for years, he knew his body language. But, Jared understood. What Juda didn't know was his little brother was trying to keep him from really messing up.

Viv was amazing. If Juda let their dad's plan play out, he could lose her. Even though the kid wasn't privy to the plan, he could guess it wasn't out and out honesty. Their dad had an idea of what truth meant, that no one else had. Jared needed to figure out how to keep his big brother from running off the best chance of real love he'd ever have. Callen, she wasn't the right girl for his brother. But Jared knew better then to try and stop them out right. Besides, Juda didn't seem like he'd accepted the betrothal. He wanted things to work with Viv.

"I need to tell you something, but I want it to be between us only. Can you do that?" asked Viv.

Jared smiled at his cousin. No matter what had been found out about her, Jared knew, bone deep, she was trust worthy. There were very few people the kid felt that way about.

"Viv, I promise, just between us." He meant it. He prepared for her to ask what was happening. He didn't know what all she'd experienced, but if it was a spell, he'd know the signs.

"Okay. I want to leave and find my father. But I know Callen and Juda are supposed to get married. She came to my apartment this morning. The thing is, I saw her with someone in a car, doing stuff." Viv pushed up her arm sleeves then pulled them down again. "Anyway, I need your advice. If I go, will I lose a chance with Juda?"

The dark made it hard for humans to see, but Jared could see his cousin fine. Her face was blank, her eyes wide; she blinked a few times before she spoke.

"I like your brother, a lot. We're cool, right?" The night air blew past the two of them. This part of the trail was wider giving them space to walk with ease. They both shivered from the coolness of a big gust of wind.

"Viv, I am and always will be your friend, we are super green." A wide smile broke the stone mold of her face. Her arms embraced his lower chest. Trapping his arms by the elbows.

"Okay, awesome," she said with full understanding. That was one of the reasons he really liked her.

"Well, my advice, take him with you." The words shot out of Jared's mouth fast. The idea had barely solidified in his thoughts. But if Juda left, he's be able to avoid whatever it was their dad had planned. Plus, maybe get the girl.

"Take him? I wouldn't think he'd leave here."

"Viv, he has ten years to find a suitable wife. Trust me, he likes you a lot, too." Jared had to laugh as he watched her brows shoot up. Even in the low moonlight, he could see her cheeks warming. "You should tell him tomorrow, get him to agree and leave. He's the prince, he can do what he wants." This would work; this would be perfect. By the time they came back, Juda would be head over hills in love, and their dad wouldn't be able to stop that.

"Okay, but…"

"What? You said you like him and…"

"No, it's not that. I'm a wanted killer remember? Maybe you and I could do some crash course lessons on shifting before I approach him about this?

Jared thought a moment. That would be a good idea. Plus, he'd perfected the art of shifting, a real self-proclaimed Rembrandt. Jared held in his laugh, he was pretty bad at shifting, but he knew enough.

"Okay, first thing tomorrow, you tell him and you guys leave." She frowned at him, then turned and started back down the trail.

"You're not telling me everything are you?" Well, she'd know if he lied, so he told her what he could.

"I want to see you and Juda really get a shot, and there is too much going against that here." They stopped speaking, he hoped he'd said enough to motivate her to really try, but he got the feeling she wasn't sharing anymore tonight.

Chapter Twenty-One

Shifting

The knocking at the door interrupts my dreams. I think there was kissing involved, but the clock says 7:50 am, and I'm struggling to remember how to sit up. Maybe if I lay here and make no noise, whoever it is will leave and come back later? Who was I kissing?

The knock came again.

Dang it. The cover flops off me. Wait, where are my clothes? I must have really been hot last night. After a second, I find my night shirt crumpled under the blanket. The ratty Alice Cooper tee and pair of old school gym short with the white strips on either side are pushed into the sheets. A third knock amps up my frustration and with it my adrenalin levels.

Great, I won't be able to get back to sleep now.

"Coming..." please stop knocking.

A quick look, and its Jared? The door flies open, and I almost clock myself in the forehead.

"Who died?"

His mouth falls open slightly and his brow sinks in a question. "Huh?"

"You're awake before me? Something bad has to be going on." Now I regret not getting to the door sooner.

"No! Oh sorry. Juda went in with our dat early. I figured we should start on your lessons as soon as possible." He looks a little too awake. "Sorry 'Dad' I forget English with you."

"You can say dat, I've picked up on some terms, sort of." Instead of sitting, the teen paces the room.

"How much caffeine have you had already?" I figure it's a staple for all the Dacian.

"Ah, only a cup, I usually do black teas. Coffee's bitter no matter how much sugar I add. I drank some this morning though. I wanted to be awake for this." Jared mindlessly moves things around the shelves. Putting things in order, the way they'd been when I first came to the apartment. When he slides the remaining three frames back where they'd been, one spot is left empty. That had been the one I'd taken. His long fingers trace the vacant spot.

Something is off with him today, it's not just the over caffeination. His eyes stick in one place too long, like something is on his mind.

"Juda said no one else had been in here for seventeen years?" My voice broke the silence in the room, it makes him jerk slightly.

He blows out a long breath, then sits down on the sofa. As he does, a thin gold chain falls out of his loose T-shirt. He sits at on the edge of the sofa and mindlessly shakes a leg. In order to keep things casual, I toss the small handmade throw, hanging over the couch, over my shoulders. Leaning into the door-less frame that separates the kitchen from the living room I wait for his response.

"I never told anyone I came here. When my best friend died, I was nine. I needed to be somewhere no one would look for me."

His hands fidget with the gold chain; it emerges out from his blue T-shirt completely. A small golden medallion hangs from the necklace. That million-mile stare is back in his eyes. He's sad, that's part of what I'm missing.

"Is that a saint?" I ask to break up the awkwardness. He looks at his fingers, which rubbed the small disk.

"Yeah, I haven't taken it off since David died. He'd given it to me after we made our blood brothers packet." Jared's eyes move over the room. Just when I think he's going to speak, his brows crease and he looks someplace new. He wants to tell me something, forcing him to speak may not get me all the info I need. I'll let him tell me when he's ready.

"English breakfast tea, okay?" I turn to put the kettle on. Out of the corner of my eye, I see him reach up and wipe his cheek. There's a somber look to him, except I suspect more. Loneliness coupled with frustration maybe. How could a kid like Jared get that way with such a big family around him?

I pull down two small china cups, white with dainty blue flowers painted on them. Since I'm being domestic, I put out a miniature ceramic pitcher with milk and add a platter of shortbread cookies, that I'm sure will disappear first. The little plastic bear with the golden honey looks out of place on the silver platter. The steam whistles out of the kettle. May as well amp up the caffeine, I plop four tea bags into the water and turn off the fire. Jared walks into the kitchen and sits at the small table. As I'm putting the platter down, he grabs up two cookies, of course. His eyes look distant, time for plan B.

"I'm thinking you came so early for more than one reason." Jared turns his head, avoiding my eyes, he needs to be snapped out of this funk. "What's the what kid?" Direct. Loners hate being manipulated. I understand that feeling very well.

"You're in danger, Viv." He dumped three spoons of honey into his tea, with some milk. I watch the brown swirl with the white, and let his words sink in. Hadn't Callen been trying to take my head off one way or the other for the past few days? What could be worse than a jealous, insecure teenager? Okay, I'm technically still a teenager, but I've been self-sufficient since I was eight. Come to think of it, I shouldn't let Callen bug me as much. Mean girls. Ugh.

"Okay, I know Callen's intense and she did try to use my head for a bear toy, but I'm handling myself alright." He sits down the cup in his hands.

166

My own porcelain cup has my attention, but mostly because I sense there is way more to his story that I don't want to hear.

"Viv, I know you saw me following you guys yesterday. There's something going on, I'm not sure what though. It's because you're not normal." I let the question show on my face, WTF?

"Oh, sorry I didn't mean, well not that way." His fumbling words help smooth nothing over, but I let it go. He's struggling to tell me something, and anger won't help that get out faster.

"Jared, you don't have to say anything you don't want to. I trust you, more than anyone else here." My gut unclenches, I hadn't realized I was tense. "I mean, I really like Juda, but he's not easy to get a read on." And there it is, I don't trust Juda. Lusted for yes, was crushing on for sure, but not one hundred percent trusted him. The thought makes me a little sad. Also, confused. Is it my own issues blocking the connection, or am I picking up on something else?

Jared's long leg shook as he studies my face. His head bobs with one decisive nod.

"It's time for you to learn how to shift."

He's right, but I hadn't expected him to say that. Butterflies do a disco dance in my stomach. If I can shift. No, I'm not human and I won't let anyone stop me, not even me.

"Okay, but let me go change really quick." I slept with a workout bra on, but the mini gym shorts are way too short. While I'm changing into jeans and a different shirt, I take out my contacts and clean my eyes out. The new pair settles much better after I get each eye moisturized well. The mustard yellow of the shower curtain and rug look vivid this morning. I shouldn't keep contacts in that long. Jared hasn't moved from the kitchen table.

"How do we start?"

In one gulp, he finishes his tea, then leads me to the living room. All ten cookies, gone. The caffeine pumping through my veins only adds to my growing angst.

"Help me move the sofa and stuff to make space." Jared says. He moves the table, and I work on the chair. He continues to explain our exercise, like we're talking about baking a cake. "I can turn into a bob cat. I mean, we can shift into anything living, I like bob cats and stick to that form." Everyday occurrences don't include changing into other living things, I'd prefer the cake. The space is empty, and I'm starting to realize what I'm about to attempt. The disco is over, now the butterflies have sky scrapers for wings, and seem to be fighting for space in my stomach.

"Watch." He stands in the middle of the room, in a blink he's a large gray and white cat.

"Wow!" I stumble back a few steps, and my heart jumps into high gear. The fluttering pulse in my throat sends sweat to the creases of my arms and legs. The cat opens its mouth and a feral growl comes out; seriously pointy teeth, add a murderous effect the growl wasn't missing.

I've seen the others change, but seeing someone shift two feet from me, rattles me a bit more then I'd expected. My survival instincts are screaming at me to leave, now. My feet move slightly, but I catch myself. This is still Jared, and I am not human.

"You okay?" Jared says, that quickly he'd turned back into the tall, lanky teen. His normal dark brown shaggy hair has a bit of gray, like the cats, in it.

When I don't answer, he approaches me, with caution. His arms rise, palms facing me. Our eyes hold as he places his open hand on my heart.

"It beats because of magic. The Aunts told me once when I was little 'we're the keepers of life.' I have no idea what that means, but I think it means

168

we're a part of everything." Most of the time I see Jared as a kid, but right now, he's the experienced shifter.

"Viv, don't forget, we're not human."

"I know, but..." His words do help, but my human logic clings to the insides of my head. "What if I attack you? I mean your cat didn't, but you've been turning into it for a while right?" He snorts out a single note that sounds like a laugh. If he tells me I'm not normal one more time, I may bite him before I shift.

"You're still you, but you can do all the things that the animal does. It's like a copy. You don't have an animal; you ARE the animal. But, only on the outside. Try it, it's not difficult, it's in our nature. Just focus on the animal you want to be."

Alceade and his pack pop in my mind, "Is there a trick to keeping my clothes on, like you did when you shifted? Shift? Shifts? I don't wanna be naked in front of anyone." Dang TV land brain. Not that I minded seeing Alceade naked.

"The magic takes care of that. Just concentrate on shifting your form."

I'm sure there's a lot to understand about magic, but right now I need to accept it for face value. I'll take his word for it.

With a nod, I step to the center of the room. Now or never, shit, or get off the pot, jump or, okay, enough stalling. My stomach churns. I'm not human. Focus, I must focus my thoughts on the animal I want to become. Each breath dissolves my initial reaction, though my hands tremble with the anticipation.

"Don't worry, just pick something easy. Keep the image in your head."

Jared's face is set in determination. He believes I can do it, it's part of who I am, he'd said. A cooling sensation spreads from my chest to the rest of my body, and like that, I know it will be fine. The Aunts spell, I assume.

The cat would be easiest since I'd just seen it, but my mind doesn't want to settle on that. Images of the roosters in the compound swim into my mind. My eyes are squeezed closed, and the memory of the little feathery crowing bird pops up again, despite my intention to see the cat. Seems I will have to go with the bird. There'd been so many roosters around, fighting for territory and keeping the hens in line.

Sharp tingles start to run down my head to my toes. Not letting the sensations distract me from seeing the bird is difficult. The other times I've manipulated the things in my environment, hadn't been like this. Red, brown, stiff feathers, short stubby legs, my long arms and legs feel wrong, like they are balloons and the air is being let out. The sensation of falling, or rather shrinking fills in the void, I stay focused.

The body I'm used to is gone. I move my arms and legs, except they are not so long anymore. My lips are gone, instead there's a stiffness to my face. Prickles move over my skin, the best way I can describe it, there seems to be popcorn bursting from my head to my butt where all the feathers grew. Then it stops. My breathing is calmer. Stretching causes each and every feather to move. My eyes open, the room is huge. Jared is standing above me. And I thought I couldn't get any shorter.

"Great Viv!" My wings go up, as though I'm trying to say, how is this great? He bursts into laughter. My beak opens and closes, I want to tell him to shut up, but instead a shrill cry fills the room. With my agitation, my feathers ruffle, which causes me to wiggle side to side. Each step measuring the weight of my body, the smallness of it is too foreign. Complete helplessness fills me up. The movement really brings home the new form, I'm a freaking rooster!

"How do I turn back? You didn't tell me how to turn back!" My crazy rooster cry gets louder. Jared's laughter doubles. Great.

"Okay, okay I get it, you want to turn back. Stop trying to talk cause I'm gonna have to leave to stop laughing!"

He wipes at his face and I try to give him a stern look with my little black beady eyes.

"Are you trying to make me pee my pants?" He burst into laughter again. Pressure in my chest is building. My tiny body starts to puff up. A shrill monster-ish crow escapes my pointy beak. The sound jerks Jared out of his fit and he wipes away his tears once again.

"Yes, sorry... okay." He gets up and switches back into instructor mode. "You turn back the same way you shifted. You must concentrate on who you are, your skin, hair, feet, hands, stuff like that."

Okay maybe instructor isn't the right word.

"You know all the things that make up Vivian." He is obviously barely holding it together. Rolling my eyes, or at least trying to, I get back into the frame of mind that had transformed me into a foot-tall rooster. Male, really? Just in case I turn my back to him, if I end up naked, at least I'd be saved some embarrassment.

Calling up the images of my hands, arms, legs, and hair; the tingles start, each toe, each finger, my eyes, my lips and nose. This time, the change starts at my feet, and rushes up towards my head. The sensation however is very different this time.

I'm not just a body anymore, I'm everything. Vast amounts of energy, strength, love and understanding of the world fills me. A great power, very near, connected to others, seeing them, knowing them, understanding them. Simultaneously, I am aware of the feathers melting, becoming my soft, normal skin and my feet and hands coming back. Each strand of my own hair pushing through my scalp. Warmth spreads through each limb. The bigger connection shirks down becoming a single strong link. This magic pools into my stomach, like hot soup. But it doesn't stop, it travels to my forming hands, and up into the back of my neck; then, finally spreads over my face. The heat moves down my spine, and into each muscle as they grow human shape again. A deep breath, and the magic of life moves my lungs; I'd never realized how magical this is, breathing. The magic, my link, makes everything vivid and less overwhelming. Though the sharpness of my sight, smell, hearing, and knowingness logically should freak me out. There's no way of explaining how natural the new sensations are, like the way I was before had been the wrong way and this is right.

"I did it!" Elation pumps through me, and I do a little snoopy dance. I'm not naked either. Relieved, I jump around and face Jared. He is motionless. I can't tell if he's even breathing. My joyful jig comes to an abrupt halt.

"Jared?"

"Viv, don't ever transform in front of anyone else." My muscles tighten, and my gut twists.

"Why?"

He answers by shifting back into his cat form; shrinking down into the little gray fluff ball. His eyes hold mine. Then, he turns back, this time I notice the shapes his body goes through during his change. Before my own shift it had been like watching something blurry, kinda human-ish form in front of me. Now, I see the shapes, see his spark of magic. The strange magical connection that had let me feel the change is gone, but I can see it clearly.

"Did you see, I looked out'ta focus right?" He doesn't let me answer. "When you transformed back, it was like molecules from the thin air appeared to make your body. I've never seen it before. It was amazing but not normal." His face looks caught between amazement and horror, very strange combo.

The anxiety I'd been feeling non-stop since I came here, tries to sneak back into my gut. My shift had flipped something on inside of me. The power

172

gave me a kind of high. So, Jared's strange reaction isn't bringing me down completely, even if he called me abnormal again.

The kid nodded once more, making another inner decision. "It's cool, we'll figure it out." His boy grin warms the room. Maybe my elation is contagious. Trusting him is the right thing to do, it feels right.

"That wasn't funny, by the way."

"Sorry, I wasn't expecting you to be a rooster. I thought you may try something less, meek." I give him a well-practiced eye roll, he laughs.

Over the next hour we shift into various animals. Each time, the magic sings to me through my changes, no matter how fast I go. He manages to become the rooster too, but he prefers the bob cat. Each time he turned, the cat would have more details, longer, fuller tale or black thick eyeliner, and sharper teeth. By his fifth shift, a thin layer of sweat covers his face. I think I've gone through half the alphabet, and I haven't started feeling tired. The worried look comes back over Jared, adding five years to his appearance.

"Okay, I need a break." His hair and neck are damp.

"I'll make us some lunch." We move to the kitchen; his movements are sluggish.

"When you turned eighteen, you connected to the Source of Magic, but normal shifters can't do what you're doing. It's like your connection is as strong if not stronger then my dat's."

More of how 'I'm not normal' talk. A girl can get self-esteem issues this way. The busy work of pulling out ham and cheese and laying it on mayo covered bread, keeps my hands from wrapping around his neck. My silence must be giving him a clue. I get it already.

"Is that why you think I'm in danger?" I balance the sandwich plate, stacked six deep, with two cans of DP and a large bag of potato chips. I set it all down, he helps by taking two sandwiches from the top. After a minute, he notices I'm not eating, only waiting for his answer.

"Yeah it is. I'm under instruction to report whatever we do together. I trust you Viv, I have since we met in the library. Whatever is going on with you, I wanna help you figure it out. And I don't really know if that is what they want." He finishes the first two he'd grabbed, and goes for another ham and cheese. I decide I better get one before he eats the whole plate. We eat quietly for another minute.

"Maybe it's like the Aunts said, my connection is stronger because I'm a part of the women power thingy?" Jared pauses in mid bite to raise his brows. I know he's right, I'm not normal. I give him a warning look not to say it again. He nods in understanding and finishes his mouth full of food.

"I CAN say I am the ONLY one who trusts you here. Which is why I think I should go with you instead of my brother." This statement bothers me, enough that I put my half eaten lunch down.

"You think Juda doesn't trust me?" Jeez, I sound like a stupid middle school girl.

"He does, but not like I do. I don't want to see you get hurt. I love my brother, more than anyone from my life, but he is the eldest son. Don't forget that."

"I don't get that eldest thing, really, or The Source of Magic for that matter."

He drains his soda then swipes my untouched can, *brat*. "I can only tell you what I've heard in the legends and a few overheard conversations by my uncles and dat. The eldest of the eldest is the only one connected directly to the source of magic. Which is what all magical things are connected to, no matter what form they are in. The rest of us only get a fine thread. No one knows what the full power can do. Even the eldest only holds the magic, he doesn't manipulate it. The power to shift ourselves into any living thing, and a few other tricks, is all the magic an average shifter gets."

Watching Jared speak of his history I expected some kind of pride like Juda had shown. But he looks as if it aged him with each sentence. He may believe it, but he doesn't like it. Not at all. The connection I felt earlier would probably fall into the *not normal* category, I think I'll keep it to myself for now.

"You seem like you'd rather be a part of anything else but this, magical source thing. What's the down side you're not telling me?"

"Look, Juda and I are close, but he's the important one in this family. I remember having a brother, and then I didn't. I guess that's why I was close to David." He sits back into the chair. Defeated, he absently fiddles with his chain.

"What happen to him?" He's quiet so long, I start to eat again thinking he won't answer.

"David was close to my age. His father and mother had stopped here for a couple of months. It was about the time Juda started doing his preparation to become the next king. I was happy having someone to play with, since Juda wasn't allowed to anymore. David told me they were going to stay here, that my father had offered to let them join our vitsa." He pauses for a drink, and continues. "The third month they were here a bad storm came through. They went out and never came back. Juda told me a week later, their car was found in the lake, and they were still in it. I ran away for two weeks. I came here and would sneak into the house late at night for food. My mother kept Father from sending out search parties. I think she knew I wasn't far. The only way I went back was when the tin shed showed up and my first computer." He let the gold medallion drop and closed his eyes.

"I'm so sorry. I guess it was like losing your brother, twice." Part of me wanted to comfort Jared, but he wasn't used to that, what loner is? If I do, he may think I'm making him into a victim, and people like us, don't want that kind of treatment, ever.

"There's a lot of stuff I see when no one thinks I'm looking. I'm glad you can shift now." He straightens up, and grabs another sandwich. "When do we leave?"

Chapter Twenty-Two

Getting to Know You

The sun is up before I crack an eye open. The weather must be cooler outside. My comforter is too warm and cozy to pull out from under. After finishing off the chili, Jared left before five. I'd finished shifting the alphabet in animals, only slowing when I had to use an old set of encyclopedias to find things to shift into. I'd washed the dinner dishes, put furniture back in order, and took a long hot shower before fatigue hit. Jared's voice calling me a freak is the hardest thing to shake about today.

With some apprehension, I stretch under my tent of down feathers, but there is no stiffness or sourness. We'd decided to get out of the compound today. For some reason we'd never really solidified our plan of action, maybe he's intending on talking me into staying. I think my strange shifting bothers him more than he'd said.

Dressing in my favorite black shirt, and tight jeans brings me back down to earth. What makes me feel human is seeing the wrinkles in my outfit from sitting in the dryer all night. Guess there is no shifting those away. A knock at the door has me glancing at the red numbers of the alarm clock which says, it's eight a.m. on the dot. Jared got up a second day before nine?

"Wow, showered and all!" Juda says. For a moment I recall Jared's warning, but the smell of Juda, coffee and cloves, lights up my body. I forget to take a breath as I take in his presences; he looks amazing. His tall lean body pushes at the cotton shirt and jeans like it wants to be free. Oh, how I want to assist in its escape. He brought me homemade sweet bread and fruit. Can't turn away a guy with gifts.

"Thanks for the breakfast. How was your meeting yesterday?" I'd given him his usual cup of mud I'd brewed. My tea looks ready for honey and milk.

"Great, I got a special project. It's a big deal, my first grown up responsibility that will bring money for the vitsa; it's boring shop talk though. I want to hear what you and my bro did yesterday? Did he take you to his tin-can as a hostage?"

I swirl the milk into the tan colored water and watch as the dairy becomes cloudy for a brief moment. Part of me wants to confess the story Jared had shared with me, but I know it would betray our budding connection. A deep clench in my gut tells me I'd regret losing that friendship. The smell of Juda invades my senses again. I have to blink a few times to regain my focus.

Instead, I tell him what I can, without lying, "He was great, we stayed here." That sounds a little risqué. So I add, "He taught me how to shift."

Juda lifts his brows close to his perfectly combed hair line, pretty boy, umm pretty boy.

"I didn't think he'd do, *that*. I thought you'd be bored to tears and I'd have to take you out on a date tonight to make up for it." He puts his coffee cup down and tosses a piece of bread in his mouth, totally acting as if he'd not just done a drive-by-date invite.

His blatant and unexpected words make my face hot. The sexy boy flashes me a devilish smile. Okay I'll bite, but only a little.

"Well... the day was pretty great. Think you can do better?" Shameless flirting.

Juda reaches across the table; his smile growing. I froze, not sure I can trust my own reactions to whatever it is he's intending to do to me. Juda's hand grabs mine. He lifts it to his lips. His soft kiss sends every nerve ending in my body into over drive. Turning my hand over, he kisses the inside of my wrist

178

and inhaled the aroma of my skin. I almost throw the table to the floor to get to him, but a knock on the door saves the table.

"I, uh...door, I better get..." My mouth stumbles on my words, and my feet follow their example. Lucky for me, the table is stable enough to help me catch my balance. The strange dizzy spell passes over me before I can let go of the table. Jared stood in the doorway with his friendly smile. The tingling from Juda's kiss resonates over my entire body. There's real effort involved in me pulling my mind out of the gutter.

"Hey Jared, what's up?" I'm trying too hard to make it seem like all is normal. I sound like a twelve-year-old at a boy band concert. Jared gives me a look that says, okay..., to which I simply smile.

"Hey, Viv. Can I... talk to Juda?" In spite my obvious giddiness, I step aside, keeping my mouth clamped. Perhaps I should gather what's left of my dignity in this situation.

"I'm gonna go to my room and give you guys some privacy. Good to see you, Jared." Not waiting for their replies, and looking anywhere but at Juda. I hurry to the back bedroom. If I could, I'd turn into a small mouse and scurry away. Of course the possibility of me humping Juda's leg as any kind of wild animal is all too real. Instead, once in the bedroom, there's plenty to keep me busy. Making the bed, cleaning the bathroom and even arranging my shoes. Finally, calm enough, my mind can focus on getting ready for a day with Juda. Not what I was expecting to do with my day, but at some point, I can ask him about coming on the trip with Jared and me. I mean, since Jared wants to go, why can't I invite Juda too?

I put on some make-up, pull my hair out of its tie, and run a brush through the tangled mess. My mothers' jewelry is simple. I choose a one-inch-long silver pendant that's been cut to look like a braid. The chain is also silver and the perfect length for the simple thin braid to rest at my throat. The cool metal against my chest soothes me, further. Okay, I'm ready to face them.

When I emerge from my calming chamber, I find the house is silent. Have they both left? Making my way into the living room, I find Juda standing there alone reading my mother's Bible. My hot becomes cold in an instant. Though I know this is good, I'm kinda annoyed. Well, we need to know more about each other first. Maybe today will help me solidify how I really feel for Juda, not just how my lady parts react to him.

"Jared left?"

He looks up and puts the book back on the shelf, "Yep, it's just us." He says softly. "I was thinking we'd take a drive around town. I'm not sure if I'll be called away later. How about we start our date now?" He approaches me, a shadow of the evil grin that'd started up my engines earlier, plays on his lips. I can't let that happen again. I need to stay focused on my goal here. And the best way to do that is to not let my eyes linger on any part of him besides his eyes.

A few steps before he reaches me, I turn and open the door, and step out into the sunlight.

"Let's go." Finally, I'm getting a full day with Juda.

We did a drive around town, he points out some places he finds interesting or places that are prominent to the area. About the third land mark, I inform him I've been to McAllen many times.

"Of course. I didn't think of that," He laughs at himself.

"It's cool. I haven't shared the experience with someone else. I like seeing them with you." There is no controlling myself with him. He'd taken my hand in the truck and hadn't let it go. I know what Jared, my mom, and the Aunts said. But when we are together, it's like I can't find the will to care.

"Well Ms. Most Wanted, what sounds good next?" He cracks a smile at me, but his words clear my head a bit. What else can we do? He could sneak me into a movie? But I'd rather spend time looking at him not sitting in silence. The beach?

"Too bad we can't go across the border and run away to Cancun together." I wasn't expecting to say that out loud. Juda has on his sly smile; he likes the idea.

"But we don't have our swim suits." He teases me.

"I'm sure I can weave us some out of palm leaves." My silly comment makes his brows shoot up and gets a short chuckle too.

Juda squeezes my hand gently. I hope he knows I really am happiest with him. I wish I could say the right thing that would finalize us being mates. He said he wants me. His clean truck is nice; the cool air is perfect. Some of the trees we pass have started to turn into their autumn colors. All of this perfection with the perfect guy. I really want Juda. I need him.

"Okay, there are some great tacos at a little stand on the next street. I'm going to get us lunch. You stay in the truck out of sight."

"What a perfect idea." To my ears I sound like a love struck nit. But, isn't that what I am? He is so amazing

"I thought so, too." Juda found a parking space and turns off the truck. He lifts our hands and kisses my bent fingers. The flesh sizzles from the act. He looks me in the eye and kisses each finger deliberately. His soft lips bring a wave of electricity with each peck.

"Okay, if you don't want us to draw attention, I'd save that for later." He grins and leaves the cab. If he hadn't done that, I would have pulled a Callen in the middle of the day for sure. No, even my amped up libido could never make me behave like a skank. I watch Juda walk to the taco stand. Maybe the validity of that statement will be tested, soon.

181

The tacos are great. He drives me around as we eat. I point out some of the places I'd worked. Juda rubs my shoulder and holds my hand when possible. We joke about Cancun more. He seems to think he can train monkeys for a living. I want to tell him about the weird stuff going on with my magic, but the words literally won't come out. No matter, I don't want to ruin our day anyhow.

On the drive back to the compound, I decide I want to ask him to go north with Jared and me. Before I can, he starts to rub my knee. The small motion drives me insane with need for him. I put my right hand on his, and lay my head on his arm. His skin smells savory and sweet from the cloves. He'd put up the armrest, I'm closer then I was when we left this morning. I place my left hand close to his thigh. His fingers grip my leg. With intended slowness, I run my fingers down the side of his leg to his knee. His breathing picks up.

The truck slows and pull over to the side of the road. My lips want his, but then I remember he may not be pulling over to make out. I look around to see we are at the hidden entrance of his home. Instantly I regret having to sit up and give him his hand back. But I don't want him running into a tree.

Leaving the small space of the cab is difficult. Juda grabs my hand the second he's around the truck. He starts to head up the path towards my apartment, but stops.

"Let's take a walk and enjoy the sun a little more." He kisses my hand. I'd walk into an oncoming mac truck if he asked.

Instead of taking a right, we go left. I can't tell if I've been down this path, the trees seem denser. But, with Juda holding my hand, walking close to me, I really don't care. He wraps his arm around me, getting his hand into my left jean pocket. His thumb rubs my hip. All the sizzle from the truck remains, I can't figure out why he'd want to stay out of the apartment? I mean, we are old enough to decide what we want; sex is part of life. But, am I ready for that

with him though? Things get too confusing the more I try and work it out. I'm
going to go along with him and see where we end up.

"I know you've heard Callen and the others talking about me getting
engaged soon. I don't want to freak you out, but I'm required to marry within
my first ruling year. I mean that's ten years in human time. I'm willing to court
you all ten, if you'd consider the idea of staying and mar..." he stops the
obvious end of his sentence.

Miraculously, I don't break out in a run or simply pass out right where
we stand. Getting a proposal, though technically it wouldn't be for ten years,
hadn't been a part of the plan for the day. We'd come through thick trees to a
small clearing. The area looks undisturbed. Juda pulls his hand out of my
pocket, and tugs me gently until we face one another. Our eyes lock, I must be
crazy for considering all this, but I think I have to do just that.

For the past week, Juda had said how life only felt right with family. I
never had that. I know the Aunts, and even the spirit of my mother, all seemed
to say something opposing Juda, but here and now with him, it all seems
pointless. Marring anyone, especially my fist cousin, is overwhelming. I want
to answer him, but part of me resists forming the words. I want to find my
father, and if I'm betrothed to Juda, he'd have to wait for me to come back or
leave with me. Besides, I won't be agreeing to marriage just agreeing to the
possibility of it. Right?

"You're pretty quiet over there, you thinking of a way to let me down
easy?" His nervous laugh tells me he isn't sure of how I will react. Could he not
know how much I need him? He reaches up and lets the tips of his fingers run
along the side of my face.

"Feel like letting me know what's going on in there?" He pulls me
right up to him, our bodies touch. Juda grabs my waist with both hands.

Looking into his violet eyes, all I want to do is wrap my arms around his neck and give into his advances.

"I do want you. I just, I need, or maybe I want you except... I'm messing this up." For some reason, my mind is too foggy to make the words come out right. Why can't he see it in my eyes? Determined to show him, I lock my eyes on his. The look between us changes, Juda starts breathing hard. Speaking of hard, his jeans have grown considerably tighter.

We haven't been this close before, and the spark between us jumps past fire, directly into a blaze. He bends down and kisses my neck, letting his breath dance on my bare skin. I melt into him further. He pulls back, holding my face inches away.

"A yes or a no is all I need here."

"Juda, I," the words stick. The pull from his eyes is as strong as the pull from his hands on my lower back. I need to show him not tell him. My head tilts up and my lips move towards his.

A sound breaks the trance we're in, but before I can look, something heavy hits my left temple. A blossom of pain follows the blow. The world buzzes like a snowy TV, while more pain registers in my knees and palms. I've fallen to the ground. Everything is spinning around me. My fingers are covered in blood, I touch my head, and my palm comes away, bloodier then before. Is my hand bleeding or my head? When had I touched my head, wait, am I bleeding? My stomach is twisting from nausea and fear. Something hot and wet is starting to drip down my forehead, past my eyes. That's right, my head is bleeding.

There's yelling, running, a hand grabs my arm. With my bloody hand, I grab the arm back to keep from falling into the gaping black hole I feel pulling me down. The static in my head makes the voices swarming about,

184

hard to understand. Warmth pours down my back and face. I think I'm bleeding, but I can't remember where.

"Stop... blood...pain." The voice sounds too close, but familiar. The nausea is starting to take over and I don't want to start puking while gravity sucks me into the earth.

"What did you say? OH!" Her voice is next to me. My stomach stops convulsing, but I hear retching. My head, it's bleeding, yes, I am holding it to stop the bleeding. There's a girl next to me, she's the one vomiting. Call my magic, I need to focus and connect. The noises around me fades, picturing me, healthy, whole, there's a tingling on my head. Warmth spreads over my scalp, this time from the inside. Some of the noises around me make since, I can tell Juda is scaring someone. Gravity pulls at my arm, wait, it's the girl next to me. A few feet away, I see a rock with blood on it, there may even be some skin as well. That's what hit me, the blood is bright red.

I am healthy, whole. All the bewildering things happening around me start to separate into their own categories. Juda yells and tries to order someone to move. My eyes finally regained their focus and I see the back of Callen. Next to me is Danya, her sister, who looks pale. Her hand is on my forearm, while my hand holds onto her forearm too, with a vise grip. There is a trickle of blood coming from her forehead, I let go, and she falls to the ground.

Another wave of dizziness comes over me, but after a few seconds it's easier to breathe through. I know the damage isn't completely gone, but now it's more like I'd fallen out of bed and whacked my head on the night stand. There are birds and stars circling, but I know I will be fine.

"I can fix it please stop! King Shea will kill me! Please, I didn't mean to hit her. I just wanted her away from you! Juda, listen you are acting crazy!" Callen is really wigging out.

She is half shifted into what looks like a bull's lower body. Her hooves half dug into the ground, as if she's being pushed hard. Juda is wrestling with her human arms that are also bulky with bigger than usual muscle mass. His skin shimmers with magic. Callen's hair looks as if she's touching a light socket.

"I'm okay, it's okay." Getting up isn't that easy, but I manage. Once I'm on my feet, I reach for Danya. She withdraws into the grass from my hand. She's breathing hard, and more blood has leaked out of a pretty good sized cut on her forehead.

Automatically, I reach for my head, my own wound is no longer gushing, but the cut remains with a small bit of blood coming out. The one on Danya's head looks worse than my cut feels. However, the brightness of the sun makes my eyes water, and the slight tilt of the world tells me the effects of the blow aren't completely gone.

"Danya, what happened?" Callen turns, shifting back into her slim figure. She pushes past me and reaches for her sister. Danya's stomach fluids are near where I step, the smell sends me in the other direction. My foot stumbles, somehow I don't fall. But I reach down and pick up the bloody rock that had almost tripped me.

"Viv, you're okay? Thank God!" Juda runs to me, taking a minute to examine the cut on my head. A few feet to the left, Callen's cousin with the bright red hair kneels over the other cousin, who is lying on the ground. The unconscious girl comes too; the red head helps her up. They are a good fifteen feet from where Juda and Callen had been. The half-conscious girl's arm looks odd. She's holding onto it, she'd gotten injured. Callen looks from her sister, who leaned on her slightly as she stood up, to me. I can't help but notice Callen looks shocked and possibly more afraid then she did when Juda magically electrifying her.

"Good, thank God, I'm so sorry." Her voice sounds sincere, but her eyes are cold. The urge to show her just how strong of a shifter I'm becoming, flashes through each muscle, but I can play her game. Smiling, I wipe my forehead to show the small amount of blood. Her eyes round. She knew she'd hit me, hard. In theory, I think my magic gave Dayna some of the wound. But, I don't think it's normal that my magic did that. I'm going to keep the theory to myself, for now. With that thought, my gut clenches, a sure sign I'm right.

"I had the wind knocked out of me, but its passing. Danya hit this rock here when she tried to help me. Better take her to get looked at." The medium sized rock falls to the ground out of my hand. Not waiting to see if they bought that, I step next to Juda.

He stares as wide eyed at me, but only for a second. If he believes me or not, I can't tell. He grabs my hand though, and I weave my finger though his. Callen can't hide the pure hate that washes over her face, and impregnates every word she speaks next.

"See, she's fine Juda. Let's go girls; we don't want to stop the prince from his duties." She turns and twitches away so fast that her long crazy curls whip in the air behind her. Juda looks at me, his smile says he's relived I'm not hurt, but his eyes hold suspicion. Jared's warnings whisper in my mind. Don't let people know what I'm capable of when it comes to magic, and not to trust anyone. In spite of the warning, I don't let go. Juda's touch makes it all too hard to believe. He is more than some guy, though I haven't figured out just how much more yet.

Danya hadn't followed the others, instead she stood for a minute longer, staring at me. Her long hair pulled back into a pony tail, making it easy to see the cut we both knew hadn't been done by the rock. For the first time, I realize the cut is in the exact spot my own cut is in, on my own forehead. A

187

look of disgust paints her face, she may not know what I am, but she clearly loathes me.

My heart speeds up. My bag of tricks isn't completely exposed, but her knowing I'd lied isn't good either. Things have taken a turn in a direction I don't want. She won't be able to prove it. It's her word against my own, but still, in this world, I have no idea what can be done to prove things real or not real. I have no idea what's real or not real these days, anyway. I need to say something to smooth this over with Juda. There's no way a powerful shifter like him doesn't sense more out of this then he's saying.

"The Aunts told me my magic is stronger since I'm a part of the monarchy for the females of our family." Danya takes a piece of cloth out of her pocket, and puts it to her head to stop the bleeding. Without any response, she walks past us to the red headed cousin who waited for her. They walk off, but I'm too busy watching Juda. The little tension in his shoulders loosens, as my words filter through the information he'd been processing in him mind. His free hand reaches over and tucks my hair behind my ear. Juda must not know the details from the thunder dome, face-off between me and his dad. A calmer, more confidant look comes over his face.

After a moment he says, "That would make a lot of since. They have their own connection to the magic. A direct line helps speed up healing and protects our health. Do you know what this means? We'd be the most powerful leaders who have ever been in our lands. There is much more for you to discover about your magic. Together, we could truly rule our kind." His speech doesn't settle right for me; it's too power hungry. The image of a wolf lingered behind his irises, a wild animal that'd do anything to get what he wants pops into my head. Do I look like the sacrificial lamb to him? Or a shallow, unethical shrewd like Callen?

Juda pulls me close into a long embrace. The strange speech and its effects evaporate. I'm a fighter. Maybe I can fix his selfish tendencies? Juda had gotten a peek into my freak show and hadn't run away. I can be strong enough for the both of us. Love concerns all, right?

Chapter Twenty-Three

Danya

Tannie accompanied Danya back to their trailer. Danya's head ached, but at least the vomiting had stopped. Callen and Gonya hadn't waited. Danya was sure the younger cousin had to listen to Callen complain all the way back, which would have been extra hard holding onto your own broken arm. Their father, Nick, hadn't left his brother's house since the Naming. No one else knew him and a few of the king's brothers had stuck around. Finding out Viv was the daughter of their dead sister had changed things dramatically.

"Danya, come to my room, I will clean your cut," Tannie said. The girl had no idea how beautiful she was, thanks to Callen. Danya knew she should have told her cousin years ago to stay away from her little sister. But Tannie's father's vitsa was not a good place for a girl like her. Her father knew it too, which is why she'd lived with her uncle Nick since she was eleven. Next year the girl would turn eighteen and hopefully marry someone who deserved her.

"Wow, its healing well, the bleeding has slowed," Tannie said as she patted her cousin's head with alcohol. Danya didn't show how much it stung. Instead she looked out of the window of the back part of the trailer the four girls had been lodging in all week. From here she could see Jared. He reminded her of herself, when she was his age. The kid sat back and watched, never over reacting and never showing his emotions.

"Look, your dat came out of the house to help Gonya." Tannie pointed at the scene playing out. Her father came up to look at Gonya's arm, then a second later, King Shea was there, along with the rest of the brothers that had been in hiding. Danya couldn't read lips, but she thought they asked about the incident. The surprised look on the king's face cued Danya in on what Callen was probably blabbing. Juda did this. Dayna was sure the little brat would manipulate the situation. Clearly Juda wanted Viv, no matter how complicated it would be for them to be together, but Callen would not give up that easily.

"Tannie, why don't you go keep Jared busy for a while. Tell him what happened, I'm sure he'd find it interesting." Danya looked at the girl fast enough to catch the look on her face before she had time to compose herself. She had been smiling, she liked the kid huh? Danya thought that would be a good match, she added, "Maybe you should brush your hair first." Tannie smiled and went to the bathroom to freshen up.

Danya's bandage was secure. She knew she'd have to tell them the truth. She didn't want to see Juda end up with Callen, but she knew what she'd tell them would take away the possibilities for Viv to be his bride. At the age of nineteen, Danya wasn't a candidate to marry the prince. But, she'd hoped she could at least keep Callen off the throne.

Danya waited till Tannie approached Jared, making sure he'd not over hear what she needed to tell her uncles and father. Once the girl started twisting the end of her long red hair, she got up and left the trailer. The contingency of men and the two girls sat at the smaller version of the commons. No one else had come around.

"Danya, let me see your head, girl," her father called. She stepped up, ignoring the look of control on Callen's face. She knew she had to keep up the facade of being on Callen's side, but that wasn't as important at the moment.

"How did you hit the rock so hard rakli?" Danya wasn't a girl anymore, but her father insisted on treating her like one. Every time she tried to say something about it, he replied, no daughter of mine will be an old maid; I will get you a husband.

"I didn't." That changed Callen's face. Danya looked at her sister, watching her face go from shock to triumph in a split second. A small part of Danya shivered knowing her words would seal Callen's fate, and worse, Juda's. It would also break his heart.

"Callen, Gonya, leave us." King Shea commanded. Callen didn't let her mask slip, but Danya knew her eyes held the outrage of being ordered around. Not even their father could do that to the girl. Gonya got to her feet. Danya could hardly see the bruises from the break on her arm, but it was set in a splint, and that would need to stay on for at least a week to make sure the bone had healed correctly. After the two were back in the trailer, the king moved Danya to the bench.

"I can't say Viv understood what happened. To be completely honest, it's a bit of a blur for me too." Here's the part Callen probably left out, thank the Fates the king had sent her inside. "We'd seen them pull up in the lot, Juda looked, excited." Awkward thing to describe to five grown men. "Anyhow, we saw them walk off towards the old trail, and Callen wanted to follow." The king looked at her father, who didn't look at him back. Did King Shea suspect Callen to be a liar? Perhaps Danya's words would keep the young girl off the throne after all.

"I will speak to her, brother. Danya, continue." Nick hadn't looked at his older brother. Danya was sure this was something the two men had discussed before.

"Well, they held hands, and said things to one another as they walked that suggested their relationship is starting to solidify. Callen became, upset..."

"The truth, women." The king said. Danya didn't have Callen's flair for using the truth to tell a good lie.

"She was outraged. Callen started to talk about what we could do to permanently get rid of Viv." Danya looked up at the king, but the confession

192

didn't bring his anger. In fact, he looked, approving. Danya's heart rate picked up, she suspected Viv of being different, and even after what had occurred, she didn't know for sure if what she suspected was true. If the king was already aware of what she suspected, she'd be the one sentencing Viv to death.

"Well, when it looked like the two would kiss, Callen lost it. She grabbed the largest rock by our feet and used her full strength to send the rock right into Viv's temple."

"The girl stopped the kiss?" This time it was Nate who spoke. Her father closed his eyes, his nose flared with his breathing. All the men were agitated, Danya kept still, afraid to be the receiver of the anger Callen had caused them. Crazy thing, none of them cared that her psycho little sister had meant to kill Viv and would have if what happened next hadn't occurred.

"It's fine brother, she didn't know," The king said. "Danya, get to the part about you and the rock, now." The power of the king nearly made Danya drop off the bench from fear. Shaking slightly, she continued.

"I didn't want Callen to get into trouble, so I went directly to Viv. Everything happened quickly. Juda hadn't understood what had happened, and he fought to see if Viv was injured. As soon as Viv touched my arm, I felt stuck to her, like a current had seized me. She said some words I really couldn't make them out. Next thing I knew, I was seeing things sideways, and nausea hit me strong. I was vomiting and trying not to pass out from the pain that was in my forehead. I never once hit a rock, I did fall onto the ground when Viv let me go, but there weren't any rocks, just grass."

The king pulled the bandage off Danya's head. She sat unmoving as he looked it over. He put it back on, the second stick wasn't as tight, and she'd need to replace it when she went back inside.

"Your connection is strong, I am surprised." The king said. The strange statement made Danya uncomfortable, like she'd been exposed.

"Brother, I will accept her engagement to Lu's son. Danya, go get prepared to leave." What? She looked at her father questioningly.

"I will tell you soon, now go do as the king said. And thank you for the truth my daughter." Her father smiled, not a sign of stress on his face. Had they not just heard what she'd said? And now she was being sent away? Danya couldn't put it all together, but she did as she was told. Her trailer was the opposite direction from the others, she never went back in to be questioned by Callen. The little liar would not come out until King Shea was gone.

Danya left in the yellow bug. She'd been betrothed to her cousin Bo. Out of all that drama, the king had realized her potential. Still, Danya worried about what would happen. What Viv was had never been before. No one really knew what she'd be able to do to defend herself. Danya tried to shake the bad feeling in the pit of her stomach. She'd been betrothed, her life would change dramatically. Bo was her age, he'd never wanted to marry, but now he would be. No one had a say in these things.

Except, the lingering stress from the confrontation wouldn't leave. The only thing that finally made Danya relax, smile even, was the thought of what Callen's face would look like when their father told her why Danya had been sent away. No more covering up for her. If there was one thing her little sister hated, it was to have what she thought belonged to her, taken away.

The meat cooking, potatoes boiling and the bacon crisping in the oven, frees me up to clean the blood off the meat grinder, Danya's bloody wound comes back into my mind. How had I done it, sent her my nausea, wound and most of my symptoms? When it had happened with Todd Hamon, I'd been dying. Really thinking about it, I had wanted to stop the pain, and not be injured. Jared said we had to concentrate on what we wanted to shift into, which fits. But Danya looked at me like I was disgusting. Whatever it meant, I don't think it's something shifters can do. I know it is magic, but, and I hate to say it, it's not normal magic. Even I can see the irony in my own words. Only days ago I wouldn't accept the human, non-human thing. Now I'm comparing magical powers?

My mother would've been a great ally. Don't they have to love you no matter how many skanks you almost kill? With the meat grinder cleaned and put up, I get to concentrating on cooking instead. Right as the food is done, Juda stood at the door.

"Good timing, the food is ready." His large upper body looks as if it may pop the buttons of the black shirt he's wearing. The jeans he chose define his thighs and other bulging areas, well. I need to busy my hands with serving dinner, before I start liberating his body from the confining clothing. But his hands found their way to my waist, and he's not permitting me to move from the closed front door just yet.

"It smells great." He leans down and kisses my check. In one of his hands, I notice a handled paper bag dangling. There is something at the bottom and it catches my attention.

"This is for you. You can open it now if you like, it's not a gift. Just stuff your mom had in the main house..." He says, but he doesn't hand it to me. Juda steps past me and sets the bag down on the coffee table and makes his way into the kitchen. Why would he say I can open it now but not offer it to

197

me? And why would anything of my mother's be in the main house? Juda turns and looks at me from the kitchen doorway.

"You look very lovely, by the way." His sly smile appears. I'll worry about the bag later.

"Thank you, sir." I say and make my way into the kitchen to start loading our plates. Juda pours us tea. I'd had time to make a fresh pitcher. We eat for a few minutes before he says anything else.

"Viv, I'm sorry about everything that happened today. The whole 'King' thing is new to me. I promise things will be less crazy from now on. You know you can trust me right?"

"Juda, I've gotta be honest, I don't know who to trust. So much is going on, there are things I'm discovering about who I am, which make me wonder if I can trust myself, much less anyone else." And that is exactly how I feel. Saying that out loud, kind of clears my thoughts. The root of my hesitation is simple as having him means one day I could lose him. The Aunts said I would have to… something about choices or decisions? My mind is a bit fuzzy on those details. The harder I try and see it, the more my head fills up with cotton.

"Hey, you can trust me; I am here, now and for years to come." Juda reaches up, taking both my shoulders in his hands. His touch calms the storm in my mind, solidifying my thoughts once more about him. I'd never been in love, and it seems odd that I may be now, but when I look at him, everything makes since. The truth is, I'm sick of the running, sick of the denial that I'm falling for Juda. He is here, and I want him.

He gets up and walks into the living room and comes back with the paper bag.

"I wanted to give this to you later, but I think you need it now." He holds the bag out to me. Inside is a small wooden box. The box is light in my hands, and covered in a pattern that only decorates the lid. A circular design was etched into the wood. There are small leaves at the ends of each line. A simple design, but nice. Holding it fully, the part of me that had been struggling with accepting magic, clicks into place, things stop spinning. I look at Juda, but he isn't looking at my face, only at the box in my hands. He looks up and pulls his lips into a small grin, then sits on one of the kitchen chairs. His movements are awkward, almost clumsy. I sit to switch the attention back onto me, to take away from his embarrassment.

"What is it?"

"It was your mother's when she was here." Juda scoots up in his chair, coming as close to me as he can. Tracing the pattern with my fingertips, the box starts to warm in my hands. A small metal clamp holds it shut. I turn the clasp and flip it open. The inside lid is smooth, light colored wood. A few hair clips, a gray rock, some broken costume jewelry and other small treasures lay inside. These are things she must have collected as a child. This is, was, who she had been. Not just some apartment with things people had gifted her or made with her. Juda had given me a part of who she was.

"Thank you," I breathe. He reaches over and touches the hand that holds the box. The urge for his hands to touch more of me are overwhelming. My plan from earlier lingers in the back of my head. Claim him, then he will want to help me, need to help me like I need to touch him now. Placing the box down, I lace my fingers through his. He lifts our clasped hands and I get up, letting him guide me to the front of his chair. He lets go, freeing me to run my palms over his upper chest. Both his hands slide up my hips to my waist and he tugs me onto his lap. My body's reaction to his touch is unlike any kind of pleasure any guy has ever given to me. There's no way to not give into this need.

My legs part, as I step on either side of his chair, to straddle him. His hands slip under my T-shirt, onto my back. My lips brush his neck and a soft moan leaves him. He tastes like cloves. His hands pull off my shirt, and I let him. He grabs my head with one hand, guiding me to his lips. I don't want to stop tasting him just yet. Instead of following his lead, I reach down and unbutton his shirt, and pull myself away from his wanting mouth. The shirt lay open, giving me a full view of his perfect bronzed skin and defined chest.

My lips follow the trail of my fingers, kissing each dip and crevasse of his pecks. As my teeth and tongue work, I let my fingers run down his lower sculpted abs. Perfect, he is perfect. Touching, tasting, pleasing him, makes me light headed.

More moans fill the room the closer my fingertips get to his man cleavage. He pulls my face up for a kiss, but I bite his lower lip instead. My body is flushed pink with the heat from my bashfulness; I've never been this forward. Okay, mostly I think I'm being slutty, but if there has ever been real electricity between two people, this is how it would feel.

He gives up on kissing me, and instead he lowers his mouth to my breast. His warm lips arouse me, my hips move in small circles on his lap, he responds by pulling the left side of my bra down, giving him more sensitive areas to tease.

There's no stopping this train now. One of my slutty girl hands starts on his belt, while the other takes action on his stiff, well, jeans. They are so tight I don't understand how he's not in pain.

"Oh, Viv…," He says, and then his entire mouth is on my nipple. His teeth push me past the point of caring if he will call me in the morning. I let a few moans of my own out.

"Bed," I command. There's no hesitation in his execution of my order. Queen, yes, the idea is very seductive at the moment. My legs wrap around his

200

waist. As he carries me to the bedroom, I place small bites on that little dip between the jaw and the ear. His breathing picks up, and his fingers dig into my backside. We make it to the bedroom. My legs start to fall towards the floor. As I stand there, he goes for my jeans, every time his flesh brushes my belly, a shock fills my body. As he pulls the jeans down, I take off the bra.

"Wow, you are so sexy," Juda says. Bending down, his mouth starts on the right breast, as more moans escape my lips. His right hand moves down. His fingers find the most sensitive areas a girl has. Looking around, I can't figure out how to get onto the bed without him stopping. I go with it, lifting up one leg, so he can get to the right spots. Sensation spreads through my body, his touch inside of me and outside of me, his lips and tongue continue to work on my breasts. I can't stop my deep release. Standing awkwardly with half my body in his grip, and the other half climbing him like a tree, my body trembles, as I ride the wave of ecstasy.

"Lay down, open your legs for me baby." The rough touch to his voice makes me tremble with the need for him to fully enter me. I do as he commands, taking off the last bit of clothing I have on. My eyes can't stop watching his tan full body move.

He strips off his top, then his jeans. His thighs are thick and sculpted perfectly. The deep lines of his lower stomach muscles go down into his groin. Dark soft hair shows from the top of his boxer's.

"Take them off," I say, his sly smile appears. His hands pull at the elastic of his boxer briefs. A part of my mind reminds me I'm past skank territory, but the hum of my body won't be ignored. A deep need for him surges over my skin. I spread my legs further, as he climbs over the top of me.

His mouth kisses my neck. With the strength of, *I so want you right now*, I flip him over. His boxers aren't completely off, as I straddle his nearly bare lap, trying to kiss him all over and pull them down. He catches my head and gently tugs my mouth towards him, but just then I free little Juda, which beats him for attention. His sudden stiffness against my own bare sex sends me into another fit. I need him, needed him from the moment our eyes met, and he is here, finally here. I push my pelvis down, he pushes up. Our bodies aren't lined up for him to enter me, but the move finally breaks him.

Juda flips me over onto the pillows and grabs both my wrists. Both of my hands are fully gripped in one of his. With his free hand, he traces a line down between my breasts to my hips. The slowness that he's using to get rid of his boxers makes me squirm. My feet try and assist him, to which he laughs, and then he sucks up my left nipple into his mouth sending ripples of pleasure through my body. My moans are higher pitched with desire.

Temporarily I forget everything else. But his boxers are gone, and he aligns his body with mine. My hands grip the slats of wood that make up the headboard, and I brace for his next move.

"Do you want me Viv?" His words drip with desire. My pelvis rises towards his, he pulls his hardness from me, more teasing.

"Please, I want you." And I do, every part of my body craves him. He looks at me while his free hand slides up and down my side, and moves over the soft perfectly shaped patch of hair I'd left earlier. The sensation makes my stomach flip. A little noise leaves my lips. He continues to stroke the soft hair. Not getting any closer no matter how much I arc my back towards his touch.

"Not just the sex. Do you want me? Can you give yourself to me?" His fingers briefly tease the spot he'd worked earlier. My breathing becomes pants. It's hard to focus on what he's saying. His hand moves back to my hip, and rests there. Finally, I realize what he's asking of me. He lets go of my wrists. Looking at him open and exposed I realize, I do want all of him, not just the sex.

"I want you. I give myself to you Juda." I can hear the surrender in my voice. The truth is the truth, having a guy like this for the rest of my life, I want that. Some of the lust evaporates, our eyes lock. After a moment, his hands both tighten on my hips and he moves his pelvis back towards me. My grip tightens on the bars.

"Kiss me." He lowers his body onto mine. I wrap a leg around his waist, as he lingers so I can feel his hardness close to its goal. His lips touch mine softly, everything becomes about the kiss. The lust evaporates, it's only the kiss, our only and true connection. My tongue moves past his lips, and the kiss deepens. A different kind of heat grows between us.

Everything seems wrong, as if an actual fire has been set above me. The heat is all wrong, painful instead of wanting. Somewhere there's a tug at my conscience, but it's as if the kiss has trapped me. There is nothing but the kiss, nothing else but our tongues, mouths and heat. Images are flying past my closed eyes. I can't make them out. A pair of brilliant crystal-blue eyes appear. They are like my own, but more masculine.

A load crack fills the room. Pain sears my lips, and Juda is thrown off me, back into the wall at the foot of the bed. For a moment the pain blinds me, I taste blood coming from a gash on my lip. The smell of burnt flesh is in the air. Not a smell you can mistake for anything else. The pain slowly subsides and my mind starts to clear. Juda is on the floor, back against the wall, holding his hand to his own mouth. Realizing I'm completely naked, I grab the crumpled blanket we'd pushed over, and cover myself. Juda gets up without a word and gathers his clothes, then disappears in the restroom, door closing behind him.

Shame and embarrassment color my skin. I need to get up, but my body's weak and distant. Taking a few breathes helps clear away the chaos further, and steadies my heart beat. I don't want him to see me like this.

The strength to get up and get dressed lasts until I get into the kitchen. I take a glass down and fill it with tap water, drinking it down in one long pull, which helps a lot. The food on our plates is uneaten and cold. The sight disturbs me. After another minute, I'm able to start clearing the table, trashing the dinner because it reminds me of him. The dizziness stops once the food and drinks are cleaned up. Had he drugged me? That doesn't seem right, we hadn't touched the dinner. I drink another glass of tap water, hoping to flush my system of anything that could've caused me to be so, crazy.

My mother's wooden box is the only thing left on the table. An urge to hide it hits me hard. I quickly place it in a cabinet, tossing the paper bag to keep him from thinking about the gift. The bathroom door opens, I start wiping the counters again to look busy. Juda comes into the room, I stop and face him.

He looks into my eyes. A wave of energy moves over my skin, is he trying to knock me down or scare me? The smell of sulfur tells me he's more like this father than I want to believe. Part of me wants to be offended, but the majority wants to show him I wasn't that dispensable. His lips are red and swollen.

"I think we better call it a night." He doesn't bother to smile or call up an ounce of the charm he's so good at playing up. A normal girl might find this crippling, he's rejecting me. But that consuming need for him is gone, along with that dopey puppy love, none of it was real. That little bit of me that first found him attractive and had found some affection for him, is easy enough to silence with the thought of his false advances. I won't let his cruelness back me down.

"Yeah, okay." I want him to leave, which is exactly what he does. No good bye or see you tomorrow. Once the door closes, I go to it and secure the locks.

"Shit." The honeymoon is definitely over.

Chapter Twenty-Five

Inheritance

The tea kettle whistles behind me. Standing still, I let the steam screech out my pain. How stupid I'd been. All my life I protected myself. Not just from criminals and possible life threating situations, but from making dumb choices. I'd trusted Juda. I'm not sure what happened. He must've used magic on me, it's the only thing that makes since. What the spell told him, I don't know. The odd image of blue eyes is a clue, but I had no idea who that was. And, being shocked by my lips, and then tossed across the room, is a bad sign. The way he looked at me, my stomach clenches at the thought.

My skin tingles with the need to shift and do something bad to Juda. But, I'm just as guilty, and that's really why I'm pissed. I'd let him get past my barriers.

The screeching steam isn't calming anymore, so I turn the fire off, and pour my cup of tea. If I could cry, scream, or run away and hide under something big, but what good would that do? For all I know, the shock must've meant I'm not the right mate for him. Ugh, I actually got super slutty with a guy that used the word 'mate.' The crazy thing, I can't ever remember being slutty, ever. What had come over me?

I don't need to worry about his approval of my trip now. Jared will probably go with me, but in truth, I need a break from all things Dacian. It's night outside, I could slip out. But, others had seen me last time. Would they stop me? I could stay and leave first thing. The deep tug in my gut disagrees. Alright, I will wait till after midnight and go. Until then, I need something to do. My mother's box would be a great distraction right now. There's magic with-in it, which must be hers since it's her box. I know she can't be here physically, but some part of her presence would be comforting right now.

The need to understand why my mother had chosen to leave is a question I had no one to ask but her. The box, now on the kitchen table next to my tea cup, possibly held an answer. My chest tightens as the thought of finding my mother's family, my family, comes into the equation. If I'm not his true mate, fine, but these people are my blood too. Would they not accept me now? What if the shock meant something worse? The king had said he'd protect me; I'd be as safe as my mother would have been. I wonder if he'd used magic on her? There seemed to be no trouble in doing that exact thing to me. An ache in my heart reminds me Juda had gotten my permission, just in the most despicable way possible. My hormones had walked me right into that one.

Except secretly I have to admit, I'd wanted to love him. I can't help but think he wanted the same thing.

If I am going to find my way out of this, I have to be willing to live with the truth. Juda had looked at me like I was his enemy. The same look Danya had given me, as well as some of the other shifters, my family, since I'd been here. Jared had said I can't trust anyone, more like shouldn't. Well, let's see what my mom left; I sure hope there are answers to why she'd taken us away from here.

My fingers trace the strange design of the vines with only one leaf on each end. She had left, no one tricked her, and she'd gone on her own. My intuition says I'm right. But, what if my mother had done something really bad and no one had told me because they're trying to see if I'm here to finish whatever it is she'd started? Or maybe it's not that at all, why should I think my mother was a bad person? All these years on my own, anger made me believe she was, but now, being here with them, maybe she was trying to protect me? There's another ping in the back of my mind with that thought. What could've possibly happened to make her leave her entire family? Given their track record with me, they don't seem very respectful towards even their own.

My fingers move to the small metallic ring. The metal is smooth and warm to the touch. Normally metal is cool. Strange, there's nothing else out of the ordinary about the simple wooden box. I turn the ring to the vertical open position, the lid, now free of its lock, lifts easily. No squeak or protest. Another odd thing, this metal is at least eighteen years old. Wouldn't there be some rust? Magic, it's gotta be magic.

The air fills with electricity. There's a taste of lilac and honey dew. The smell and flavor reminds me of the ranch in Mexico. A woman's laugh gives me a start, but I don't know if it's in the apartment or in my memory. Inside the small box sits the same dozen normal looking things I'd seen earlier, scattered without care. The old watch is made by Guess, a few loose bits of tarnished jewelry, hair pins, a red ribbon, a small dark gray rock, a pair of dice and a photo of girls, none of them my mother. Just normal things a child would have. Maybe there's nothing here, but the presence of magic gives me the impression there is something, I only have to look.

One after the other, I pick up each item and lay it on the table. None of them set off my gut, strange how well magic and I are starting to get to know one another. The watch is last to come out, but the sense of magic within the now empty box, remains. The box itself feels the same weight in my hand, even with everything out of it, interesting. Jared had taught me to allow the magic to lead me, I need to focus. The best place to focus would be on the other side of the border. However, away from the front part of the apartment, with as many locked doors I can get between me and the world will be just fine for tonight.

I don't want to leave her things out here. I put them all back in the box and head to the bedroom. The smell of burnt skin lingers, but the smell of my mother's magic is stronger. Carefully, I put the box on the bed and lay next to it, closing my eyes. I focus on my mother's energy. The meditation begins to draw out the stress from each part of my body.

I hear her before I see her. The shrill cry of the little girl I used to be fills the air. A woman towers over me, a field of green spreads out around us. We walk hand in hand in the bright green grass. My small plump hand latches onto her middle finger. She smiles down at me, she looks happy and pleased. A shadow moves across her eyes, the smile on her face widened. I'm being picked up and embraced. But, I can only see my mother standing in front of me. Who is holding me then? I fly into the air, admiring the green fields with each toss-up. My laugh fills the air again; joy seems to be emanating from me.

He embraces me gently, kissing the top of my head. The stubble of his chin pricks my tiny fingers as I grab at his face. He pulls me back and I get a good look at him. The blue luminous light shines in his eyes, making the ordinary brown of the pupil appear to be floating. Like an island in a crystal blue ocean. He is making funny faces at me, laughter bubbles up out of my throat. My little heart is happy to see him.

Daddy, he kisses my face, calling me his baby girl. My mother comes over to peer at me, the two of them make me laugh, but they look different. My mother's magic, like an ocean wave, moves over my soft child skin. But his magic, is very different, not like my mother's at all. Cold, but not a bitter cold, more of the relief that ice water brings on a hot summer day. And like cold frosty air, his magic hovers in the air, wrapping around us, protecting us from all the bad in the world.

I sit up in the bed. My hand grips the box, causing its sharp edges to bite into the fleshy part of my palm. I try and release the box, but it seems super glued to my skin. The wood starts to heat up. A surge of urgency zips through my body. I need to be safer, I jump up and lock myself inside the bathroom. Once the door shuts, the wooden box falls to the floor. All the contents rattle about, but nothing breaks. I look at the door and down at the simple box.

"I wonder..." Kneeling, I place my hand along the side of the box, nothing. I keep my hand on the side of the box, and reach for the door knob. The second I touch the handle; the box digs its self into my hand as if I'm a powerful magnet for wood. The sharp edges painfully bite into my palm. I let go of the door and the box sits in my hand normally. I place the empty thing on to the shaggy bathroom rug. Why would the magic in this thing react like that? Unless it wasn't safe in the other room? Was someone watching me out there?

I hate people who get paranoid. Which is why I never cared to do drugs, I've seen enough druggies thinking everyone is out to get them, no thank you. But my gut is telling me I'm right, I am being watched. The way the king had treated me, for sure he doesn't trust me. I mean, the way he treats Jared, like property, and not his youngest son. He'd have no problem invading my privacy. In fact, he'd proved that only two nights ago.

If so, he had one hell of a show earlier. I'd be embarrassed, but I'm too damn mad to care what they saw. No wonder Juda had no problem leaving me all alone, they'd seen the meals I'd made and ate with Jared and all the shifting I'd done. Did they have audio? Was Jared going to be in trouble? There's no way he knew about it. He'd asked me to keep stuff to myself. Poor guy's in the dark as much as I'd been. Bugged isn't that what the spy shows call it? Asses all of them are giant asses. There's no window in here, they must not have put cameras in this room.

My eyes land on the box that sits in front of me. My mother's magic wanted me to be alone with it, let's find out why. First, just in case there is a bug, I turn on the shower. Sitting on the toilet I bend down and pick up the box, and look closer at the wood. The underneath is rose colored. When I pass my fingers over the smooth bottom, it's warm. The center, however, is the hottest. Turning it upside down, I inspect the wood closer. The thick legs of the box cover most of the edges, but something is off. The box should be deeper than it appears. There's a hidden compartment.

Taking calming breathes, I close my eyes and think, *softer*. My hand presses up into the bottom, and the wood gives way, first to my fingers, and then my entire hand. I open my eyes to see my hand move into the wood further than it should if there had been a simple hidden compartment. From the top of the box nothing looks strange. My hand isn't there or some weird wooden bubble. Actually it is as if my hand has disappeared entirely, though it's still at the end of my arm.

My fingers find something large and cool to the touch. I enclose it in my palm and pull. There's no resistance, and a large jewel attached to a thick chain of silver appears as my hand comes back into view. The jewel is an odd color. The overall impression I get is like a living opal. Red with green and light blue dust that hovers in its milky surface. The chain and back of the piece is a light silver, maybe even white gold.

A surge of energy moves from the jewel into my skin. If I had felt connected before, the memory pales in comparison to how amplified my magic is now. Every drop of water hitting the porcelain tub echoes off the walls. The collecting liquid swirling into the pipes and flowing under my very feet, sounds like a running river. Out in the bed room I hear the clock on the night stand ticking and into the kitchen I hear the drip of the faucet. Inside the walls, I hear the buzz of the cameras, one in each room. Air fills my lungs, I can smell the chlorine and ammonia used to clean the bathroom.

This jewel belongs to me. This is my inheritance from my real family. The room settles around me like I'd been in the middle of a storm and hadn't realized it.

Standing up I place the long thick chain over my head, instantly it shrinks to the perfect size, right above my collar bone. A strong sense of love surrounds me, all the years of loneliness and fear slip out from under my skin. I'd never known unconditional love, but from what I hear, that's how it's supposed to be. An acceptance no matter what I have done or become. A whispering sound catches my attention. After a moment, I realize it's coming from the box.

I move my hand back into the portal, there is a piece of folded paper that must've been pressed down by the jewel before. I pull it out and the liquid wood, re-hardened. The papers folded into four sections. My name is written across one of the sides. I open it.

Dear Vivian,

If you have found this letter, I'm afraid I'm not alive. I don't know if my plan to hide us has worked. I can think of a thousand ways you have come by this letter. I hope it is in a way that leaves you to follow in my foot steps and get away from my family.

I pray to the Fates that you are safe. As I write this, I am only a month pregnant but the thought of you older makes me happy! My daughter, I don't know how much time we had together, if I ever got to see you grow or if I had to leave you somewhere. Know, you are important to me!

The knot in my chest is too hard to ignore, I have to put the letter down. I've never read anything my mother had written, my anger for her had shrunk, but her words banish the old heat that had kept me going so long. All

212

that's left is a longing for her. My hand lifts up to the necklace, warmth spread though my tight chest. A soft breeze caresses my cheeks. The gift of the Aunts lends me the strength I need to continue reading. But as I start, tears spill down my face. I'm helpless to stop them. Instead, I'm careful the drops don't fall onto her delicate writing.

I could go on and on, but I fear I am already out of time to write this. I have chosen to leave you this letter along with a box of things I've kept since I was a child. The things in the box are only a child's view of the world, but our family is easily fooled by "things." I knew it would be the right way to get you this note under their very noses. I also left you my diaries; I pray no one found them. If you are can get into my bedroom you will find them in the bathroom under the floor in between the sink and wall. Your father, the one time he recklessly came to the compound, put them there. If the room still stands, only you can retrieve them, just do what you did in finding this letter.

By now you may know you are not a normal shifter child, you are a breed all of your own. If any are like you on this earth, they are hidden for their safety. More than likely though, they're dead, as you will be if I don't provide the blood line of your father. You see my family found out I am pregnant, and I have until sunrise to tell them who the father is, and he's not a shifter, or a boy from town, he is a Weaver. Well, that's what our kind calls them. You are half Weaver, this is how you are able to manipulate non-living things.

My mind is racing. I reread the last paragraph over again, flashes of all the glares from the vitsa pop into my mind. They suspected me, they were all playing me. Had Juda known? Had his affection only been a rouse? If he lied, I never caught it, but I can't think about that now. I must finish the letter.

Your father was happy to know you had lasted a month, but then we both realized you would last no longer if I was to stay here with my clan. His vitsa would not allow me anywhere near their camp grounds. If either knew of your existence, they'd terminate my pregnancy. Even after you are born, if it was discovered you are a cross breed, you'd be executed. I can't let this happen. So tonight I will leave my home, in search of a safe place. We will try to stay together, but chances are we will be discovered as a pair.

Vivian, my brother, the king, is strong and fierce, I am afraid I will not find cover thick enough from his eyes. I hope you do find this, that's what I will tell myself. It would mean you are alive and able to live on. If your father wasn't with us, go to him. I can't tell you his ways. I don't know how the Weavers live, or how my shifter blood will be affected by his. We are both direct descendants from our lines; the magic will work strong inside of you.

Remember, a shifter only changes form into other LIVING creatures. You are not supposed to be able to shift things outside of your own body. The thought is amazing, but your father and I speculate you may have this gift. He must say incantations and shed blood to get nonliving things to bend to his will. Oh honey, you must be so beautiful.

I can't give you your father's name in case somehow my family found this letter first. But, the necklace will lead you to him if you keep it close to your heart. He said it would know you; he said you will know it. Wear it, it will never abandon you and no one can remove it once you have accepted it.

Daughter, be safe and leave my family. Don't do it in a way they will follow you, but leave. I must go, oh one more thing, your father can send out his thoughts. That's the best way I can explain it. His kind are a mystery to me, but that didn't stop us from falling in love. You are the only thing to show for that love, and we will both protect you with our lives.

I wish I could hold you while you read this my love. However, I trust the amulet will keep my note safe for your eyes only, and one day you will understand the sacrifice I had to make. I will forever find my happiness in the thought that you lived, and I hope you keep me in your heart.

I love you Vivian.

Her last words bring out the sobs. I allow myself a full minute in my grief. But I know it's not safe to fall too deep into myself just now. The answers she'd left me check off as I lay on the rug and look at ceiling tiles to pull myself out of the sadness. I'm a hybrid, possibly the only one. If they knew they'd kill me. Is that what the spell was about earlier? I'm all kinds of screwed if so. All the things people had said to me make since now. My mother had sacrificed her life to give me life. All those years, all the anger I'd had, was directed at the wrong person.

Quietly I get to my knees and grab the edge of the sink. Spanish print decorated each tile. I move my left hand over the cool surface. Though it's very clean, I can see it's old. That gives me hope it's the same floor my father had hidden the diaries under. There is a two inch gap between the sink and the

215

wall. I place my palm on the tiles, not a speck of dust or grim. The tile begins to grow warm. My hand lingers over the warm spot. Shutting my eyes, and concentrating, I will it to be soft. In my thoughts I project the image of the liquid surface the wood had become. The tile instantly begins to move under my hand, becoming the same constancy as water. My hand moves down then stops on a large bulky object. My fingers run over a knotted string tied over the bundle. I grip it and pull the thing up and out of the floor. The tiles solidified as it clears the hole.

Righting myself, I place the bundle down on the floor in front of me. The string is tied around a stack of thin notebooks. I count eight. They are a bit dusty, but other than that there's no damage. I can't chance looking at them now. I refold the letter and push it under the top flap of one of the first diaries. I really do need to shower and I've already been sitting here for fifteen minutes or so. I hide the books under the sink and do a quick shower, making sure to wash my hair, maybe they'll think I was crying over Juda's rejection. To help, I rub my eyes a bit.

Once done, I grab the box and toss the items back in it from the floor, then grab the books to leave. My hand seizes when I grab the door handle. Of course, the books will be seen if I walk out with them. Well, if I can do what my father's people can do, maybe it's time to put that theory to the test. I turn and place the diaries on the sink and lift the box up. Thinking of a loaf of bread, I will the box to change. Before my eyes, the solid wood morphs itself into plastic covered sliced bread. My breath catches in my throat.

"Good. Now back again," I whisper. Once again, I concentrate on the image of the box. This time the wood pops back into place, the noise sounds like popping something plastic back into place. The sizzle of this magic lingers on my skin. If I had more time, I'd go around changing things all over the apartment, well time and privacy.

216

How will I keep the books with me where ever I go? The amulet. I reach up and pull it up over my head. The thick necklace lengthens on its own, so I can remove it with ease. Holding it in one hand, I pick up the five by four inch books. The thing has life of its own, so I know I can't force it to accept the notebooks.

"Please keep these within yourself and they will stay close to me. Use my magic if you need."

The stone opened and the stack of books are tugged out of my hand and swallowed up into the stone. The magic tickled my hand like I'm holding pop-rocks. I pull on my clothes from before.

"Thank you." In response, the heat of it stops. I place it back over my neck, and under my shirt. Time to face the music, I open the bathroom door.

Chapter Twenty-Six

It's Now or Never

My paranoid-ness comes back in full swing. Recently I'd stopped dressing in the closet, but I can hear the cameras buzz. I decide to change in the tight space of the closet. Juda's spell has been working on breaking me for a while. After all, my entire life I've lived watching my back from every angle possible. I had lusted for him from the first time I'd seen him. I guess tipping that over into falling for him wasn't too hard to do, pretty sly. I wonder if he'd come up with it or his father. I should leave, but they would see it through the feed and I'm sure I'd run into shifts waiting for me to make a run for it. They know this area way better than me, I need the light of day to make the right moves. Perhaps I can seal the room tight, and wait on the sun to rise?

The amulet nestled close to my skin under my shirt. I know it won't show itself. I sure hope it can lead me to my father. Other sources of magic have felt wrong or offensive. This amulet, my father's magic, is a part of me, there's nothing threating about it or scary.

I'd left my gap shirt and jeans folded on my mother's dresser in her closet. I change, using my own undies, which I'd also left with my pile. Usually I sleep in my clothes, hopefully they won't find that strange. My mother's boots are in hand, trying to make it look repetitious, I stuff some clean soaks into one of the docs and toss them close to the bed. The fake yawn I had planned turns into a real one. I can't fall asleep. But I want them to think that's exactly what I am doing.

Stepping by the door, I reach up to flip the light switch off. At the same time, I call my magic and project an image of the metal knob solidifying. The image of each small space that allowed each piece to function all

218

becoming one, fills my mind. Quickly I test the knob, it won't budge. I flop
onto the bed, too tired to get under the covers. I need to stay awake. My limbs
are too heavy, my eyelids droop and blackness takes me away.

The banging on the window pulls me out of my deep sleep. My eyes
are very heavy. I try to open them, but when I do, a wave of nausea washes
over me. I stop fighting and give into the hovering blackness.

I sit up in bed, sweat covers my face like I'd been running. The taste in
my mouth makes me gage. The more I try to catch my breath, the sicker I
become. My legs are like weights, but I get them over the side of the bed. The
one window in the room is usually covered with a dark curtain, but now the
window is slightly open, and the curtains pulled to the side.

I keep my breathing shallow. Each step pulls at my legs as if I'm
sloshing through water, but I know it's just air. At the window I manage to
push the frame, but it won't go up more than the two inches that someone else
had opened it to. I take a couple of deep breathes through the crack, which
helps clear my head. The frame must be nailed from the outside. Something
moves in the bushes directly in front of the window, at the same time my legs
stop supporting me.

I fall to my knees, catching the windowsill to keep myself up right.
The taste in my mouth intensifies, I gage. There's smoke all around me on the
floor. I need air. I looked out the window, Jared's chain sways on a branch,
David's little saint watched me in deep prayer. The smoke starts to rise, if I
don't get the window open, it will knock me out again, maybe even kill me.

That's when I hear them, hearts beating in the apartment. They aren't
taking chances. My trick with the knob kept them out, but they'd found a way
to get to me anyway. I'm not going out like this.

My hand touches the glass, "Wat...wa...wat...water!" The word finally forms correctly between my gages, the glass becomes liquid and harmlessly splashes my face.

"Air." A strong breeze pushes fresh air into the room, carrying away the sickening smoke. Vomit comes out of my throat and onto the carpet. The taste of poison, and sour stomach pass my lips leaving only a stench of chemical and pile of yellow stomach fluids on the cream colored floor.

If Jared hadn't come and opened the window, I wouldn't have woken up. That had to have been who I'd heard tapping the glass before. His necklace moved with the breeze, I sure hope he's okay. However, if I don't get up off this floor, I'll be the one in trouble.

Getting up, my legs feel like a water hose, but I manage to stumble back to the bed. No one has tried to come in, which means they aren't here to take me alive. They've been waiting to take out a body. The heat of my anger clears my head more, and I reach down for my boots. I take my time in placing them up, letting my courage catch up to my anger.

I walk to the open window and lean out. The medallion is cool and comforting to the touch. Jared would never have taken this off. A sure sign of how much danger I'm in. I grab it, and head for the bedroom door. If the king wants me dead, he's going to have to look me in the eye. Juda had tricked me to discover what I was. But, we connected on some level. No matter how angry I am at him for deceiving me, I can't believe he'd go along with his father's old fashioned beliefs. I mean, look at me, I'm not blowing things up or causing diseases, what's the big deal that I am mixed? I need to make a plea, I can't spend my life running.

The metal of the door pops noisily back into its original form, six hearts speed up at the same time in the front of the apartment. My gut is churning a little.

The only light on is in the living room. I slip Jared's necklace into my pocket as I start to walk. The next few steps I take sends wooziness through my body, I know the poison is gone, but the sick left my stomach uneasy. Crackers, there are crackers in the cabinet.

The box of saltines is sealed. I opened them up, and get out three white squares and stuff them in my mouth. The dryness in my mouth combined with the crackers is a problem. Trying to chew, and not start coughing, I grab a bottle of water. Yummy, cracker paste. Finally, the mix goes down. After a couple more, my stomach settles. Apparently being poisoned makes you thirsty, or it could've been the puking? Whatever the reason, I finish the water and put the bottle in the recycle and the crackers back in the cupboard. No reason to be messy.

No one had interrupted me, and from the sound of their heart beats, they are scared. I walk into the living room, and see Juda sitting on the sofa, and my heart sinks. I had hoped he'd be far away, refusing to watch me be executed. Or at least locked up in the house or something. But he'd come here and sat in the room next to my gas chamber. Bastard.

"I guess you've been lying to me since you met me?" I ignore the other five shifters in the room and speak only to Juda.

"Like you've been completely honest yourself." I wasn't prepared for the harsh edge of his voice but I let it cut me, so I'll know its sting.

"What's the plan then?" My arms cross over my chest. I relax against the door frame, in between the kitchen and living room to give them the impression I'm not freaking out. I won't run, I know they'd chase me down. No, I need to use my head to get out of this, if getting out is an option.

"You are summoned to the court for a trial." The air around me tightens for a second, he's lying.

"Don't you mean more magic will be forced on me and your father will do his best to kill me? Seeing as the gas chamber didn't really work out." Wow, even I'm surprised I'd said exactly what I was thinking. Juda's eyes widened, but just for a second. He stands and I mimic his body posture. Facing each other a wave of power pushes towards me. I push back. His magic has a sickening sweet smell, like jasmine going sour. My magic is sharp and cooling like mint.

Juda's brows scrunch down on his face, his energy shoves me. The amulet under my shirt heats up and the pushing is gone. No more, I mentally yell at the invisible force, the more Juda is shoved. Stumbling back, he barely catches his balance by grabbing the edge of the sofa. I didn't even call my magic and his attach was swatted away like an annoying fly.

"He will do more than try," Juda says, not acknowledging the invisible exchange between us. But his words are hollow. For the first time since I've known him, Juda is not that confident, strong leader. He's a scared, unsure boy. And even better, his mere presence doesn't have me swimming in self-doubt. I don't want to figure out how my heart really feels at the moment. I will work that out later. For now, I have to get the upper hand here.

"Alright, I'll go see what he has to say." I move to the door, and look back at the six men. "You guys coming?" They follow me out the door, but don't try to touch me.

Their heart beats aren't slowing. Good, I want them to be scared, even if that's my only advantage. Scared people hesitate, make mistakes. I can't afford to do that.

The king sits on his throne in the middle of his patch work stage. All the old bleachers were moved into a small circle around the platform. To his right is his brother Nate, and the left side, Callen. I don't think it's possible for her to look crazier then she does at the moment. Of course the queen of evil has a front row seat to my "trial."

The bleachers are filled with the shifters of the clan. Some look on with curiosity and others give me cold and angry glares.

The shifters step aside one by one, leaving me a direct line to the stage. King Shea's face has the same politician smile I'd seen Juda wear a few times. I don't see Jared anywhere, a small flip in my stomach makes my pulse speed up. I'm alone, with forty or more people that want to see me dead. A small weight presses into my chest, it's the amulet. I guess I'm not alone after all.

Readying myself for whatever may come next, I start to climb the steps. I don't know any fighting styles, but I can improvise. Secretly I send up a prayer to the Aunt's 'Fates' that I come out of this alive or at least take a few with me. Juda comes up the stairs with me, but stops by Callen. Wow, he went there. I don't stand by the king; he's moved to the front of the stage. Instead I walk to the edge of the crushed car platform, ten feet from the king.

Jared is there, dashing up the opposite side of the stage. His chest heaves up and down. He looks at me and I pull his necklace out of my pocket, but only enough to show him I'd gotten the message. The teen looks confused but understanding smooths his brow. His warning hadn't stopped me from coming, because I won't run no matter what the threat. His chest moves up and down; however, he bows his head down, and I don't really know what he's thinking. Both his hands ball up at his sides. My stomach drops. I hate letting him down. If I live, I'll have to thank him for trying.

"King Shea I have brought Vivian as you asked." Juda spat the words out. He must be trying to prove to his father how much he hates me. What he proves most of all, how big of an ass he is, another cut I let form, so I'll know the pain. How could I have gotten naked with him?

"My people, we've been deceived," the Kings voice echoes throughout the court. "She is the daughter of my sister, but my sister's sin lives within her blood." This causes loud cries of anger and fear throughout the crowd. I don't flinch or take my eyes off the king. Juda walks over and stands behind me, his way of being in control, but the King holds the real power here.

King Shea's arm goes up and the crowd falls silent.

"The prince has put his own life on the line, and spilled his essence to combine with hers, a few hours ago. He found himself injured as you can see on his lips. The essence of Weaver lingers within her blood." Some pointed to Juda and others to me. My lips had healed at, another sign of my guilt in their eyes.

"Do you deny this Vivian?" No way am I agreeing to anything he says. A wave of his magic hits me. The pungent smell of rot fills my nose. NO I DON'T, my eyes say. I push back, but just enough to get his taste and smell away from me.

"She is sentenced to death." The nice guy act was gone, the king's face is full of hate and disgust.

"Wait, you're going to kill her!" Jared steps towards his father. The king holds out a hand, three men grab Jared. Juda seizes my arms and shoves me back. Before I can stop it, I'm on my backside, to the back of the king's chair. Callen turns towards me, in one hand I see a long sharp knife held down at her side.

Jared screams and struggles to get free while the king and Juda walk toward him. Callen steps in front of me, one of her hands reaches up into the back of my head where she twists my hair into her fingers and pulls back. The other hand raises the knife and jabs it towards my exposed throat. With all my strength, I push back in time and the blade misses my throat, but the tip punctures my left eye.

224

Pain explodes across my face. Hot blood runs down my cheek, soaking my shirt. My hand flies to my face. Jelly like fluids cover my cheek. The instant the tip dug deep into my iris, everything became bright lights, turning black a second later. Everything turns on its side. Callen has my hair in her hand, but just then Jared screams my name. The king and Juda turn to see what is happening. The king simply stands there, but Juda, grabs the knife out of Callen's hand. The evil skank pushes my head down as she lets go. My balance is lost, I fall to the mats. Each muscle seizes, I don't want to die. There is blood all over me, but vertigo hits and I put my forehead down to try and stop the spinning.

"Callen, my dear she will die soon enough. Juda, calm your brother." I turn my head in time to see the king hold out his hand for the knife. Juda places the weapon in his father's hand then puts himself between the king and Jared. Callen moves a few steps from where I lay.

I want to cry out for help, but who would help me? No one. I'm back in the woods, under the C-boy, or hiding in the alley from the cops to keep from being taken back to the orphanage. If I am going to live through this, I'll fight fire with fire, and use my magic. Ignoring the pain in my head, I focus on what I want.

"Why, why are you doing this? We're not murders, father don't do this!" Juda put his hand over his younger brother's mouth, but not fast enough.

"Hush your mouth, boy or I will be forced to mark and shun you from your own family!" He waved the knife, making the threat worse. I try to heal my eye, but nothing changes. I need more energy, like when the rock hit me, I need life energy.

Callen is inching towards me. I watch her with my good eye. I'll have to act fast for this to work.

"We are not to allow abominations to live! We didn't allow David to live, nor his traitorous parents." The king says to the crowd, as well as to his youngest son. Jared stops struggling. The king had killed Jared's childhood friend; it hadn't been an accident at all. David had been the only person his lost son had ever connected to. Jared sags in Juda's arms.

"She will die tonight. No one is to grieve for her. She is an abomination." Cheers fill the arena and Callen takes another step closer, near enough for me to grab.

The king is center stage, basking in the approval of the crowd. Jared stood trapped in Juda's arms. Juda looks between his broken little brother and his father. If I want to escape, I have to do it now. Gathering all my strength and magic, I imagine the air is thicker, slowing everyone around me down, but allowing me to move through it swiftly.

The crowd of shifters is my first clue that my plan is working. Their hands and faces move, but they've slowed down, slower than slow motion. From what I can tell, they don't even notice anything is different.

My chest heaves up and down with my struggle to stay conscious. No time to waist, I reach out and grab Callen's arm from behind. In small increments of time a tightness travels up her arm. The amulet is hot under my shirt, but after a moment, it becomes cool and calming.

In my mind I see myself whole, healthy, with two eyes. A sharp pain sears up my face. Blotches of light start swirling where I could only see blackness a moment ago. As sight returns, I spot the king. His movements are jerky, not as slow as the others. His face is confused and he's saying something, but way too slow for me to understand. With my fingers, I touch the injured eye. There is no more stuff oozing out, it's completely healed. I run my finger up and down, and discover the cut on the bridge of my nose and upper brow remain, but not as deep as they'd been. I remove the contact from my other eye, no use hiding them now.

I push Callen, even with my shifter strength, it feels like we're in a deep water. The king has taken two steps towards me. Juda and the other shifters are starting to notice something isn't right. Callen hasn't made contact with the ground. Her hand moves towards her bloody eye.

I run down the steps, dodging hands and bodies in various states of frozen movement. I make it to the gates, and realize the fire in the barrels are moving faster. Time is unfreezing. Shouts are sounding like words. The more I try and stop it, the weaker I feel.

Amulet, if you have a little extra, I could use a boost. Energy shoots through my body, and I feel like I've downed ten Red Bulls, without the jitters. My steps pick up.

At some point I'd let go of the others. The snap of the twigs and dry leaves sound behind me, let's me know they are following. Their feet pound in time with my own. The woods are never ending and thicker. I need to hide, so I can figure out how to get out of here alive. My feet zig and zag through thick tree trunks. I call a little speed to my step in hopes it blurs me out. Ahead is a dense patch of trees that I duck into. A couple minutes later six or more men run past my hiding spot. More are passing to the left, but they are at least thirty feet away from me. Doubled over, I work on getting my breathing under control.

I don't hear anymore footsteps coming my way. The shouts are a good distance away too. I'm alone. I can run the opposite direction, maybe I'd be able to get close to the highway and hitch a ride. I'm pretty sure I kept east when I ran. My breathing sounds like jet engines against the still forest. No more time to waist. I get up and start to go.

A twelve-foot black grizzly bear stands directly in my path. The bear's huge paw with six-inch razor sharp claws, comes directly at me. I move back, but I'm too slow. The hit to the right side of my face makes everything disappear for an instant. The world's noise is nothing more than mumbles. A sharp cold prick in my throat jolts me back to the moment. The warmth flowing down my chest and arms makes this confusing. The warm fluid is my blood, and it's choking me. Something hits my chest. I reach up and feel my jaw. That had been the popping noise. Woozy, I reach out, trying to find something, but I don't know what. The sounds start to quiet once more, except my slowing heartbeat. For the second time in my life, I know I'm going to die.

Chapter Twenty-Seven

Fight or Flight

Someone lifts me up off the ground. I don't even remember falling. My eyes crack open to see the king. His hand is wrapped around my throat. I'm dangling in midair, like a rag doll.

"You may know your magic, but you don't know ours. The great bear would never let you live. He led me to you." His spit flies towards my face. I can't tell where it lands. The cool night breeze makes me aware of how much damage my face and neck have taken. The pain nearly knocks me out, but the king shakes me, making me stay conscious.

"I am going to watch the light leave your eyes." His words wake me further. Someplace way down inside of me, anger ignites. Desperate for the strength, I focus on that fire.

Focus, I need to focus. Me, healthy, whole. My hands move towards his arm, batting at his grip. He laughs at my weak attempts. His face is close enough for me to touch. Instead, I move my hands to his throat. My fingers cling to his neck. There's no feeling in my fingers, I push with all my might to keep my skin on his skin. His laugh gets louder. He doesn't even bother to pull my hands away.

The amulet's searing heat is hard to bare. I try to ask the elements to help me, but there's no way to form the words. The small movement of my facial muscles sends pain through my face and neck.

Then I feel it, the connection. I hadn't felt it with the C-boy, or with Danya or Callen. The king's direct connection to the Source of Magic is incredible. This is the boost I need to come back into the world of the living

229

fully and fight to live. Somehow, I need to channel this tidal wave of energy and reform my body.

The king stops laughing. My pull on his connection has registered for him finally. My feet touch the ground. His hand is at my throat, but he is pushing weakly instead of choking. The tops of the trees are coming into focus as well as more pain of my injuries. Mentally, I feel strong, but my body isn't there yet.

We fall, I land on top of him. Silver light, luminous and bright like the color of silver glitter, spread around us in a mist. My facial bones shift into place and began to reset themselves. There's a crackling noise as the bones of the king crumble in the same places my own had reset. The flesh on my cheek starts to close. The pains in my face are replaced by a agonizing numbness that vanishes fast. Tingles are next, as blood starts to flow normally through my face, jaw, and neck.

The same way it had happened with the bones, as my own wounds finish healing, the king's face rips open. His cheek sinks in, ripping lose his lower jaw bone, which lays on his upper chest. The back of his throat is visible, yet somehow he screams.

Another noise cuts through the horrific cries of the king. A whistling sound, zips past my head, followed by a small explosion in a nearby tree. Small pieces of tree debris lands over us. Only high caliber bullets can destroy like that. In shielding myself from the mini bark shower, I'd let go of the king. He lays on his side, eyes blinking, but dazed. Large amounts of blood had pooled on the ground. One of his large hands is holding up his broken jaw bone. I see parts of the flesh starting to heal on his cheek. The bright glitter like mist has turned purple, and is surrounding the injured shifter. The smell of sulfur is strong; I'd forgotten how his magic smelled.

If he heals as fast as I did, the bullets will be the last of my problems. With that thought, another bullet hits a tree trunk two feet from me, further, but not far enough. The amount of blood coming from his wound has doubled. If he's able to heal himself, it won't be fast enough. I want to help him, he's my uncle after all. At that moment the king looks at me, hate is in his eyes, but more importantly, it really hits home. My face had been the exact same way less than three minutes ago, and he'd meant for it to kill me. Shouts from the others get me to my feet.

"I'm sorry this is happening to you. I'm sorrier that...!" King Shea lifts a limp hand, but his body jerks, more blood comes out, and his eyes slack and go still.

"There! I see her!" I don't know if he was reaching towards me for help or to try and throw his power at me, but it's time to go.

The metal slugs cut through the air, hitting the ground and trees near me. My feet pound through mud, leaves and low brush. The image of the king's motionless body, and open, blank staring eyes keep popping in my head. More shouts, closer, easier to understand, pursue me.

A blaze of fire slides across my upper arm, more bullets splinter a tree I am passing by. The fire is gone, but warmth lingers. The surge of energy I'd drawn out of the king flares up, a second later, my arm feels normal, but damp. If I look I'm sure I'd see blood, but no wound from the bullet has grazed my arm.

Overhead the migrating birds take flight from their resting spots, distracting me from forming a plan. A large hawk catches my eye, unless the birds are the plan. I don't feel the shift, only the thrill of the change.

The large wings beat sure and steady, climbing the sky with all the other frightened birds. Below, voices shout out coordination for their search, but they are lost as the night sky fills my vision. I follow the hawk, trying to blend with the rest. He turns sharply. Even in the commotion he can't resist looking for prey. Small animals ran through trees and over the wooded ground. Against my survival instinct, I follow the hawk's need for prey, which is what the other birds do in the nearby trees. But the bullets below are too loud and there's no way to swoop close enough to the ground, and all my fellow winged friends push up. The pressure of the air being moved under and away from my small body is exhilarating. For the moment, I give into the relief and joy of my escape.

The night sky welcomes me into her arms. I don't want to break away from the other birds. If someone else flew up with us, they'd know I'm not with the rest if I attempt to go off on my own. I keep up with the crowd of birds, and let the cool breeze take away the horrors of the night. After a while, I see the mountain tops of my home land, Mexico.

Chapter Twenty-Eight

Juda

Juda came out of the guest house. He'd run all the way there with
Callen in his arms, to get her help for her eye. Juda had no idea how Viv had
gotten the knife away from Callen and used it on her. For that matter, he had
no idea how she'd gotten away period. When he thought back, he recalled
seeing a blur, then Callen was down screaming in pain. Before he could get to
the fallen girl, Viv was gone. His father had followed her. They'd both been
moving incredibly fast. Juda knew Viv had Weaver blood, but he had no idea
how that made her so powerful.

He didn't know if they'd caught and killed Viv, a thought he tried to
accept. As much as he hated to find out about Viv's blood sin, he also hated
losing her. But their law was solid, there was no saving the girl now.

Juda moved faster to his house to get some answers. His father should
be there by now. There was no way Viv would escape the great bear. His uncle
Nate stood in the doorway when he approached. The look on his face made
Juda's heart ache. Someone was hurt or dead. He just didn't know who he
wanted that to be right now.

"What happened?" Juda asked still ten feet from Nate.

"You need to find that bitch! She attacked your father."

Nate's skin paled when he turned his head to look at the goings on in
the house. "I will stand watch over him until you return. Go find her!"

Juda gave him a nod and ran to find the men who were out in the
woods. A thousand things moved through his head. She'd seriously injured his
father, how? Juda felt ashamed for the microscopic part of him that was glad

she wasn't dead. As he came to the picnic area, the men ran out of the woods towards him.

"She got away, she isn't anywhere in the woods," one man said. Juda started to pass them, thinking he'd turn into a large wolf and sniff her out.

"There were many animals in the trees. She could have shifted." The prince stopped, and they all followed his lead.

"Did anyone shift to follow the animals?" If you added up the years this group of men had lived, it would be in the thousands, but not one had thought to do this? There were shakes of heads, but no eye met his gaze.

Juda opened his mouth to yell at them. His mother's cries filled the night, and all words left his mind. The group of men followed but fell behind, as Juda tore towards the house. He slid to a stop. His mother shook with grief in Nate's arms.

Juda knew his father was dead. Ice filled his heart. The little speck of love that had been there turned black becoming pure hate. No one would stop him from finding and killing Vivian with his bare hands. The roar that left the young king made those around fall to their knees under its power.

Chapter Twenty-Nine

<u>Belonging</u>

The birds that traveled with me start to fall out of the sky. We'd flown for miles. I assume due to the fright of the gun shots. The flat terrain of Texas had turned into the rough mountains of Mexico. My mother and I had three years together here. This land holds my heart.

A cave in the nearest mountain comes into view. As I drop down, a few other birds follow my lead, I land on the rock, perching for a moment. A hand full of various types of birds settle down. What if they are shifters? I stay until each bird leaves or drops further down the mountain side. The other hawk is there, but further up the ridge. He takes off and the last few birds follow.

The sun rise lights up the sky. In case any of them held out, I let the sun rise over the peeks. Seeing nothing around, I move sluggishly into the cave. I guess birds get sore too because my wings feel stiff like cardboard. The air carries me down. The shift takes away some of the soreness, but fatigue hits me. Picking a wall, I lay against it and close my eyes.

What now? I can try and go back to my life in the shadows, but it won't be the same. How long can you live around people who'd age faster than you? The Romani way of living fits perfectly with the shifters. Jared had been the one thing that'd made me feel normal. Jared, what would happen to him?

My mind spins, I can't tell if I'm angry or deeply sad, the tears coming out of my eyes overtake me. For several minutes, I am lost in the grief and confusion. But feeling sorry for myself won't do anything to help me figure things out.

Had my mother fled and given up? No she'd found a way to protect me, so that I can live. The loving nudges received in her apartment may be gone, but in my heart I know it was her. On cue the amulet warms my skin, reminding me, it too is on my side. Plus, my father is out there waiting for me to find him.

My mind automatically starts to center my thoughts. I pull strength from the earth surrounding me. Each moment that passes makes me relax. The cold night air coming through my thin cotton clothes, makes me shiver. I must be higher up than I'd thought. Throughout the cave along the walls, there's dried branches or maybe they used to be small roots. I pull some down, and pile them up a little further into the nook. After a minute, a decent sized pile of dry wood is piled in the center of the space.

Thinking of my mother's letter, I grab up a hand full of dirt and say, *Fire.* As the grains of earth fall from my hand, in midair it transforms into flames, before landing on the roots.

"Wow."

I shoot up to my feet, ready to fight, when Jared steps out of the shadows.

"Sorry I didn't mean to scare you." He holds up his hands, palms facing me.

"I was in the cave opening watching, I followed you." My instincts say strike before he has a chance. The magic in me is ready to do as I ask. But Jared wouldn't hurt me. I'd thought the same of Juda. Except Jared had tried to warn me, opened a window, probably risking his own life in the process. I can trust him, unless he's here to revenge his father's death.

"Vivian, I couldn't let you be alone again. And I..." There are tears coming down his face, "I don't belong there anymore." His openness douses out my suspicion, he is broken, even more so then me. His hands and arms shake. At first I think it's because of his tears, but I see the trembles are all over him. He's fatigued. There are bruises on his face and arms, I recall his father's men pulling him off the stage. The red alert switches off.

"Are you alone?" I know the answer, but I need to ask. He bobs his head, and collapses to the ground. Jared hugs himself with his own arms, letting the sadness take control. I'm pulled to him, silently I maneuver myself behind his shaking body. His height makes it awkward, but I do my best to embrace him as he cries. Five minutes later, he falls fast asleep.

Taking out the medallion from my pocket, I hold it high, so I can stare at the golden saint. The king had killed the entire family of the boy this necklace had belonged to, just because his father and mother were different types of shifters. Look at me, I'd turned eighteen and gotten my powers or most of them. Had the world come to an end? No. Had fire shot out of my eyeballs and horns grown on my head? No. I latch it back around Jared's neck. He's sleeping too hard to notice. Everything that had happened had really sucked for me, but it had sucked as much for Jared.

Here we are. Jared with a dead best friend and me with a death sentence; to add to that, I'd now killed two people, even if it was in self-defense. How can this magic be so great?

For a brief moment I'd had family, friends and a future that didn't include hiding. All of it gone because of the blood that runs through my veins.

I can see why he feels betrayed by his people, mostly his father. In many ways, Jared had lived his life alone like me. In his tin-can, trapped under the thumb of a dictator. Me, hidden away to protect my very life from that same tyrant.

Jared knows what I am, and not only had he accepted me, but he'd leapt into the air and followed me here not knowing how I'd react to him. He trusts me. We are family, blood related yes, but closer than that. My mother was the last person to accept me for my differences, until now.

The back of my mind rattles with many emotions, none of them good. I'm way too exhausted to sort through them. My eyes start to droop, the blood soaked face of the king peeks out from behind the mental door in my head. I barely control the jerk of my arms willing themselves to my throat. Only a ghost. Jared twitches a moment. I slide down to lay next to him, letting his back drape over me. After a few seconds, he goes limper than before. I need to work harder to seal shut that mental door, except I know that's going to be difficult. All this death will haunt me, and worse, Jared has no idea his father is dead. Like it or not, I'll have to tell him what I've done, but not tonight.

The fire and my Jared blanket, help me move towards sleep. I don't know what comes next. Having Jared with me makes it less horrible. That is if he stays once he knows about his father. The comfort of his presence fills up the perpetual emptiness I've lived with my entire life. I know this won't last, but he's here for now. I have a place in the world that I belong, even if it's with one person and for only one night. That's one more person than I had before.

BELONGING

Acknowledgments

You know how you have that pair of stretchy pants you can't toss out? The ones with the big hole in the waist line that you keep sticking your leg through every time you put them on? That was this story for me. It hung around and became a part of my life. It refused to be a poem, or a simple short tale. But, a decade ago, I had no idea how to write a book. Thus began my quest to learn.

Three years ago, I met a group of writers who helped me realize three pages of description of a field was not exactly how to keep a reader's attention. The fact that they helped me week after week learn how to do this, was so amazing. I try every day to help other writers because of that kindness. Thanks to you Dan Krueger. Your selfless giving of time and knowledge truly changed me as a writer. Here I also say thank you to: Tom Waltz Sr., Kate Koen Landers, Amy Golober, Jan, Eugene Denham, Belinda King, J-Mag, Betty Welch, Charles Henderson, and many others I just don't recall.

Among those above, I met a great kid, well young man really, who truly helped ignite the passion for writing in me, because he lived, breathed and dreamed of it himself. He pushed me into making an honest effort with "Belonging." Thanks to you Julian (Veggies) Kindred. And those in his group: Fernanda Brady, Sherry Hill, Melissa Algood, Mathew Shields, and Louis Allen Epstein. A special shout out goes to Mel Algood. We pushed each other every week for better and we both have it now. Love you girl.

There have been so many people who helped with critiques. A few more are: Patty Flaherty Pagan, Pamela Fagan Hutchins, Jessica Raney, Enos Russell, David Welling, and Tom Brownscombe. Thank you all!

There is so much more that goes into a book, like beta readers. Alicia Ying helped put our hearts in knots with Juda and Viv, thank you for that much needed drama!

All those who have helped me with technical things, like understanding this whole self-publishing stuff, George Weir, Pamela Fagan Hutchins, and Enos Russell. My web designer Jessica Conley Potter, who lovingly puts up with my crazy ideas when I have no clue how web building works. My wonderful cover art designer, the very talented Elizabeth Mackey. The pro editors, Johnnie Bernhard and Elizabeth White-Olsen. My copy-editor Michelle Hedderman, so glad you're picky! Sometimes an expert is needed, even in fantasy. Tina Briere thank you for sharing the knowledge that helped ground my tales in reality. And a special thanks to Kathryn Falk who continues to help me understand the book industry.

Others help you in ways that they don't realize. Either by believing in you, which is vital, or by supporting you even if they think you're crazy. Thanks to you Cora Fisher, your words kept me from deleting the heck out of this story! Margaret Elmore and Debra Brown a big thank you. You girls inspire me all the time. My loving boyfriend, David Franco. Thanks for putting up with no dinners and my late night 80's music! My family: Angela Velasquez (sis sis), Wanda Maldonado, Molly Smith, Hope Morehead and my mother Cindy King. Honorary family members: Becky Marez, Circe Marez, and Yvonne Russo. My cousins and their family. Special thanks to Victoria Sjoberg who kept me young and now gives me grey hair. And my cousin Michael Stout, your love of reading pushed me to see this through to the end.

Love you all.

These last few people really shaped me as a person there for as the writer I've become. Veronica Devoreaux, you were the very first writer I knew in person. If it wasn't for your talent I may never have thought it possible to go from a simple poet, to a full blown novelist. Your work continues to inspire me daily. Thank you my friend. My sis sis, though I already thanked her, she really pitched in at the end of the process to make sure any last minute edits got done, plus, she is an amazing artist and all around go getter. This girl moved to NYC and made her life there on her own. I admire you every day kido, love you. Those I've lost, Bradley Page Guillory and my father Tito Velasquez. The love I had from you both was epic, and I know you are with me every step I take.

Lastly, the person I dedicated this book to, Tomas Cantu, my grandmother. She raised me and taught me above all else, education is the key. She was right. As a child she only got a grade school education. But that didn't stop her from having five children, two husbands, seven grandchildren, ten great grandchildren, and an eternal spot in all our hearts. Thank you grandma for pushing me to stay in school and become an adult. You are a part of me like no other.

In conclusion, I hope you have enjoyed this story. If so, say it in an honest review via the platform you purchased this from. Or go to www.amazon.com and leave it there. Thank you for the consideration.

Vivian's story has only begun. I do hope to have you until the very end. You won't want to miss it. Thank you for reading. May the Impala's lights shine on you until next we meet!

BELONGING

Preview

Book Two: Shifter Series

It's hard to buy groceries when everyone you know wants to kill you. Okay, maybe not everyone. Jared, the younger brother of the guy I almost broke up with, seems to be firmly on the side of Vivian the Destroyer. My words, not his. I'm afraid to ask his opinion of all that's happened in the last several weeks since we met. Though, I'm sure its worlds better than it will be when I tell him what I did to his father. At that point, everyone I know will want to kill me.

The rain outside seems to be slowing. It's almost night out, but there is still some sun-light coming through the one window of the small room. The little shack we're in sprung some leaks while the storm passed. Most of them are along the edges of the ceiling. No actual drips, just a constant stream down the rough cut wooden walls. Since there's more dirt than wood for flooring, I can't do much but let it make muddy puddles. Just like my life, surrounded by messes.

I've tried to put Juda, the almost ex, out of my head for the past couple weeks since I escaped the initial death sentence. He probably has a battalion of murderous shape shifters hunting me down as I sit on this cot. At the lead, no doubt, will be Callen. Who could blame her for wanting Juda too, and that's the only slack I'll allow her. She tried to harm or kill me almost every day after we met. But, Juda could drive a girl crazy. For example, I know as real as that mud is on the floor, it can never soak completely into the wood. They are two different types of things, like Juda and I, in his eyes. The thought of how he tricked me into almost sex to perform some stupid spell to learn the truth of my blood line, pisses me off to no end. And I wanted to stay mad, but

244

in truth, I did really like him, and still do, which sucks. It's hard to believe if we ever see each other again, he will try to kill me.

I'm sick of my situation, and I have no idea what to do to change it one bit. Maybe I need a new perspective? The two steps it takes to perch myself on a box that's under the only window of our cabin seems promising. Watching the bursts of lightening in the evening sky calms me a bit. Grey clouds with black trim still move above, even though the storm subsides. Just because the rain stopped, doesn't mean it won't come back. Great, this only reminds me of the other problem I've been battling with: coming clean with Jared about the king, his father. He already had a shaky relationship with the man before the king announced having killed Jared's best boyhood friend in front of all the clan for being like me, mixed blood. The idea of telling Jared the truth has kept me awake most nights listening to the coyote's howl.

The door pushes open, Jared is here, finally.

"Hey, I got you some tacos." Luckily, Jared had money stashed. He's a freakin' computer genius. At fourteen he'd taken his weekly ten bucks, invested wisely; and that's just the legal money. He says he's not a millionaire yet, and I don't want to ask about the rest. He'd found us this place, a shack in the middle of the Mexican desert, but better than a cave high up in the Mexican mountain tops.

"No steaks?" Our joke. I'm under house arrest. My face is all over TV for the murder of Todd Hamon, the College boy/C-boy as I call them, I'd killed. In self-defense my magic had saved my life after he'd started to choke me to death. The first of many regrets.

"Barbacoa actually! I know we agreed nothing too crazy, but it's beef and from what I hear, it's tender." Jared sits on his small cot two feet from my own. I refuse to sleep on the floor, so the cots are the only furnishing in the place. Barbacoa is good, but I know his understanding of Spanish is bad. It's tender because of the cow tongue. No matter, I like it, if I can eat at all.

Jared starts to pull out the food and I do what I've been doing for two weeks now. Try to decide how to mention what I did to his father. King Shea, the leader of a large proud clan of shape shifters, well over five hundred years old, dead by my hand.

"You call him yet?" This is our normal routine. He brings me stuff from town, I ask if he's called his skunk brother, Juda, and try not to look heartbroken.

"Viv, I'm not going to call him. He would've let our dad kill you. You may be forgiving, but I'm not."

"I don't forgive him. He used that crazy love spell on me." Jared looks at me, holding my eyes with his. I'm sure this is drudging up bad memories, which is why I shouldn't tell him. Except I know I should. How do you explain to your only friend that you accidentally, on purpose had to kill their father?

"I can't imagine how violating that was. I was hoping my father was exaggerating." He takes a breath and blows it out. "I never thought he'd do that to someone. I mean I've heard of it happening, but and I hate to say this, I really thought he fell hard for you." What? That's not what I expected to hear. A little ping in my stomach vibrates as his words ignite a flame I've been trying to put out. *Damn it.*

"It's my father. He is, just so, EVIL!" Jared stomps his foot on the muddy wooden floor.

"No, Jared, he was trying to protect you guys is all." I don't even believe my weak attempt at stopping his sudden anger, but I can't let him say things like that. It will make what I did worse when he calls home and finds out. No, I will tell him. *Maybe.*

"How can you say that? My father wants you dead just because your father has different blood than our clan. When will you stop letting bastards like him and my brother walk all over you?" My head gives a jerk. I know he saw my flinch, but it's not because I'm getting upset with what he's saying.

"I'm sorry but my father, he has no right to do what he's doing! He is such a fu..."

"I killed him."

My hands shake, I don't know why, but I can't let him speak ill of his dead father.

"What?"

I watch his eyes. Is he seeing me for the monster that I am? Tears come down my face. Why did I say it?

There's no taking it back now.

"I killed him, the king...your father."

My words come out soft, but he's not human like me, he hears them easily. A loud hum fills my ears. Wait, no it's just that quiet in the room. "I'm so sorry, I should have told you sooner Jared. I..." What? I hate myself for not saying anything? I should have let him kill me instead? I think he was a big jerk, but he didn't deserve to die? What can I possibly say? Nothing.

I can still see the blood; the full moon illuminated the dying king. He'd shifted into a giant black bear and hit me with his long sharp claws seconds before. The blow knocked my jaw off. It dangled by a single piece of skin, every movement punctuated by the weight of the bone hitting my chest. The king tried to choke the life out of me. Our skin to skin contact allowed my magic to transfer the injuries back to him, saving my life, but taking his.

A few rain drops hit the flat roof, breaking the deafening silence. Coming out of my vision I realize Jared is gone. Had I spoken all of it out loud? *Will he come back? Should he come back? Would I go back to the person*

247

that killed my own blood? I know I'd only reacted to save myself, but would that matter to him? His father was dead, and I caused that. No, I couldn't return to someone like me... He will keep going all the way back to Juda.

A searing pain seizes my chest. It's difficult to breathe. My heart squeezes and my grief erupts with loud sobs that I've held in for too long. My hands grab the shirt over my chest, as if they want to stop the pressure from the outside. I can't tell if it's my fit or more rain making the loud noises that echo off the walls around me. My hands give up on my heart and fly to my ears to block out the sounds, but I know I can't keep the reality out. I stop fighting it and give into the dark of the room. My father's amulet warms around my neck, but even that can't chase away the sadness crushing me from the inside out. Though my world seems shattered, underneath, way down, there is a glint of relief that I finally told him. But that is soon smothered by a single realization.

I am alone, again.

***

BELONGING

About the Author

Chantell Renee writes urban fantasy with a paranormal romance twist. She takes you to a world that, if you let it, can enhance your senses and open your eyes to possibilities. A good story well told can change a person. It is this author's hope that the readers thirst for words never diminishes.

Chantell Renee was born and raised in Houston, where she currently resides. Her muses are Rugby the beagle, Kevin Jello the mutt, and her two fussy cats, Ella and Ovo; who often try to add their own text while she's working.

You can keep up with her blog, be up to date on the latest installments of *The Shifter Series* and much more. Become a part of her community at www.chantellrenee.com

You can follower her on:

Twitter: @chantellrenee1

Facebook: https://www.facebook.com/Chantell-Renee

Instagram: CRrenee_

Made in the USA
San Bernardino, CA
20 January 2016